dark future

AMERICAN MEAT

AMERICA, TOMORROW. A world laced with paranoia, dominated by the entertainment industry and ruled by the corporations. A future where the ordinary man is an enslaved underclass and politics is just a branch of show-biz. Welcome to the Dark Future.

Zoologist-turned-investigator Batton MacKay has got an insane bunch of animal rights bikers on his tail and the corporations are threatening to repossess his beloved car. All he wants to do is get out of Florida, but a seem-ingly routine job for 'Fuzzies Inc.' will give MacKay a disturbing insight into the American Meat industry.

American Meat – it will put you off those steaks forever.

dark future

AMERICAN MEAT

stuart moore

BLACK FLAME

A Black Flame Publication
www.blackflame.com

First published in Great Britain in 2005 by BL Publishing, Games
Workshop Ltd., Willow Road, Nottingham NG7 2WS, UK.

Distributed in the US by Simon & Schuster, 1230 Avenue of the
Americas, New York, NY 10020, USA.

10 9 8 7 6 5 4 3 2 1

Cover illustration by Jaime Jones.

Copyright © Games Workshop Limited, 2005. All rights reserved.

Black Flame, the Black Flame logo, BL Publishing, the BL Publishing logo, Dark Future, the Dark Future logo and all associated
marks, names, characters, illustrations and images from the Dark
Future universe are either ®, TM and/or © Games Workshop Ltd
1988-2005, variably registered in the UK and other countries
around the world. All rights reserved.

ISBN 13: 978 184416 299 4
ISBN 10: 1 84416 299 0

A CIP record for this book is available from the British Library.

Printed in the UK by Bookmarque, Surrey, UK.

No part of this publication may be reproduced, stored in a retrieval
system, or transmitted in any form or by any means, electronic,
mechanical, photocopying, recording or otherwise, without the
prior permission of the publishers.

Publisher's note: This is a work of fiction, detailing an alternative and
decidedly imaginary future. All the characters, actions and events
portrayed in this book are not real, and are not based on real events
or actions.

AMERICA, TOMORROW

My fellow Americans —

I am speaking to you today from the Oval Office, to bring you hope and cheer in these troubling times. The succession of catastrophes that have assailed our once-great nation continue to threaten us, but we are resolute.

The negative fertility zone that is the desolation of the mid-west divides east from west, but life is returning. The plucky pioneers of the new Church of Joseph are reclaiming Salt Lake City from the poisonous deserts just as their forefathers once did, and our prayers are with them. And New Orleans may be under eight feet of water, but they don't call it New Venice for nothing.

Here at the heart of government, we continue to work closely with the MegaCorps who made this country the economic miracle it is today, to bring prosperity and opportunity to all who will join us. All those unfortunate or unwilling citizens who exercise their democratic right to live how they will, no matter how far away from the comfort and security of the corporate cities, may once more

rest easy in their shacks knowing that the new swathes of
Sanctioned Operatives work tirelessly to protect them from
the biker gangs and NoGo hoodlums.

The succession of apparently inexplicable or occult
manifestations and events we have recently witnessed have
unnerved many of us, it is true. Even our own Government
scientists are unable to account for much of what is
happening. Our church leaders tell us they have the unknown
entities which have infested the datanets in the guise of
viruses at bay.

A concerned **citizen** asked me the other day whether
I thought we were entering the Last Times, when Our Lord
God will return to us and visit His Rapture upon us, or
whether we were just being tested as He once tested his
own son. My friends, I cannot answer that. But I am
resolute that with God's help, we shall work, as ever, to
create a glorious future in this most beautiful land.

Thank you, and God Bless America.

President Estevez

Brought to you in conjunction with the GenTech
Corporation.

Serving America right.

[Script for proposed Presidential address, July 3rd
2021. Never transmitted.]

proLogue
xenotrans plantation

1

PROFESSOR WAN'S LONG, bony frame shivered, despite his best effort of will. He could stand the strong smells wafting out of the adjacent laboratory: meatballs, baconburgers and, of course, the pigs. He could handle the high whine of computers that permeated this entire facility. He could even stand the odour of the workers – vile, uncouth, seemingly unwashed for weeks. What he couldn't stand was their chatter.

"You crazy, ese? You dissin' my man Borges?"

"Shit yeah, man. That Borges is some weak shit – baby shit, man. You wan' literature, you need you some Cortazar, man!"

"Cortazar? The hell's that?"

"Cortazar, asshole! You know – *Hopscotch*? *62 a Model Kit*? *Blow-Up*, ese!"

"*Blow-Up*? With Travolta?"

Wan squeezed his eyes shut momentarily, then focused back on the machine in front of him. A sleek ApNext datanet terminal, it had been specially configured with extra magnetic RAM to compute rapid DFM results. A useful tool, but time was running out. He'd have to leave it behind.

"Grad student," Wan called, softly.

A slim, attractive young man dressed all in black, with pale pink hair, appeared at his shoulder. "Professor?"

"Take only the portable gene sequencer. Leave all else in this room."

"Yes, professor."

The rows of test tubes and Petri dishes would have to stay behind as well; there was no time to determine which of them might be contaminated. Wan sighed. He hated to waste material. But, he reminded himself, he'd abandoned labs before, sometimes in a much greater rush than this.

Professor Wan had just come from a meeting of the Greater Islamist Conference of Allah (East Coast US), up in Raleigh-Durham. The Islamic movement had made great strides in recent years, as Americans struggled to make sense of the chaos all around them. Very few of them seemed to be able to grasp the concept that they'd brought it all on themselves.

Wan admired the Islamists' discipline. It reminded him of his native China, of the ceaseless hard work that had made that country the world's leader in genetic research. But the Islamists were too backwards, too confined by outmoded ideas. When it came to a choice between reshaping the world and blowing things up, they always opted for explosions.

From the other room, the workers' argument grew louder, cutting into Wan's thoughts.

"I should kick your ass, dissin' Borges."

"You should read somethin' real, you should. Two words, man: Carlos Fuentes."

"Uh-uh. No way. You sold me some'a that Fuentes shit before – I couldn' get through fifty pages, man. You need a goddamn degree in Mexican history to read that shit."

Wan raised his voice a bit – a rare occurrence – hoping to drown out the men. "Where is other grad student?"

The pink-haired young man paused in his task of packing the sequencer into a small box. "She's in the front office, calling Thalamus."

"Fine." Wan frowned, glanced at the open doorway. "All is loaded aboard the Interceptor?"

"Yes, professor."

"Then let us say our goodbyes."

The pink-haired man grimaced, hefting the sequencer box under his arm. His eyes darted to the doorway. "The pig room?"

Wan raised an eyebrow. "Try not to judge what you see too harshly, grad student. All is permissible in the pursuit of DNA-Based Faunic Manipulation."

"I do not find the experiments objectionable, professor. I merely prefer not to deal with… commoners… unless absolutely necessary."

"One day, we will all be equal in our satiety," Wan said. "Come."

As they walked into the pig room, the two workers – one small and wearing a Havana Chigoes baseball cap, the other chunky and moustached – continued their literary debate. "Vargas Llosa! Are you fuckin' *high?*"

The big one looked up, held out his gigantic meatball sandwich. "Professor Juan! You want a bite?"

Wan felt the saliva rise in the back of his mouth, swallowed a shiver of desire, and grimaced. "No thank you, American."

"Suit yourself. You gonna take some of these babies off our hands?"

He gestured towards the pigs.

They looked even worse than they smelled: gigantic, bloated, two hundred pounds apiece minimum, all sitting on their asses like humans in front of a big screen TV. They couldn't have moved even if there'd been room enough in their cramped cages, which stretched all around the high-ceilinged room. Their grunts mingled with high-pitched wheezing; their sinuses were a perpetual problem, unable to cope with the creatures' bulk. Their faces seemed almost pleading in their dullness, and food particles covered the walls of the cages. They were gluttony personified.

But their size was no accident. The pigs had been grown to monstrous proportions not for eating or breeding purposes, but to strengthen their hearts. At maturity, the plan went, those hearts would be carved out and transplanted into humans. A small part of Professor Wan's glorious vision of the future.

One of the pigs was twitching, Wan noticed, and whimpering louder than the others. He moved nearer and saw that its misshapen, bloated foot was trying to scratch at a scabby, purplish patch on its face. The pig couldn't even stand – its leg flopped through the air, unable to reach the sore spot. Wan allowed himself a slight grimace.

"Nurgle's rot," he murmured. The contagion had gone farther than he'd realised.

The pink-haired young man stepped up next to him, and Wan warned him away from the cages with a sharp gesture. The room's floor was covered with dried blood, particularly in the area surrounding the bone saw. There'd been a lot of impromptu slaughters lately, and Wan knew why.

"Professor Juan?"

"I'm afraid I won't be taking any of these lovely specimens with me, gentlemen. But you shouldn't have to worry about them much longer."

Baseball Cap leaned forwards, a touch of fear in his eye. "Is it true they got some kinda disease?"

"As I say, nothing that will cause you grief for long."

Moustache took a big bite of meatball, squinted at Wan suspiciously. "We don't see you down here too much, Juan."

"A consequence of my busy schedule, I fear."

A slim young woman with ice-blue hair entered the room and grimaced briefly at the smell of the pigs.

"Grad student," Wan said to her. "Are the Mad Cows coming?"

"Yes, professor." She smiled shyly, exchanged a glance with the pink-haired boy. They wore identical black outfits. "They're already on the road."

"And MacKay?"

"Thalamus says he just left their office. He'll be here sooner."

"Then we must leave soonest." Wan turned to the moustached worker, who was preoccupied with dabbing ketchup off his jumper. "Americans… I wish you good day. Try not to make too big a stain on the cages when he kills you."

Wan strode quickly out of the room, flanked by the two young people. He ignored the workers' questions, knowing their meatball sandwiches would soon, once again, be the focus of their attention.

Professor Wan walked in silence through the lobby, glancing briefly at the corporate logo on the wall: I HEART FLORIDA. One of many companies he'd founded or been associated with in his long life. This one had shown real promise, and the data he'd just recovered would serve him well in the years to come. Someday the hold the animal kingdom held over humanity would be lifted, and Wan's name would be hailed as mankind's saviour.

Then, perhaps, he would allow himself the sublime pleasure of eating meat.

But for now, this was just another place to be left behind. To the bloodshed and carnage that would surely come soon.

At least, karmically, the building was prepared.

In its former life it had been an All-Mart.

part one
mad cows
and englishmen

I

BATTON MACKAY SQUATTED in birdshit, frowning and waiting. He'd taken up position behind an odd, disused structure that had once been some kind of parking-lot security booth. It was the ideal location, shielded from the main building by palm trees; but apparently it doubled as some sort of avian outhouse. Bad luck.

MacKay loved animals, but he'd never liked their faeces.

He checked his HanHeld; no picture yet. He peered around the booth at the former All-Mart, which was ringed by a laser-fence and bore a small, hostile-looking sign reading "I HEART FLORIDA / Research & Development". The sun had just set, and most of the workers had gone home; it was hard to tell, because few of them could afford cars, but MacKay figured there couldn't be more than a handful of people left inside the building.

MacKay's gleaming black G-Mek Interceptor sat in the parking-lot, along with two other, much older and shoddier cars. MacKay suspected they'd been there for weeks. He frowned at the Interceptor, its chain guns gleaming in the bright sunlight; he loved that car. In fact, that was why he was here.

Dog should be inside now. Soon he'd begin broadcasting, and the fun would begin.

This, though… this wasn't fun. The stink was getting worse. MacKay hated Florida, and the fact that this town was amusingly named Hollywood only added insult to nasal injury. Florida was hot and sweaty, even at night, and odours seemed to linger and grow wherever they sprang up. MacKay found his finger inching towards his MiniShredder, eager to shoot something.

Stupid Thalamus Corporation. They'd basically blackmailed him down here; he owed them some serious cash for a deal that had gone wrong, and when he initially refused to come down to Whore-ida, they'd threatened to repossess his Interceptor. A Sanctioned Operative isn't much without his car, and MacKay knew they could do it. So he'd agreed.

And Thalamus had gotten themselves into some deep birdshit this time. Apparently they'd hired this little outfit to grow giant pigs for heart transplants, and made a nice little profit on it for years. But now the pigs had some weird kind of retrovirus. It wasn't transmissible by air, but each of those pigs could wipe out a small city if their body parts ever got mixed in with a batch of T-Bone meat. I Heart Florida had guaranteed it would never happen; the pigs were routinely incinerated after their hearts were removed. But Thalamus had decided they couldn't take the chance. The hearts were no good now, anyway.

So they'd hired MacKay – the Ratcatcher. The only Sanctioned Op in the country known to be a soft touch when it came to animal problems.

Well, the only reputable one, anyway.

MacKay kept his mind on the upcoming violence, trying not to think about the fact that he wasn't getting paid for this. According to the Thalamus briefing, there were thirty-five giant, bloated pigs inside. On the minus side, MacKay would be killing defenceless creatures that had never had a real chance at a decent life. The plus: they'd probably explode entertainingly.

And he'd get to keep his car.

The HanHeld buzzed to life. A blurry grey shot of a maintenance duct faded into view, wobbling and blurring as Dog scurried through it.

"Receiving you, Dog," MacKay said softly.

Keek! Keek! the monkey replied.

Dog was MacKay's secret weapon and only partner. He was almost as stealthy as an organic monkey, except for the slight metallic *tik tik* his paws made when he scampered through small spaces.

"Go left," MacKay said. "I think I see a dataport."

The monkey scuttled down the small crawlspace, stopped before a round machine-port in the wall. The picture bobbed up and down for a moment as Dog jumped excitedly. Then, keeping his camera focused so MacKay could see, Dog extruded a connector from his paw and jacked into the wall.

"You should be in the intranet now," MacKay said. "Can you access the security system?"

Keek! Keek! MacKay knew that tone of voice; it meant Dog had found his task easier than expected. A series of pops and clicks came over the connection, and MacKay looked up sharply as the laser-fence hummed once and went dark.

"Thanks, buddy. On my way."

Smiling, he pulled out his MiniShredder and ran to the fence, then vaulted it harmlessly. He felt his blood rising as he reached for the door.

He was inside before the bikes screamed their way into the parking lot.

THE LOBBY AREA was dark, deserted, and very plainly furnished. IHF had done a lousy job of converting it; the receptionist's booth still had the faded words "Customer Service" visible on the front, and the guest chairs looked vaguely like stripped-down checkout stands. MacKay thumbed the HanHeld to life as he crept across the lobby, looking around nervously.

"Dog? You still jacked in?" *Keek!* "Check for backup generator systems. I want to make sure we—"

Suddenly the room lit up with a loud *clang! clang!* A high-powered laser beam sliced down next to him, burning a patch in the floor. "EXCUSE ME, SIR," a firm yet kindly voice said very, very loudly. "I BELIEVE YOU FORGOT TO PAY FOR THAT ITEM."

MacKay frowned in disgust. They were still using the store's old security systems! Four more lasers stabbed down, forming a ring around him and scorching the tiles. They weren't meant to be deadly – just to warn him – and presumably there were supposed to be absorption patches on the floor. I Heart Florida had opted for a less obviously customer-hostile décor for their lobby, and they were paying for it now.

Not that it would matter soon. MacKay raised his Shredder, took aim at the ceiling…

"YOUR PATRONAGE IS IMPORTANT TO US. ALLOW US TO ESCORT YOU BACK TO CUSTOMER SERVICE, WHERE YOU MAY PAY FOR YOUR ITEMS."

MacKay fired, knocking out two of the laser projectors. He threw himself sideways through the opening in the beams, and the rest of them winked off as their target moved out of range. Apparently they were only programmed to operate in the area near the checkout lanes.

Then, suddenly, MacKay ducked down as a hail of ordinary bullets sliced over his head. He quickly found shelter behind a display of magazines, which he suspected had once been a candy counter.

"MacKay! I saw your ugly ve-hickle outside, ya dumb bastard. Get out here!"

MacKay groaned, poked his head out a little. "Brutus?"

Two muscular men stood near the outer doorway, small guns lifted and smoking. They wore snug black jeans, boots, and pleather jackets with a distinctive insignia: a furious, snorting bull clenching its teeth down on a stalk of celery, as if it were a cigar.

MacKay recognized the sign immediately: the Mad Cows. Militant vegetarians. One of the nastiest gangcults in the southeastern US.

"I ain't gonna shoot you," the bigger of the two men replied. "Not if ya give up, anyway."

MacKay stepped out, pointing his gun upwards to match the men's stance. "Brutus Diamond. I can't believe it," he said. "You running with these losers now?"

Brutus grinned, and MacKay flinched even before he saw the man's teeth. Brutus's dental work, or lack of same, was legendary. The few teeth he still had seemed to be held together by unusually strong fungus. His breath could force a spider-copter down.

"Killin' animals is wrong, MacKay," Brutus said. He'd developed some creative methods to avoid lisping, MacKay noticed. "It's against the laws of God and Man. Experimentin' on 'em is even worse."

MacKay glanced at the security beam-projectors on the ceiling and sidled towards the back of the lobby. "So you're... what? Going to adopt thirty-five gigantic, diseased pigs?"

"Set 'em free, more like," Brutus said. "To live amongst nature."

"They couldn't survive 'amongst nature', you moron. They can't even walk."

"I don't think you're fit to judge God's creatures, MacKay."

"You're a hypocrite, Brutus. You used to fill up at Sizzler on Sunday night with the rest of us. You just don't eat meat now 'cause you can't chew it anymore." MacKay took another step back.

The other Mad Cow moved forwards, laughing. "Where you think you're goin', little man?"

Brutus's gun didn't waver. "Be a sin to kill you too, MacKay. But I will if I have to."

"I'll spare you the spiritual soul-searching." MacKay broke and sprinted to the back of the store. The second Mad Cow ran after him – straight into the shop's laser-barrage, as it flared back to life.

"*Aaaaaaahhhh!*"

"PLEASE DO NOT ATTEMPT TO LEAVE THE PREMISES WITHOUT PAYING, SIR. SHOULD YOU

ENTER YOUR VEHICLE, IT WILL BE TARGETED BY THE PARKING TOWER AND DESTROYED."

The man smoked and burned; his arm had a hole straight through it. He stared at it in shock, writhing around, sticking his legs and head in and out of the deadly lasers, flinching and screaming as they burned him everywhere. MacKay wished he had time to admire the slapstick. It was almost as good as a Miko D cartoon.

But he had other problems – like Brutus Diamond, the only friend of his who'd ever beaten him senseless just for fun. That had been a pretty tough-living group back at the Washington DC Zoo. No wonder they'd all become killers.

MacKay made for a doorway at the back of the lobby. Ignoring his screaming gang mate, Brutus grinned his toxic grin and followed, firing off a few shots.

"Where you goin', MacKay?"

"Got some pigs to put down, Brutus. And come to think of it–"

MacKay emptied his clip right into Brutus's heart, punching deep holes in the snorting, celery-smoking bull on his jacket.

"–this isn't a bad start."

Brutus went down, writhed and frothed blood, and died.

MacKay looked down at Brutus's body for a second, shook his head. "You always were too soft on the animals, Brutus. Makes the herd weak."

A few bullets shot out wildly, ricocheting around the room. The other Mad Cow was now burned on most of his body, firing crazily at all angles and howling like an animal as the lasers tightened their circle on him.

The security speaker laid it down.

"ALL-MART IS AUTHORIZED TO EMPLOY LETHAL FORCE AGAINST BOTH SHOPLIFTERS AND EMPLOYEES. THIS ALLOWS US TO BRING YOU FINE GOODS... AND KEEP OUR PRICES AS LOW AS POSSIBLE."

MacKay sighed, reloaded, and fired three shots. Two hit the writhing figure on the arm, but the third put him out of his misery.

This wasn't going well. MacKay hadn't bargained on armed resistance — especially from ideological fanatics. How many more were there?

MacKay aimed his MiniShredder at an inner door, blasted it open. He ran through the door into a darkened corridor.

"ALL-MART HAS MANY FINE EMPLOYMENT OPTIONS. IF, AFTER YOU HAVE ATONED FOR YOUR CRIME, YOU ARE INTERESTED, PLEASE PROCEED TO CUSTOMER SERVICE AND FILL OUT A–"

Rolling his eyes, MacKay reached into his jacket and pulled out a mini Gren-Aid. He yanked the pin and tossed it back through the doorway, then ran to the far end of the corridor and hunkered down.

The lobby exploded in a toxic cloud of chemicals, gunpowder, ugly plastic furniture, and dead gangcult members. MacKay coughed as the miasma drifted into the corridor. He looked down, startled, as a roll of old All-Mart register tape clattered into the hallway.

The only thing worse than vegetarians was corporations.

MacKay flipped a button on the HanHeld, and a schematic of the building appeared. He darted down the hall, pushing open a fire door to a dingy metal stairwell. No alarm went off; apparently now the security systems really were down. He thumbed the HanHeld to his secure comm channel.

"Dog," he whispered, taking the stairs two at a time. "Meet me on level three, the pig lab. Copy?"

The screen was blank.

"Dog?"

The screen buzzed, rattled, then resolved itself into the strikingly attractive face of a woman in gang gear: spiked dark hair, dog collar, heavy Goth revival makeup, and that damn snorting-bull jacket. She looked about thirty – old for a ganger – but she had high cheekbones, hard coal eyes, and an attractive sneer. She stood in a room full of datanet consoles.

"We've got your monkey, Op," the woman said, "and we're not going to stand for this cruelty. You want him back, you'll vacate this building soonest."

MacKay felt his blood rise. Dog was his only friend.

"Who the hell are you?" he asked, keeping his tone even.

A tall, thin man stepped into view behind the woman and placed a proprietary hand on her shoulder. "You know who we are, killer." He wore the Cow jacket, but he seemed too well-groomed, too clean-shaven to be a ganger. The widow's peak haircut wasn't really working for him, either.

The woman frowned at him, then turned back to speak to MacKay through Dog's camera. "Get out of here, MacKay, and we'll mail him back to you after we've freed the pigs. Otherwise he's scrap metal."

Thumbing a button on the HanHeld, MacKay traced Dog's signal. There was too much metal in the building's structure to get an exact fix, but it was definitely coming from below him. So the rest of the Mad Cows hadn't made it to the upper floors, and the pig lab, yet.

He continued climbing the stairs.

"Listen," he said, coming to a landing and a heavy fire door. He shouldered it open. "You, lady, you're the leader of these guys? What do I call you, anyway?"

"How about Mia. It's my name."

"Mia." MacKay scanned the hallway: empty. The lab was just ahead. "You don't believe in harming animals, right? That's your code?"

"You know it, killer," Mia said. "That's what makes us different from corporate tools like you."

He pushed through a double-door into the lab.

The sight of the pigs – huge, grotesque, mewling unhappily – stopped him momentarily. Their rotting odour mixed with an odd food smell; looking down, MacKay saw a few pieces of meat and tomato-soaked bread littering the floor, along with a dog-eared book called *All Fires the Fire*. They seemed to have been left behind quickly.

He shook off the smell, looked back at the HanHeld. Dog had no display screen on his body; MacKay could see the Mad Cows, but they couldn't see him.

"Then you can't harm Dog – my monkey," MacKay said.

"After all, he's an animal."

Mia laughed. "Nice try, you psychopath. He's a *robot* animal. There's nothing real about him."

"Oh, but there is."

Grimacing, MacKay pulled a small detection device from his belt, scanned the air. No sign of airborne pathogens. Good. That meant Thalamus hadn't lied to him, sent him on a suicide mission. Which meant he didn't have to race back to their office to infect the top execs with his final breaths by way of revenge.

"What the hell are you talking about?" Mia asked.

MacKay reached into his pack, pulled out a small, deadly dartgun. "Dog is a robot monkey," he said into the HanHeld, "but he's got a real monkey brain. Inside, he's a genuine, living creature."

On the little screen, Mia flinched. "What? Who would do a thing like that?"

Behind her, a few of the other gang members peered into the camera, curious. MacKay saw two stringy girls and a thug-faced Hispanic boy. They really were a weedy-looking bunch, he thought.

Clenching the HanHeld in his armpit, MacKay walked up to the first pig. Its whole face was discoloured, scabby, and it whined like a terminal cancer patient. Poor bastard. MacKay shot a poison dart at its heart; the dart bounced off the creature's tough, mottled skin, and rattled onto the floor.

"Have you heard of a Doctor Donovan, of GenTech?" MacKay asked.

"Sure," Mia replied. "Genius at transplanting human brains into artificial bodies. Or so they say."

"Well, Dog was one of his first experiments."

Grimacing, MacKay carefully picked up the dart, then reached through the bars and forced it by hand, inch by inch, into the boar's chest. The animal whimpered a bit louder, but seemed barely aware of the added pain. At last MacKay felt the tip hit soft tissue, and he stepped back. The pig groaned, slumped forwards, and was still.

One down.

"A monkey brain," Mia said slowly, "in a robot monkey body."

"That's right," MacKay replied, jamming a second dart into another pig's chest. "Which means, by your own charter, you may not harm him."

"And you adopted him."

MacKay held up the HanHeld just in time to see the male Cow turn to Mia. "He's right, Mia. What are we gonna—"

"Shut up, Hank." Mia frowned. "Stand by, MacKay. Don't do anything stupid." And she cut the connection.

He looked around at the roomful of deformed pigs, then down at the handful of darts that would have to be laboriously, manually jammed into each of their hearts.

"Little late for that," he murmured.

IT TOOK FIFTEEN minutes to put down all the pigs. Some of them were more diseased than others; their skin was starting to flake off. MacKay carefully avoided touching any of them. He'd worked with sick animals before.

Several times during his task, the HanHeld beeped, but MacKay didn't answer. The Mad Cows could wait. MacKay knew they wouldn't harm his monkey unless they were sure he was lying. Which he wasn't.

Finally, all three dozen plague-ridden boars lay limp, having ceased breathing, in their cramped prisons. Several of them had defecated upon dying, adding a new, thick, even more pungent smell to the grisly scene. MacKay felt a twinge of déjà vu; he remembered the gang slaughter that had ended his career as a zookeeper. Elephants, pythons, tigers – all shot down, bodies littering the habitats, dried dark brown with blood. The worst day of his life.

But that had been different – senseless, cruel.

This was mercy.

He yanked out six Gren-Aids, wired them up to the cages in a big circle around the room. Just inside the door, he attached a microtimer to the last wire. He stepped outside, reached back in, and flicked the timer on.

"So long, guys," he said.

As he ran to the stairwell, he thumbed the HanHeld on.

"Listen to me and listen good," he hissed. "I've just wired the entire third floor of this building to explode in three minutes. That means that, in about three and a half minutes, a particularly toxic combination of plaster, asbestos, discarded fast food, and diseased pig guts is going to come crashing down on your heads."

Mia appeared, frowning. "MacKay," she said. "What assurance do we have that you're telling the truth about—"

"You've got no assurance, baby — except that this building's about to go up. If I were you, I'd get out of Dodge before an entire building lands on your ass — not to mention those pigs. They don't carry airborne contagions, but I sure wouldn't want their pus-covered internal organs falling down all over *me*."

Mia stared into the camera for a moment. There was disgust on her face, and also a kind of fascination. "Do you actually *like* killing things?"

Then Hank, the other Cow, pushed his way in front of Mia. "MacKay, you bastard. No way you're getting out of this place alive—"

Mia punched him on the arm, hard. "Oh, grow up, Hank. He's got us." She turned back to the camera. "We're leaving, MacKay. But we'll see you again."

MacKay sprinted down the stairwell, three steps at a time. "Drop my monkey on the front doorstep for me, would you?"

Mia stared into the camera with tenderness, and for a startled moment, MacKay thought she was going to come on to him. Then he realised she was looking at Dog, with an animal-lover's sympathy.

"Yeah," she said softly. "Okay."

By the time MacKay made it through the lobby, the Mad Cows' cycles were already roaring off into the distance. Sure enough, Dog sat on the welcome mat, chattering agitatedly.

"You idiot," MacKay said. "C'mere."

Dog jumped onto MacKay's arm, and they ran out to the parking lot. MacKay's Interceptor stood just where he'd left it, illuminated by the building's emergency lighting. It was untouched except for a gigantic white paint-graffito across the side reading: MAD COWS WAS HERE.

"Shit," MacKay said.

Keek! Keek!

"Right – get in." MacKay opened the door, and Dog scampered inside. MacKay slammed the door, wrenched the car into high gear, and tore away.

Behind them, the pigs rained down.

II

MacKay sped up the old Florida Turnpike, past rotting towns and collapsed palm trees, at 125 mph. He'd sworn himself a solemn oath: his foot would remain pressed down tight on the gas pedal until he saw the words "Welcome to Georgia".

Thalamus hadn't been so bad. They'd thrown in a small bonus for his work, plus an affidavit releasing them from all claims on his car. They'd even thrown in a carwash from the company motor pool, erasing the Mad Cows' petty handiwork.

The exec who'd paid MacKay had no visible facial features – just a strip of blank cloth across the front of his head. Apparently this was a new fashion among corporate execs. MacKay didn't know how they managed to breathe, but he found the effect disturbing, which was probably the idea, though not quite as disturbing as the exec's voice. To MacKay it sounded for all the world like Sylvester the Cat impersonating Darth Vader.

"We're sending in a cleanup crew to decontaminate the area around the lab," the exec had said, "sending" sounding as "fending" due to the pronounced lisp. "Probably have to close the dog track in Hollywood for a few days, but that's life."

"Why didn't you just send them in to start with?" MacKay had asked. "Why did you need me?"

"We had a three-year contract with I Heart Florida," the man had replied. "Couldn't just break it. Of course, once the building was the victim of rogue Op and gangcult violence, we were able to do them a favour by stepping in."

Typical corporate shenanigans. Just one of many reasons MacKay couldn't wait to get out of Florida.

Another reason was the Mad Cows. MacKay knew he'd been lucky, back at the lab; gangcults were a serious hazard to a solo Op. His best intel said there were ten to twelve members of the gang's Miami chapter, and he'd killed two. That still left some pretty crappy odds – and some angry survivors.

And the Cows were local; MacKay wasn't. That meant they probably had allies. The last thing MacKay needed was to run up against the Bush Leaguers – the Florida Electoral Tax Police. They made the Maniax look like a puppet show. They'd do anything for money, or for power.

No, it was time for MacKay to take his own advice and get the hell out of Dodge, hopefully spend a few days on a ranch in North Carolina. Horses, pretty girls; maybe he'd finally learn how to play golf. And the bonus would buy him a nice supply of extra water.

Still, something about the past day nagged at him. He glanced over at Dog, who was fiddling with the cigarette lighter. MacKay had tried to break him of the habit, but figured that, sooner or later, the monkey would burn a vital system. That would teach him a lesson.

"I don't know," MacKay said aloud. "Something about all this doesn't add up. The Mad Cows are fanatics... but how did they happen to show up at the exact same time I did?"

Ignoring his master, Dog braced his feet on the dash and pulled the lighter free. He made a triumphant noise.

"And that woman... their leader. She called me 'MacKay.' I haven't been in Florida for seven years, and I'm not exactly a household name. Were they *waiting* for me?"

The monkey waved the hot-tipped lighter around, screeching happily.

"I guess it doesn't matter." MacKay snatched the lighter and plugged it back into the dash, then patted the disappointed monkey on the head. "You kind of liked her, didn't you? That little hottie, Mia?"

Dog shrugged and scratched under his armpit.

"She was something. Seemed pretty smart, too. How does a woman like that get mixed up with a gangcult?"

Dog turned to him. *Keek! Keek!*

"Yeah, I know. How does a zoologist wind up killing animals for a living? Pretty fucked-up world."

Suddenly the dashboard went *beep beep beep*, indicating an incoming call on the satellite line. MacKay raised an eyebrow. He wasn't supposed to have a satellite booster, and very few people knew the codes to reach him on it. This one showed no caller ID.

Shrugging, he pressed the talk button. "Raspler's Pet Emporium."

"Mister MacKay?" No picture – the sat traffic must be heavy today – but the voice had a heavy, hard-to-place accent. "Allow me to introduce myself. Alastair Henry Patrick Wellington, Chief Executive Officer of Fuzzies, Inc."

MacKay frowned into the phone. "Never heard of it. How did you get this number?"

"Ahem – we are, you might say, affiliated with GenTech Industries. I believe you've done some ruddy business with them before."

Ruddy? "Are you English?"

The voice laughed, a broken noise on the static-distorted connection. "By Jove, sir, you've found me out. Might I persuade you to drop by our offices in Belle Glade? We'd heard you were visiting Florida and hoped to avail ourselves of your services."

"Not interested, thanks. I believe it's in my best interest to *un*-visit Florida as quickly as possible."

"I quite understand, sir. Oh, bloody hell, yes." Something was odd here – the man sounded more like a Mary Poppins character than any Englishman MacKay had ever met. "But I assure you this job would take you out of state very quickly."

"Sorry. I need a vacation."

"And we need an animal expert… a ruthless, trained Op who'll stop at nothing to get the bloody job done. Which means you."

"I'm flattered. No."

"We are prepared to pay…"

And Wellington said a number. MacKay blinked.

"Could you repeat that, please?"

Wellington repeated the number.

It was a very, very large number.

Dog looked at MacKay, shaking his head. *Keek! Keek!*

MacKay frowned.

"I'm not accepting – yet. But I think I can detour by your offices to discuss it."

"Good show, old chap. You're coming up on Haverhill, I believe… just take a left and follow the carrion-strewn motorway."

MacKay called up a transparent Gazetteer NavMap, which superimposed itself on the windshield. "Copy that. Be there in forty-five minutes."

"Capital, sir. I'll be here with bells on!"

MacKay cut the connection.

He kept his eyes on the road, refusing to look at the monkey, whom he knew was rebuking him with his eyes. "Don't start," he said. "With that much money, we could retire."

Dog's *keek keek* was soft, admonishing, like an old woman's *tut tut*.

"And this Wellington… well, he's gotta be an anecdote in the making, right?"

The monkey was silent.

MacKay leaned over the wheel, glumly. "At least he sounds like he has a face."

▥

WHATEVER FUZZIES, INC was, it didn't want attention. When MacKay drew near Belle Glade, he found himself driving along a single-lane road with swampland all around. He had to call the Fuzzies office and have a secretary talk him down a hidden driveway to a huge, nondescript, grey office building surrounded by desolate swamp.

Inside, the place was lush but uninformative. No plaques on the walls, no magazine write-ups in the lobby; just bare couches and bullet-proof glass with a double-security lock separating MacKay from the inside offices. At first the horn-rimmed receptionist refused to let Dog come through with him – MacKay had to threaten to walk – but soon the pair found themselves seated in comfortable, real-leather chairs before a huge oak conference table. A lit-up, detailed relief map of the United States hung on the wall, with red overlays for serious no-go zones; the largest was Utah, which, word had it, had actually seceded recently under the control of some large religious cult. Other extremist groups were reportedly pushing similar agendas in a number of states.

Leaning back, MacKay realised how tired he was. He forced himself to stay alert.

"Mister Wellington will be right with you," the receptionist said, smiling a plastic smile. MacKay nodded, pulled out his HanHeld, and started watching an old Marko Sharko cartoon. Dog sat perched on his shoulder, watching intently. When the shark ate a bank robber whole, MacKay chuckled.

Then Wellington entered the room, and the cartoon seemed suddenly tame.

The exec was tall, stout, and dressed in a foppish Victorian suit – all ruffles and frills everywhere. He sported a large handlebar moustache and, incredibly, a monocle. An old-style, curved pipe was clenched in his mouth; when he caught sight of MacKay, he reached up to remove it.

"Dear boy! I say – what an honour. You look frightfully good!" He pumped MacKay's hand with enthusiasm. "Welcome to our most humble establishment."

MacKay rose to his feet, running disbelieving eyes down the man's body. He'd already decided he had nothing to lose here, so he might as well be honest. "Mister Wellington. May I ask you a question?"

"Anything, old boy. Tea?"

"No thanks. On the phone – you said you were British."

"And so I am, sir."

"Bullshit. You're not from England."

Wellington dropped two sugar cubes into a small china teacup, then looked up, smiling sharply. "Ah, my dear man. You have indeed snared me in a technicality. Strictly speaking, I do not hail from the blessed shores of Blighty. Through a quirk of fate, I found myself born in *this* hemisphere instead. One of life's little misfortunes, don't you know.

"But make no mistake, sir: I *am* English – through and through. The mighty blood of Robert the Bruce and the Bard himself burns in my veins. The fires of old empire stoke my every move, provide the motive force that propels me through the savage jungle of the business world. Were I other than English, I should never have survived – let alone thrived – in this dark future we must all navigate, every day of our wretched, misbegotten lives."

"Old empire." MacKay glanced up at the map on the wall, pocked with red. "I hear you, Limey. Just where exactly *are* you from?"

Wellington frowned, took a long draw off his pipe. "Newark," he muttered.

"Capital," MacKay replied.

Wellington looked up, smiled again. "Well, my boy, it is good to finally meet you. I've heard tales of your exploits for years. What is it they call you?"

"That depends on how well they know me."

"Ha! Gracious, lad, your wit is – ah, but I recall now. Rat-catcher. They call you the *Ratcatchah*."

On MacKay's shoulder, Dog suddenly jumped up and down. *Keek! Keek!*

"He doesn't like that name," MacKay said softly.

"I see," Wellington said. "And do you?"

MacKay shrugged. "It's a name. What exactly do you do around here, Mister Wellington?"

Wellington leaned across the table, grinning past his huge moustache. "Direct and to the point. I like that, dear boy. I only wish I were in a position to tell you everything."

"What *can* you tell me?"

Wellington rose, started pacing, oblivious to MacKay's question. "Everything's so official these days – all security checks and need-to-know. Why, twenty years ago, when I founded this company, I'd have just taken you on a tour of the whole bol-locks. We'd have drunk champagne while you peered in wonder at the faunic chambers – but I've already said too much."

MacKay was inclined to agree, though for different reasons.

"I hope you'll forgive me, old boy, but – in matters of this sensitivity, I'm required to defer to GenTech security." He gestured towards the door. "Allow me to introduce Mister Five-A."

A tall man appeared in the doorway. He wore a crisp black suit, stood ramrod straight, and his face was a blur of static and pixels. The current fad on this floor no doubt.

MacKay sighed.

"Pleased to meet you," Five-A said in a booming voice, leaning down to shake MacKay's hand. MacKay shrank away from the man's sparkling, iridescent face. He noticed an odd logo on Five-A's shirt, in garish orange and green: the Miami Snake-heads. He remembered that GenTech employees often wore the colours of sports teams the company sponsored. It clashed a bit with the impassive, faceless, men-in-black look Five-A was trying for.

Five-A strode theatrically to the front of the room, stood behind a small holo-projector mounted on the table. "You're an interesting man, MacKay. The only Op in the States prepared to take on animal cases, I believe."

"There's one other, but he's a complete idiot." MacKay turned to Wellington. "*Twat*, you might say."

"Ha!" said Wellington. "Quite so."

Five-A soldiered on, all business. MacKay noticed that his face was actually a projection from his collar, some sort of high-tech scrambling device. MacKay had heard of them – they were used by riot police and prison interrogators, to limit liability and unnerve prisoners – but he'd never seen one in action. Apparently they were part of the same corporate fashion as the Thalamus face-cloths, but higher-tech and more intimidating.

GenTech always had the best toys.

"I need to start by giving you a little background on the business Fuzzies, Inc, is in… but because of certain government contracts, I cannot be too specific. I hope you'll understand."

"I don't understand much yet, but keep going."

"Fuzzies is a leader in the field of DFM: DNA-based Faunic Manipulation. It's a broad term for a host of techniques used to manipulate the growth of animal tissue for various uses. Fuzzies has used DFM for several purposes, but its primary business has always been in manufacturing intelligent and semi-intelligent animals for very exclusive clients."

MacKay frowned. "That sounds kind of sleazy."

Wellington smiled, shook his head.

Five-A continued: "Some of our customers *have* commissioned animals for… unspecified carnal purposes. But our primary market is interested in more productive uses. The most popular categories are scientific experimentation, domestic servants, government contracts, specialized private industry, and filmed entertainment. Also, containers for AIs or AI-enhanced creatures."

"I'm having a little trouble wrapping my mind around this," MacKay said. Dog made a *Keek! Keek!* noise in agreement. "Can you give me some examples?"

"That's the tricky part." Five-A leaned forwards on the table, in what MacKay supposed was meant to be a power move. "All Fuzzies animals are produced in strict secrecy; the clients must sign a strict confidentiality agreement, and we abide by that as well."

"The law is rather, er, fuzzy on the legal status of these creatures," Wellington added.

"And you don't want a test case that might outlaw them completely," MacKay said. "I understand, though I admit I'm a little repelled. But I can't take a job without knowing what I'm hunting."

"I'm authorized to show you one sample of Fuzzies' technology."

Five-A pressed a button on the holo-projector, and an image appeared in the air. It was a squat, dwarf-like humanoid figure, with a wolf's face and paws, but with large, eyes. It looked feral and scared, but friendly. The overalls it wore gave it a kind of cartoonish look.

"This is Lobito, one of the first tests of the i-DFM process."

"i-DFM?"

"*Intelligent* DNA-based et cetera," Wellington said.

"Lobito was created here, at Fuzzies, many years ago," Five-A said. "His brain was enhanced with, by today's standards, primitive artificial intelligence technology during incubation; at birth, he could count to twenty and speak roughly as well as Scooby-Doo."

"Rimpressive," MacKay said. "How'd that work out?"

"Unfortunately, despite his intelligence, Lobito had… emotional issues. He yearned to be among his own kind. One day, he sneaked out of the Fuzzies compound and tried to make friends with a local wolf pack. They promptly ripped him to shreds."

A display appeared, superimposed over Lobito's image. It read "TOTAL LIFESPAN: FOUR DAYS, TWO HOURS."

MacKay rubbed his chin thoughtfully. "I take it he's not the creature I'll be looking for."

"The animals created using the i-DFM process have tended to be… *limited*," Five-A continued. "They have their uses, but their intelligence has rarely approximated that of human beings. Until recently, that is."

"We've made a breakthrough, don't you know," said Wellington.

"Under the corporate guidance and funding of GenTech, Fuzzies has recently developed an experimental strain of animals with far greater intelligence and range of emotional response than before. The first subjects – a dog, a cat, and a large mouse – showed enormous potential."

MacKay's head was swimming. "So what happened? They break loose and start robbing banks?"

"Not exactly. They've been kidnapped."

"Ah. A corporate raid?"

"Not this time."

Five-A pressed another button on the projector, and an image appeared of a grey-haired, squinty man with little glasses and a tight, nasty smile. "This is Donald Caisson, leader of ACTS – Advanced Covert Theological Storm. They're a survivalist military-stroke-religious group headquartered somewhere in the southern half of the United States – we haven't been able to pinpoint exactly where."

"And they're bloody barking barmy," Wellington said.

"Caisson and his followers are extremely religious. Exactly what faith they follow is a bit hazy, however. They seem to be inspired, on the one hand, by cults like Jonestown, Waco and Glen Burnie, and on the other, by more traditional fundamentalist Christianity. The common element: they really, really dislike outsiders." Five-A paused, then recited, as though by rote: "GenTech is an equal opportunity employer. We support any and all private worship on the part of our employees."

MacKay rolled his eyes.

"In any case," Five-A continued, "According to our intelligence, ACTS believe that Fuzzies' three newest animals hold the key to divine powers on Earth. The holy trinity, perhaps. So they've captured the animals and are using them in some sort of rituals… God knows what exactly."

"Holy trinity," MacKay repeated.

Five-A leaned forwards again. "ACTS is very, very dangerous. The US government had them under surveillance for years. They're a small force – no more than a hundred and ten soldiers, plus families – but their goals are nothing less than conquest of this entire country."

"Sounds a bit ambitious."

"Oh, we're not worried about having to deal with President Caisson anytime soon. If ACTS ever tries a march on Washington, that'll probably be the end of them.

"Our concern is solely with those creatures. GenTech – and Fuzzies, of course – have invested a great deal of money and resources in their development. We want them back if at all possible. But failing that– "

"We want them dead, old boy," said Wellington, with sudden fire in his voice. "This company's secrets are far too valuable to fall into the hands of religious fanatics. And if any of our AI research was to fall into the hands of a rival corporation…"

"A dog, a cat, and a large mouse," MacKay repeated. "Do you have any clues as to where they are?"

Five-A pressed another button. The holo faded, and the lights on the wall-map dimmed. A half-dozen spots along the lower half of the map lit up, stretching west from Alabama all the way to the California coast.

"All Fuzzies animals are implanted with tracking devices at birth," Five-A said. "Unfortunately, ACTS has managed to scramble the trackers' signals. We've compiled this map of possible locations, but some of them may be false readings, or other, older Fuzzies creations showing up on the grid by mistake."

Wellington handed a small electronic device to MacKay. "This tracker will alert you when you get close to one of the little buggers. When you make contact, ring us up and we'll verify your target."

MacKay stared at the machine, which had a single red light on top. "That's assuming I'm near a phone, sat uplink, or in a part of the country with working cell towers."

Wellington smiled at him. "We know you have ways, my boy."

"I need to stress one thing." Five-A's face emitted a slight hissing sound as he strode towards MacKay, looming over him menacingly. "The very existence of these animals is a deep secret. Only a few of them have ever been made – and the general public knows nothing of their existence. Your discretion, Mister MacKay, is essential." He held out a gloved hand. "Do we have a deal?"

MacKay glared at the hand. "I'm not certain. I work with animals – not freaks of nature. I'm not sure it's to my advantage to get involved with this."

The GenTech man's pixelated face was unreadable.

Dog scratched under his arm, then on his lower back.

Wellington stood, laid a hand on Five-A's shoulder. "Thank you very much, old chap. Now would you excuse us for a moment? I'd like a word with Mister MacKay in private."

Five-A aimed an expressionless look at MacKay for a moment, then strode to the door and left in silence.

Wellington smiled. "You'll have to excuse him. Personality of a teabag." As though that reminded him, Wellington sat down again and poured some more tea. "Ever since GenTech bought us out, I've had to deal with just his sort of bureaucrat. Almost a relief that they've become *literally* faceless."

MacKay sat, running the whole thing around in his mind. "Don't get me wrong, Wellington. The money here is very tempting. I'm just not sure—"

"I quite understand, dear sir. Indeed. I've felt a kinship with you since the moment you walked in the door." He fixed a strong gaze on MacKay, and MacKay suddenly saw the force of will that made Wellington an effective company exec, despite the man's clownish quirks. "In a way, we're two sides of the same halfpenny. I create animals, and you destroy them."

"That's not all I do." But MacKay heard the hesitation in his own voice.

"Quite right. And these animals are living, breathing, thinking creatures — not just blips on a vidgame. We don't want some remorseless murderer, some gangcult refugee who'll shoot first and count the blood-soaked paws later. We need a man of proven judgment, compassion, and character. We need…" he paused dramatically, and his eyes lit up, "…the *Ratcatchah*."

MacKay closed his eyes. "You'll deposit half the fee in my account up front?"

Wellington grinned. "Already done, my good man."

MacKay stood, held out his hand. "Then I guess we have a deal."

They shook hands. On the table, Dog jumped, scratched, and tossed the tracking device up in the air. Without looking, MacKay reached out a hand and caught it.

"Behave yourself," he said to Dog, waving the tracker at the lit-up map. "We've got a long trip ahead."

"Indubitably," Wellington said.

10

SHE WAS RIGHT there with them: the things that needed killing.

They hung upside-down in their hideous abattoir, a thousand headless cattle deliberately grown together in one giant, beefy mass, ripe for the slaughter. Their stubby legs hung suspended from the ceiling; the water rose in the bare-metal tank till it touched their hanging neck-stumps. Then the current – thousands of volts surging through the liquid, stunning the cow-things, paralysing them.

Then the bleeding.

They couldn't die till they were bled dry – else the meat would be ruined. Only a select few, the men who processed the world's meat, knew that juicy little detail.

She watched horrified, as paralysed as the cow-things themselves. A stench rose from their electrically-shocked flesh, a smell like the first lit coals in a new barbecue, or the only steakhouse on a hundred-mile stretch of road. She tried to turn away, to repel the assault on her senses. But it was hopeless.

To Mia Sangre's horror, she found the smell delicious.

She couldn't move; she couldn't even tell where she was. Her whole world was the slaughterhouse, this horrible nightmare-place that made her mouth water. Science had made this possible, the twisted science that turned natural creatures into pure beef, that created, in a lab, a no-headed cow-thing with four thousand legs and sixteen thousand pure, juicy ribs. She yearned to stop it, to root out and destroy the place where these horrors were developed and perpetrated on the world. But she was helpless.

Blood dripped into the tank, washed out of the room by powerful water-jets. It was an abomination, a scene from a horror film. The creatures' suffering grew by the minute, all at the whim of some unseen master. Peering into the red-water spray, Mia could almost see his reflection: a tall, gaunt, Chinese man, nodding in satisfaction.

And she could do nothing.

Then she felt a hand on hers. New strength flooded into her, and she tensed for action.

She was a Mad Cow again, an avenger of the animal kingdom. Pure, white-hot anger channelled in the service of her helpless, four-legged brethren. A primal force.

Too bad she had to wake up.

Then she was hurtling down the road at 110 mph on her tricked-out cycle, leading seven other Cows up the battered mess that had once been Route 75. Hank was chattering in her ear, as usual.

"Mi? Are you listening to me?"

She grunted, then looked down at the tracker on her board. The light still blinked a healthy green; MacKay wasn't far ahead of them.

"Mi, I'm kind of tired. Wister-Hauser's getting that hypogly-caemic paranoia he's prone to, and Cristina just got her period. What do you say we stop for the night?"

Mia sighed a sigh that held thirty years of disappointment and exasperation. Sometimes she thought she was getting too old for the gang life. This gang, anyway.

She held up a hand and motioned to the next exit. A fallen concrete divider had smashed into the centre line, but it looked like the cycles could make it around.

Despite everything, the taste of meat still lingered in her mouth.

HANK STOOD IN his briefs, T-shirt, and pleather jacket, ironing his jeans. He looked like an idiot, Mia thought, and the sheer fact of it infuriated her. What kind of gang member *ironed his jeans*?

"...did some checking on this MacKay guy," Hank was saying. "Did you know Brutus used to work with him? At some zoo?"

"Didn't stop MacKay from killing him," Mia muttered. She lay sprawled on the motel room sofa, leafing absently through a magazine.

"Yeah. Pretty cold." Hank held up the jeans, peered at them as though he were judging a prize poodle. Then he crossed to the bathroom and hung them on the shower door. "He's the kind of psycho we got into this business to eradicate."

Mia snapped her head towards him angrily. "What you mean, 'we'? You got into this 'cause you like to ride bikes."

Hank stalked back towards her. "Hey – I believe in the cause. I'm here to help free our animal brethren from the oppression of being our foodstuff. Right?"

He stood right over her now; she stared up at him. "You're here because you had a breakdown and couldn't stand being an exec anymore."

"Oh yeah? Then why are you sleeping with me?"

Mia lowered her eyes to his briefs, which dangled roughly at her level, but she said nothing.

He smiled, watching her. Her long limbs lay stretched out fetchingly. "Come on, baby," he said. "Come to bed."

Then a faint burning smell seeped into the room, and Mia glanced at the window. "Maybe later," she said. "Got to check on the little Cows first."

When she stood up to go, he followed. He was halfway out the door before he remembered his trousers.

Mia shook her head, more disgusted than amused.

OUT BACK OF the motel, on the edge of a grove of trees, the Mad Cows had built a campfire. They didn't need it for the heat; this was Florida, after all. But it gave them some primal sense of community, of fellowship.

"The kids are alright, Mia."

She ignored Hank, looking around at the group.

Shank, a mean, stocky girl, and Jefe, a skinny Cuban, sat in front of the fire, roasting mockmellows and flirting toughly, smacking each other hard on the arms. Britney and Cristina – who were inseparable, and formidable fighters despite their combined weight of 180lbs – had spilled out the contents of their purses on the ground and were trading cosmetics.

Wister-Hauser and Hauser-Wister were arguing philosophy, as usual. He'd gotten her into radical vegetarianism in the first place, but she was the one who'd really taken it on as a crusade. Of all the Cows, they gave Mia the creeps – especially the way they insisted on wearing swastikas on the sleeves of their jackets.

Nevertheless, they were all family. Mia could almost see Brutus and Chester, sitting there with the group.

Never again.

She was tired – tired of this life. But her kids needed her.

She turned and looked at Hank — really looked at him, for the first time in weeks. He was tall and handsome and strong, and a lot of things she liked. But he wasn't what she wanted anymore.

She took his hand, pressed up against him, and spoke to his chest. "Let's go to bed."

LATER, SNUGGLED UNDER the crook of Hank's arm, Mia slept, then woke again to her nightmare. The rusted hooks hung from the ceiling, the meat screamed — chickens, this time, grown to monstrous size in a long daisy-chain, linked like Siamese twins at the sides. Electrodes sparked, feathers flapped in spasms, and blood began to flow.

And once again, she felt the hand in hers, lending her strength. Righteous bloodlust flooded through her. Death in service of life; violence in defence of the helpless. And by her side…

Who?

A heavy bulk fell on her, and Mia woke, panicked. She pushed Hank's body off her, and he tumbled onto his back. Still asleep, he snorted, a contented noise.

Mia stared at the crack-strewn ceiling, listened to the laughter outside, and smelled the faint wood-burning scent of the campfire. She didn't know what was going to happen next, but she knew this much — things were about to change.

part two
the smartest
dog on earth

I

"DOG. KNOCK IT off *now* – or you're riding the rest of the way as the hood ornament."

Ever since the I Heart Florida job, the monkey had developed a particularly irritating habit of jumping up on the dash and scratching madly, sometimes under his arm, sometimes on his lower back. The experience of being held captive by vegetarian extremists seemed to have made him jumpier than usual.

Then again, MacKay reflected, maybe *he* was the one on edge. In order to make the best time to Alabama, he'd driven flat-out across Old Ten through the Florida panhandle – real Dixiecrat territory, some of the most bigoted parts of the South, the kind of places where they still, after all this time, kind of missed slavery. Not that they were far away from returning to it; indentured servitude had made a strong comeback in the South and the corps were more than happy to take advantage.

It wasn't much to look at, either: shacks, crumbling stores, roadside ice cream parlours that seemed to have melted in the heat. MacKay suspected the entire area, the entire state outside of the PZs for all he knew, had collapsed under its own hatred and hypocrisy.

Fifteen minutes ago, they'd finally crossed over into Alabama. They would have been there sooner had the car's GangBuster radar unit not picked up some gangcult activity just before the border forcing them to detour and avoid trouble. That brought with it a whole other problem; had he driven too close to Century and the NeoGen compound there, then he would have been liable for a corporate toll on the stretch of interstate they'd purchased from the State of Florida back in '17. In the end he'd decided to head west and hit the border just after Bratt. The only threat there was the faded "Vote Clinton in 2012" billboard that somebody had either forgotten, or couldn't be bothered, to take down.

MacKay was tired and bleary, and his water supply was getting low. The tracking device showed they were about three hours out from the first blip on GenTech's map.

Which gave MacKay time to think. And even more than before, things weren't quite adding up.

"I don't buy Wellington's description of Fuzzies' business," he said aloud, turning to address the fidgeting monkey. "That's an awfully big corporate headquarters for a company that churns out two or three experimental animals a year."

Keek! Keek!

"I know, he said that crap about GenTech moving some of their administrative functions there after the disaster in Narcoossee. But it still sounds wrong. And how the hell am I supposed to hunt these critters when I don't even know what they look like?"

Dog had no answer to that one.

If MacKay had been disgusted by Florida, Alabama was a different kind of horror show. Where Florida seemed rundown, abandoned, torn and tossed by hurricanes and neglect, Alabama was just *poor*. Handmade signs lined nearly every roadside exit, practically begging you to stop by and have some homemade pie or a cheap night's sleep. But the glimpses of towns MacKay saw from the highway made him shudder.

Ten miles past Montgomery, MacKay pulled off the highway and began the eight-mile trip through NoGo Alabammy to his destination. The roads here weren't even really roads — more like dirt paths with sad traces of old pavement, long since torn up or overgrown with weeds. The Interceptor's PlasTyres screeched and bumped their way along, jolting MacKay and making Dog scratch even more.

At last they came to a town. If you could call it that.

The faded sign, lettered in once-bright 1990s colours, read CRUDUP, ALABAMA — A HELL OF A NICE PLACE T'LIVE. Maybe it had been, once. Now it looked like twelve blocks of rundown houses, paint peeling and big old porches propped up unsteadily with unfinished wood pilings. MacKay's carbon-armoured Interceptor tooled slowly through the pot-holed streets, past pickups, small imports, and the occasional bike — none of them less than ten years old. A few shoeless children and obese old people sat on the porches, staring.

"Feeling conspicuous yet?" he asked Dog.

The tracker was blinking an almost-solid red, so MacKay pulled up GenTech's map on his windshield NavMap. He linked the tracker to it and zoomed in. The animal's signal was coming not from the centre of town, but just past it. Good. MacKay really didn't want to attract any more attention in this hellhole.

He pressed the pedal down further, toying with the speed limit. He didn't want to get pulled over in these parts, either. These small southern towns changed hands frequently, coming under the control of various warlords. And some of them could be downright nasty.

The centre of Crudup consisted of a half-boarded-up post office, a heavily fenced bank, a faded motel, an indenture recruitment office and an All-Mart. MacKay supposed the All-Mart had been carved up into various shops, stalls, and drinking establishments, as so many of them had down here. Who knows, if they'd not held out for so long during the corporate takeover wars of the 2010s then they might still be in business today instead of their former premises being used as hangouts for drunks and trailer trash.

As Crudup thinned out, the terrain became rougher. The tracker seemed to be leading them up one particular, steep hill, past a few abandoned shacks and a lot of dead trees. The trees grew thicker, partially shielding a few small houses from view. MacKay followed the trail up a winding driveway, over gravel pebbles the size of softballs. It ended before a house.

The house was nothing special, but it looked freshly painted. Thick bushes hid it from the road and from its neighbours; an old pickup truck sat in the driveway. As MacKay pulled the Interceptor to a halt, two figures appeared at the front door.

MacKay palmed the tracker, opened the door and got out; Dog hopped quickly onto his shoulder. They watched, curious, as a big, round man with a dull expression pushed a wheelchair down a ramp towards them. The figure in the wheelchair was mostly covered by a blanket, but MacKay saw enough of it to make his breath catch.

It was a dog – but not an ordinary dog. A dog that sat upright, in the chair, the way a person would; a dog with sharp, penetrating eyes and a limp, flaccid body. A dog that looked like all the air had been let out of it.

It opened its mouth.

"Howdy, strangers," it said. "Welcome to Crudup."

Even Dog was speechless.

II

THE WHEELCHAIR-BOUND mutt shook, trembled, and finally raised a front paw. MacKay realised the creature wanted to shake hands, and hurriedly stuck his out. The big man just watched, mute.

"Good to see you've got some manners, son," the dog said. "Do you speak too?"

"Fuck me, you're a talking dog!" Although most of the initial shock had washed off of MacKay this was about as eloquent a response as he could muster.

"I take back my previous comment. Are you always this rude to strangers?" The dog spoke in a peculiar drawn out drawl, the way he said previous sounded as if the word was spelt with about twenty "e"s.

"But... but... you're a talking dog!"

"I think we've established that I'm a talking dog. Now are you going to tell me who you are or am I going to have to ask you to leave?"

MacKay recovered himself. "Sorry, sir. Batton MacKay, Sanctioned Operative. This is my friend, Dog."

The dog – the real dog – stared at the monkey for a second. "Why d'you call him Dog?"

"Always wanted a dog."

The dog stared at him with new respect. "Well, come on inside. Any dog lover's welcome in my house."

MacKay followed, frowning.

Was this the intelligent dog the GenTech exec had described? It seemed too old for that, and its AI was kind of decrepit. When it spoke, its mouth only opened a fraction, and it had trouble with articulation. MacKay supposed a genetically enhanced animal might have some trouble with human speech, but this one seemed actively handicapped.

And while the dog's house was creepy and isolated, it didn't exactly look like a cult headquarters.

MacKay considered making some excuse, slipping away, and calling Fuzzies for confirmation. But a quick glance at his Han-Held showed no cell towers in the area, which wasn't a big surprise. He could use the car's satphone, but that would (a) cost a fortune and (b) let anyone at the corps know his location. Somehow he felt he should stay off the grid as much as possible. Dealing with GenTech *and* Thalamus in the space of two days had made him paranoid.

The dog showed him into a small, tacky but comfortable living room. Old furniture, old lamps, new MP7 player. "Sit down, stranger," he said. "Like some water?"

MacKay realised he was parched. "Thank you."

"Fluffa?"

The big man turned without a word and walked to the kitchen.

"Hang on one minute if you would, sir." MacKay pressed a button on his HanHeld and a small earpiece popped out. He placed it in his ear and pulled up the consonant adjustment screen on the HanHeld. "Would you say a few sentences, please?"

"Say a few sentences?" MacKay fiddled with the HanHeld as the dog drawled on. "You're a funny one, mister. What you want next – I should do some tricks?"

MacKay smiled. "No sir – thank you very much. Just adjusting things so I can understand you better." Then, suddenly afraid he'd offended the creature, he added, "Standard procedure."

"When you're talking to a gimp?"

MacKay looked away.

But the dog seemed to be smiling. "No problem, stranger. I'm all for enhanced communication. Name's Sputo."

The name was vaguely familiar. "Sputo… the dog who went into space?"

"My fame precedes me."

Now MacKay remembered.

Ten years ago, a company called Private Space had won Britain's coveted XXX Prize which – despite its name – was not an award for outstanding porn, but a grant to develop space-travel vehicles. As part of its PR campaign, Private Space had made a minor media celeb out of its pilot: a dog named Sputo.

All the publicity had described Sputo as "the smartest dog on Earth". MacKay, along with everyone else, had assumed it was just a catchphrase. But no.

Sputo was a Fuzzy.

"That capsule almost caught fire seven times," Sputo recalled. "An ordinary dog woulda been toast."

Fluffa came back into the room with a healthy pitcher of water. MacKay's mouth watered as the big man poured two glasses.

"'I'm ready for my supper, Fluffa," Sputo said. "Chop it up good'n'fine now. Thanks."

Fluffa returned to the kitchen.

MacKay tried not to gulp his water all at once. "What happened to Private Space?"

"Bad management, then the economy collapsed. No market for space travel. Whole thing just fell apart."

"And you?"

"Too much time in zero-G." Sputo raised a feeble paw, pointed at his lower legs. "My bones an' muscles atrophied badly. Can't chase sticks no more, that's for sure."

"So you retired here."

"This place's too poor for even the warlords to care about – probably why you had such an easy run out here. And the locals take good care of me."

Almost on cue, a wheezing, battered pickup truck pulled up outside. A wizened, pocked, black man in his fifties, with perfect teeth, poked his head in the door. He carried a big jug with XX written on the side. "Spoot? Y'alright in there?"

"Just fine, Willy. Thanks."

"Saw you had company." The man glared briefly at MacKay.

"'It's cool. We're just reminiscing about old times."

Willy dropped the jug on the coffee table. "I brung you some moonshine. Payback for last month."

"Not necessary, Willy. But that's very kind."

"No problem, buddy. You saved my ass from them indenturers."

Sputo stared a bit helplessly at the jug. Then he said to MacKay: "Would you do the honours?"

MacKay downed his water, then refilled both glasses from the jug. It smelled like battery acid. Dog sniffed at it, recoiled.

Willy looked around suspiciously. "Where's Fluffa?"

"Kitchen. Chopping my meat."

"You sure everything's okay?"

"If it wasn't, I'd have you take this cracker out back and shoot his ass."

MacKay looked up sharply.

"It's all good, Willy. Thanks again."

"Yell if ya need me, Spoot." He glanced pointedly at MacKay again, then left.

MacKay took a tentative sip of the whiskey. "I see what you mean about the locals."

"They're good folks… most of 'em. I do their taxes, keep the indenture folks away… talk the warlords out of settling here once in a while. An I got a dentist up here six months ago. Did everyone's teeth." He grinned a broken, gap-toothed grin. "Except mine."

Fluffa walked back in carrying a tray-table covered with small, finely-chopped bits of raw beef. Sputo looked up; a bit of drool escaped from his mouth. "Pardon me, Mister MacKay. It's my dinnertime."

MacKay nodded.

Sputo dived into the meat, hoovering it up with small, jerky movements. It was disturbing to watch, the sharp jaws searching for rare, bloody bits. "I love my meat," he said between bites. "Got real scarce for a few years there, when the economy went to hell. Never got a taste for shamburgers."

"Me neither." Especially, MacKay thought, after the terrorist plot that had caused them to expand violently inside their victims' stomachs, killing hundreds of people. The fast-food industry had never quite recovered.

"But did you notice? Last few years, meat's easy to find again."

MacKay realised he'd never thought about it. "Yeah. Why is that?"

"Dunno. I don't question life's little miracles."

MacKay waited while the pooch finished his one-course meal, then leaned forwards.

"Sputo… I don't want to disrupt your life here or anything. But I've gotta ask you something." He took a breath. "You're a product of Fuzzies, Inc – right?"

Sputo looked up at him suspiciously.

"Now, don't worry. I been sent to recover a few of their animals… but you don't qualify. They're only interested in the newer models."

"Professor Wan send you?"

MacKay shook his head. "What?"

"Never mind." He fished into his blanket, pulled out a small wad of bills. "Fluffa… it's getting late. Go down the town and buy me some lottery tickets. Pick-Nos, Scratch-Off, and a couple for yourself."

Fluffa took the money and smiled, for the first time.

"Hurry back now."

Fluffa practically danced his giant bulk over to the door. Outside, MacKay heard him start up the old pickup and race away.

"It's, uh, it's good of you to find employment for the mentally challenged."

Sputo looked at him, eyes twinkling. "You don't know much about Alabama, do you, stranger? Alabama fell apart long before the rest of the US. Started in '04 with the massive budget cuts… public schools closed down completely by 2010. Long before the rest of the country went to hell."

MacKay looked at him, confused.

"Fluffa ain't challenged. He just never went to school."

MacKay didn't know what to say. He picked up Dog and stroked the monkey's metal skin.

Sputo lapped at his whiskey. "So you're working for Fuzzies?"

"Contract job. Couple of their animals have been kidnapped."

"Nasty business. Usually is with Fuzzies."

MacKay leaned forwards. "You don't like them?"

"Always a strange company. But more so since GenTech took 'em over."

"You *were* one of their, uh, creations… right?"

"Yeah. Bought and paid for with Private Space's IPO money. I was one of the last ones they made before GenTech came in."

"You think that changed things? GenTech's management?"

"Yes and no. Of course GenTech's got a touch of the… dark side about them but there was always something odd about Fuzzies." Sputo paused. "Must be Professor Wan. He's got his fingers in everywhere."

It was the second time the dog had mentioned Professor Wan, and for the second time, a chill went up MacKay's back, though he'd never heard the name before.

"This Professor Wan. He made you?"

"Me, the mouse, the bird… it's hard to remember." The whiskey seemed to be hitting Sputo now. His head lolled to the side a bit.

"All I know is… there's changes coming. Big, bad changes."

MacKay sipped at the foul whiskey, feeling its fingers reach into his brain. He knew he needed to stay alert; this was red-neck territory, and while Sputo seemed friendly, it was always possible the dog was planning to rob him, to steal his monkey and his Interceptor. An Op, especially a solo, didn't last long by letting his guard down.

But as MacKay listened to the big-brained, feeble-limbed dog descend into paranoid rambling, a beautiful face in Goth revival makeup seemed to superimpose itself on his thoughts. She seemed larger than when he'd seen her on the HanHeld's screen, more vivid. More real.

Dog chittered, trying to rouse his master. But MacKay was lost in dreams of an angel.

III

THE MIDDLE-EASTERN clerk pressed his fingers against his nose, just below his eyes. It was going to be a long night.

On the other side of the counter stood Fluffa, head cocked to look up at the hanging lottery tickets. He smiled a small, dull smile. Two people stood in line behind him, staring at him. In the background a muzak version of Radiohead's "Karma Police" droned through a set of cheap speakers.

The clerk forced a smile to his face. "May I help you sir?" he asked. For the fourth time.

At last Fluffa smiled a little wider, and pointed, tentatively, to one of the tickets.

"Scratch-Off?"

Fluffa nodded.

"How many?"

Fluffa raised a hand to his chin, cocked his head again.

Four people stood behind him now.

"Four perhaps?"

Fluffa nodded.

"Very well sir. That'll be—"

Fluffa leaned forwards menacingly, pointed at another hanging ticket.

Seven people in line.

"Jack-Me-Ten." The clerk sighed. "How many?"

Hand to chin; head cocked.

"Four?"

Fluffa shook his head, violently.

"Six?"

Fluffa smiled, nodded.

The clerk moved quickly to the cash register. Without looking up, he said, "Two hundred and twelve eighteen with tax, thank you sir."

Silence.

Slowly, eyes squeezed half-shut with dread, he looked up.

Fluffa was pointing to another ticket.

FORTY-THREE FEET away, in another part of the carved-up All-Mart, the Mad Cows were occupying about a third of a small, dark, smoky drinking establishment. Mia sat at one end of the bar, morosely nursing a whiskey and soda. Tinny country music spazzed through the air all around her, jangling her nerves.

Mia was trying not to think about her dreams, which had grown more intense. Sometimes she could even see the images in the daytime: genetically enlarged turkeys, packed into concrete pens, as many as ten per square foot – no air, no room to move, just feeding tubes and electric slaughter.

Mia was also trying not to think about Hank. Which, as usual, was his cue.

"Mi," he said, sidling up next to her. "What are we doing here? We're gonna lose MacKay."

She studied her whiskey glass. "We won't lose him."

"I just don't understand why we're in here getting drunk."

"We're a *biker gang*, Hank. Bikers go to bars and get drunk." She signalled the bartender for a refill. "Besides, I'm strategising."

"That's what you call it?"

She turned to him, murder in her eye. "You got something to say to me?"

He gritted his teeth, started to shake a little. God, she hated it when he did that! "I'm just saying… you don't seem to have had a lot of time for me lately."

"Yeah, well – maybe I've got more important things on my mind." She couldn't resist. "*Bigger* things."

He glared at her for a minute, then spun and walked away.

Mia laughed bitterly.

She looked around at the rest of the Cows, all up to their usual tricks. Shank was perched a couple stools over, downing massively strong shots, while Jefe poured for her. Wister-Hauser and Hauser-Wister sat in a corner, clad in their brown shirts, glaring at everyone. And Britney and Cristina were flirting with a couple of tank-topped, acned local boys. I really should have a talk with those two, Mia thought. One of these days, they'll get themselves into a situation it'll take the whole gang to get them out of.

The whole gang. It seemed like a heavier weight every day.

In a way, Hank was right. They were wasting time. But MacKay seemed to have stopped for the night, a few miles away, and before the Cows moved in on him, Mia wanted more information about the creature he'd tracked here. The Mad Cows were a tough gangcult, but if MacKay was now allied with, say, a giant carnivorous crocodile, she wanted to know about it before she went charging up the hill with lightweight combat lasers.

Besides, sometimes a girl just needed a drink.

"Mia? Umm… Mia? Hey?"

It was Cristina. Her beret-topped fake-blonde hair flapped onto the bar.

"Keep those braids out of my drink, Cris."

"Sorry, Mia. Just thought you'd wanna know… me an' Brit been talkin' to these totally cool guys who–"

"That's nice, Cris."

"–who say there's a *dog* livin' in a house up the hill."

Mia looked up. She downed her drink.

"Strategising," she muttered, pulling herself to her feet. "Lead the way, Cris."

HANK POLEHOUSE WAS pissed off. He'd been treated like dirt all his life by parents, schoolmates, teachers, and bosses. He still remembered the day GenTech had laid him off. When they offered him "compensatory outplacement services", he'd told them to shove it up their asses. Or at least, over the years, he'd convinced himself he'd told them that.

Now his own girlfriend didn't even seem to want him anymore. And after all he'd done for her. He'd pulled strings to get the gang's bikes fitted with lightweight, detachable combat lasers; no other gangcult in the southeast had that kind of firepower. Maybe sometime soon he'd even put in a training request so the gang could actually learn how to use them properly. He'd filled out the Cows' organisational structure, creating a crucial middle management position – for himself, of course. He'd even agreed, admittedly after considerable debate, to perform mutually in the area of oral gratification.

He'd given up eating *bacon*, for God's sake! What more could you ask of a man?

"Screwdriver," he said to the bartender. The man raised an eyebrow and pulled out a carton of Tropicana Nearly Natural. The flickering holo playing on the side of the container was of a now missing girl blowing out the candles at her eighth birthday party. The incongruity of the image was lost on both Hank and the bartender.

"Rough time with your woman?"

Hank looked over at the man next to him. He was thin as a rail, hard edges all around, and his skin looked like it'd been worked over with sandpaper. But his teeth were perfect.

"You could say that," Hank replied.

"We all been there, my friend." He sighed heavily, and Hank almost passed out at the sour-liquor smell. "Women an' men… they ain't meant to be together all the time. Makes 'em both crazy."

Hank grunted.

A burst of laughter erupted from behind him, and he turned to see Britney giggling and touching a local boy's arm. No discipline at all, Hank thought. If he were running the Cows, they wouldn't be sitting in his shithole – they'd be on MacKay by now like cubicle workers on a free stapler. And he *should* be running the gang, dammit. He was the one with management experience!

"Ah miss the old days," the drunk next to him continued. "Used to be, your woman got outta line, *bap!* Quick left to the jaw. Ended the argument for good. Can't do that no more, though. FemDom gangcults would string you right up by your macadamias."

Hank grimaced. He took a big yellow sip.

"Take my woman," the man said. "She got a mouth on her! An' not in a good way. I mean, sometimes in a good way, sure. But mostly…" He leaned right into Hank, putting most of his weight on Hank's shoulder, and stage-whispered: "… mostly she got her trap flapping wide like a old woman. Yip yip yip yip!"

"I hear you," Hank hissed, pushing the man back upright.

The drunk leaned back in, touched a surprisingly gentle hand to Hank's chest. "Then she wants to *cuddle*." He unzipped Hank's Mad Cow jacket and, as Hank watched in shock, felt around inside. The other locals watched, pointing and snickering, as the drunk's voice rose to a falsetto. "Oooooh, *baaaaaa*beeee, I'm *sorrrrrrrr*eee. Of *coorrrrrrrse* y'kin put it in me now. Just make it *quiiiiiiiiick* – like *uuuuuuuu*sual."

He tweaked Hank's nipple.

"Get off me, you brain-damaged redneck!"

Hank pushed the drunk, who tottered and fell sideways into the next man at the bar – a big bruiser with a red face. Beer spilled onto the big man.

"What's your problem?" the thin drunk said.

The bruiser pulled himself up to full height, looking at the beer stain on his sleeveless Petya Tcherkassof muscle shirt. "I'd be fascinated to know that myself, friend."

Hank swallowed.

★ ★ ★

"Yeah, we started little Jayston here on the Junior Ritalin early." The man, whose name was Mr Hatter, held up a little child in a flowery bundle. "One time he spit some food on the floor, an' we figured, it's gonna happen sooner or later. Why wait?"

"Uh-huh," Mia said, shying away. Babies repulsed her.

Mrs Hatter held up a bottle proudly. "We like to mix it with Jack Daniels," she said. "Keeps the little darlin' right quiet."

"You can't go wrong with old Jack," Mr Hatter added.

"About this dog," Mia said.

Britney and Cristina had introduced her to the Hatters, and then promptly returned to flirting with the family's two teenage boys... which left Mia with a pair of drunken lunatics whose idea of a family night out, apparently, was a trip to the filthiest bar in town.

"Yeah – old *Sputo*," Mr Hatter said. He spat the dog's name like a curse. "He's some kinda astronaut hero or somethin'. They say."

"Lotta folks stick up for him," Mrs Hatter said. She poured beer from a pitcher into Mia's glass, sloshing some on her own ample jeans. "But I can't help noticing... ever since he arrived in Crudup, folks just keep getting poorer an' poorer."

"He stole our welfare check once. Dang thing just disappeared. Can't prove it, but I know it was him."

Mia took a sip of the acidic beer. She had just come to three conclusions:

One, the Hatters might not be mad, but they were powerful drunks. Their "missing" welfare check had probably long ago been converted into moonshine.

Two, she could probably talk them into absolutely anything.

And three, folks in Crudup would keep getting poorer even if the sky rained thousand-dollar bills.

"I, uh, got a beef with that dang dog too," Mia said, consciously slipping into the Hatters' accent. "How'd y'all like to–"

KA-RASSH!

Mia knew what – or rather, who – it was, even before she turned around. Sure enough, up at the bar, Hank was stepping back, trying to look brave and failing pathetically, as a gigantic man in a faded Petya Tcherkassof t-shirt menaced him with a broken bottle. A smaller, thin man stood next to him, weaving back and forth drunkenly.

"Alright,". Hatter said, swigging his beer and standing up. "A fight!"

Without a conscious thought, Mia stood up, strode to the bar, and backhanded Hank across the face. He crumpled into a heap, stunned and shocked.

The other Cows gathered in a semicircle, ready to fight. Britney took point, looking to Mia for their next move.

"Sorry about my idiot friend," Mia said to the big man.

"A gallant gesture, ma'am," the man said, flexing his biceps. "And, if I may say, an impressive left cross as well. But you'll note that the gentleman in question has soiled my collectors' item garment. It's from Comrade Tcherkassof's farewell tour of the southern states."

"I hear you," she said. "Would you take his motorcycle in return?"

Hank gaped in astonishment.

The man was only slightly less stunned, but recovered quickly. "Very generous, ma'am. I humbly accept your offer."

Dazed, Hank pulled himself upright against the bar. "My… my bike?"

Mia reached into his jacket and fished out his keys. "Be glad I didn't just let this guy fillet you." She tossed the keys to the large man.

Hank turned to her, tried to smile. "Guess this means I'll have to ride with you for a while."

"We'll draw straws. Now go outside."

Hank gave her a stunned look. Then he staggered to the door, a defeated man.

Mia turned back to the Hatters, who stood hooting and applauding.

"Ma'am," said Mr Hatter, "that was some show!"

"Thank you," Mia said. "Brit, Cris — would you arrange for the Hatters to take us to see this Sputo?"

The two girls moved, with their reluctant new boyfriends, back to the elder Hatters' table. The boys clearly didn't want to associate with their parents, but Cristina and Britney were charmers. Soon Mr Hatter took Britney by the shoulder and walked her to the bar window, which faced the inside of the shopping complex. He pointed outside, across the mall, where a long line had formed outside a cigarette counter window.

His other hand dropped perilously close to Britney's ass, but miraculously never touched it.

At the table, the Hatters' baby started to whine. Mrs Hatter fed it a nipple of Ritalin and Jack, and it quieted right down again.

Cristina and Britney were good kids, Mia thought. And the Mad Cows had been her life for as long as she could remember. She'd endured bumps in the road like Hank before.

But as she watched the Hatters feed their baby liquor, the enormity of it all descended on her. She thought of thousands of mutilated cattle hanging from hooks, of passionless sex with a man she didn't love, of miles and miles of broken road. And suddenly she knew.

She'd had enough.

"PICK-NOS?"

Fluffa twisted up his face in a grotesque parody of human thought.

Behind him, the line now stretched all the way across the tiled hallway to the bar.

The clerk was near tears. He almost wished he were back in Guantanamo Bay.

"Sir… *please*. Pick-Nos?"

Suddenly a woman's strong, lithe hand placed a firm grip on Fluffa's shoulder. She wore a biker jacket decorated with a snorting bull smoking a stick of celery. Six other bikers clustered around her, and a local family with a baby. The clerk vaguely recalled the family as frequent purchasers of beef jerky.

"Okay, Hayseed," the woman said, fixing Fluffa with a steely gaze. "Time to see a man about a dog."

Bewildered, Fluffa followed them off, lottery tickets clutched sloppily in his fist.

The clerk nearly wept with happiness.

10

"FLUFFA'S BEEN GONE a while," Sputo drawled. "Sometimes he has trouble making his consumer desires understood."

MacKay nodded drowsily. He shook his head, tried to clear it. Maybe the moonshine had been a mistake.

"Lottery's the only reliable government agency left. It's 'cos it's run by the Mafia, from up north." Sputo sighed. "South ain't got nothing left to call its own."

"Mmm," MacKay said. "North ain't got much either." He thought of his old zoo, lying in ashy ruin, the animals torn and mortar-blown to shreds. He fought back a tear.

"Where you based, McKay?"

"DC, originally. All over, these days." MacKay shrugged. "Sleep in my car, half the time."

"Wise feller," said Willy. He'd returned a while ago – an hour? two? – with another jug, anticipating Sputo's need for a refill. ("New batch, Spoot – I added a touch of nutmeg.") Willy had gotten over his suspicion of MacKay, and now the two of them sat sprawled out on the couch, side by side. Even Dog, who didn't drink, had adopted a couch potato pose in imitation of the humans. He hadn't moved in twenty minutes.

All they needed was a major sporting event. And a TV set to watch it on.

"You're a wise feller, Ratcatcher," Willy repeated.

"'It's a stupid name," MacKay said. But he laughed.

"Ratcatcher," Sputo slurred, and giggled drunkenly.

Keek! Keek!

MacKay gazed around the house, at the faded plaid furniture paid for with government benefits. He looked at the wizened old dog, lower body covered by the wheelchair's blanket, and the XXX Prize citations on the wall, half-covering cracks in the plaster. He looked at Willy, leaning sideways on the couch – a man who couldn't find work, so he devoted his considerable energies to improving his homemade moonshine.

And MacKay thought of how many people lived like this, in this once-great country. Scraping by, trying to keep the ceiling from falling in. Creating projects to keep themselves busy, convincing themselves those projects were somehow important. Numbing themselves with foul, cheap liquor to banish the hideous doubts and insecurities.

It was depressing to think about. But it was also oddly seductive. Sure seemed like a lot less work than shootouts with clinically insane Vegans.

MacKay forced himself to concentrate. "Sputo… I got to ask you something else. You seem like a pretty smart guy. Animal. Dog, I mean."

"Damn right he's smart," Willy said. "Smartest man or beast in Crudup."

"Yeah. Anyway… when I was at Fuzzies, they made it sound like all their animals were… uh, pretty limited in the thinking and speaking department. Till recently, anyway."

Sputo growled, low. "That's kind of insulting."

"Yeah. And it doesn't really add up. Were you… I mean, could the others talk as well as you? Think as well?"

"I dint really know too many of 'em… they'd get made an then shipped right off to the clients. But I think they were all pretty smart."

MacKay was trying to make sense of that when Dog jumped bolt upright. *Keek! Keek! Keek Keek Keek!*

MacKay heard the motorcycles, and was instantly alert.

"Ain't never had much trouble with bikers," Sputo said, eyeing the window. Willy moved to the door with MacKay, and they both peered outside.

"Makes one of us," MacKay said. "Can't see 'em yet."

He fingered his Shredder; he hoped it wasn't the Mad Cows outside. And then, thinking of Mia, he almost hoped it was.

A rock thumped against the door from outside, then another. MacKay motioned Willy and Sputo back, then flung the door open and tossed himself backwards, out of the line of fire. Cautiously, the three of them peered at the opening.

Then the baby crawled in.

"Why did we put the camera on his ass, again?"

Mia hated this plan. It seemed the height of cruelty to use a baby as a stalking horse against an armed killer. But the Hatters had eagerly volunteered their child —"He's a scrappy little bastard!" — and Wister-Hauser had so wanted to use his little spy-camera gadget. And Mia hadn't had a better plan to scout out the dog's house.

She hated babies, anyway. So what the hell?

"It's not on his ass," Wister-Hauser said stiffly, fiddling with the small monitor. "It's clipped to his diaper."

They stood huddled together in the thick brush outside Sputo's house: eight Mad Cows, two Hatters, and one hostage. Jefe, Shank, and Cristina guarded the gagged and trussed Fluffa, who stood propped up against a tree, sobbing softly.

The night was hot, and the ride up had been contentious. Hank had been forced to ride with Hauser-Wister, who kept threatening to cut off his roving hands with her Bowie knife. Hank had protested his innocence, but it didn't really sound any more convincing than anything else coming out of his mouth. At least the Hatter boys hadn't come along — Britney had slipped a Junior Rohyp into their underage beers, and they were still sleeping it off in the bar.

Wister-Hauser's monitor showed a fuzzy, floor-level view of throw rugs, stained wood floor, and the wheels of a wheelchair.

"That's the damn dog's chair," Mr Hatter said, fingering a big old shotgun. "You watch — li'l Jayston'll fall down pretty soon an' you'll see."

"He can't crawl for shit," Mrs Hatter laughed.

Sure enough, the camera angle shot upwards as the baby's head dropped, pitching his ass up. Mia caught a glimpse of a big-snouted dog with more wrinkles than she'd ever seen on an animal, staring fixedly into the monitor.

"This plan sucks ass," Hank said weakly, scratching at a superficial bramble-cut. "Holy Jesus – what kind of an animal is that, anyway?"

Mia ignored him.

"I can't believe you gave away my bike," Hank continued. "The Mad Cows used to be tough – we used to fight for things."

She rounded on him, and he flinched back. "Some things just aren't worth fighting for, asshole. And don't you start lecturing *me* about the old days."

Hank backed off, grumbling.

On the monitor, a distorted fish-eye image of MacKay leaned down to look at the baby. MacKay spoke, but only static came from the monitor.

"You got sound on that thing, Mister?" asked Mr Hatter.

"I'm working on it."

Mia stared at the image of MacKay. A flickering image from her dreams crossed her mind: a freakishly large cow, being milked and bled to death simultaneously.

Then voices started coming from the monitor.

"Holy shit, MacKay," a black man said, leaning down and pointing out of the screen. "I think his ass is transmitting!"

On the screen, MacKay made a sharp motion, and the robot monkey jumped into view.

The screen went blank.

"Oh my God," Mrs Hatter screamed. "My *baby*!"

DOG SAT ON the floor, back-to-back with the baby. The baby cooed and gurgled happily. The monkey's tail was raised; it emitted a small, mechanical humming noise.

"Good boy," MacKay said. Then, to Sputo and Willy: "He's jamming the signal."

"That's quite a monkey," Sputo said. Dog smiled, wagged his head.

Willy leaned down to scratch the baby under his chin. "He's a cute little feller, this one. Real little charmer, ain't you?"

The baby caught sight of Willy's XX jug on the coffee table, and reached out its arms.

Then the door blew in with a crash, and the Hatters appeared – both brandishing huge, rusty shotguns. "You sumbitch!" Mr Hatter yelled. "Get your dirty dog paws off my–"

MacKay leapt to his feet and fired automatically. MiniShredder bullets ripped through the couple. They spasmed, gurgled, and went down in the doorway.

The baby let out a small, questioning sound.

Willy rose from the couch and pulled out a concealed, old-style revolver. Sputo wheeled back a bit, towards the kitchen. "Shit," he said.

"That's far enough, MacKay." Mia appeared in the doorway, shielded by Fluffa's enormous bulk. The big man's eyes were squeezed shut, his mouth was gagged, his arms and legs tied. And Mia held a gun to his temple.

MacKay raised his gun, grimacing. "Drop it," Mia said. "Or I do him right now."

Past her, MacKay could hear the rest of the Mad Cows approaching.

Out of the corner of his eye, MacKay noticed that the baby had somehow climbed onto the coffee table and was hugging the moonshine bottle. Keeping his gaze on Mia – not an unpleasant task – he reached back and grabbed the baby in one quick, fluid motion. Then he held it up in front of him and aimed his Shredder at its head.

"You drop it," he said.

Mia's lovely face went even whiter than usual. "You're threatening to *kill* a *baby*?"

"I didn't get him into this. You did."

"You just offed his parents."

"They aimed their guns at me." The tall Cow, the one who looked like a corporate exec, had appeared at Mia's shoulder. MacKay motioned at him. "Keep that psycho back."

"Put the baby down, MacKay."

"I don't think that's what's going to happen. I think you're going to back right out of that doorway and drop Fluffa there on the lawn for us to untie later. And then I think you're going to get on your bikes and head on out of here."

The tall psycho moved forwards. "That's not how we work, killer. You're going to pay for your crimes against the animal world."

MacKay fixed him with a gaze, and pressed the gun against the baby's temple. "One more step and I ventilate this little orphan – then you."

"Tell him, MacKay," Willy said, aiming his pistol. "I got your back."

Dog jumped up and down, *keek*-ing in agreement.

"Back off, Hank," Mia said, shoving the tall Cow backwards.

The other Cows pushed in, crowding the doorway. Some of them looked down at the Hatters' bodies, blocking the way.

Fluffa whimpered.

Sputo picked that moment to wheel forwards. "Listen," he said. "You're all guests in my house. Why don't y'all just put down the guns–"

But Hank raised his gun, aimed straight at the handicapped dog. His mouth fell open. "Shit," he sneered. "That thing's even uglier in person–"

All at once, MacKay crouched down and slid the baby along the floor, towards Dog. With his other hand, he fired low, catching Hank on the leg. The tall man howled and lurched backwards, out of the door.

Mia jumped forwards and leaped onto MacKay, startling him. He tried to aim his Shredder at her, but she smacked his arm hard against his side. "You bastard!"

He pushed her back. She spat at him, and he flinched. He shook his head, looked at her rage-red face. God, she was beautiful.

Bereft of support, Fluffa tottered in the doorway, his legs still securely bound.

Mia and MacKay rolled behind the coffee table, clawing at each other madly. As soon as she was out of sight, the other Cows opened fire. MacKay was startled to notice that some of them wielded lightweight combat lasers, the kind that clipped on and off bikes; where the hell had they gotten hold of *those*? Others held M-78s, with and without ScumShredder ammo. Red beams shot around Sputo's living room, scorching spots on the walls. Bullets ricocheted madly.

Willy had positioned himself behind a big bookcase and was taking pot-shots. Dog had the baby's diaper clutched firmly in his mouth; he dragged the infant backwards across the floor, carefully avoiding the crossfire.

Little Jayston cooed happily, pointing at the red laser-trails above.

MacKay grabbed Mia's hand, knocking her gun away. She looked at his hand and jolted, as though an electric shock had gone through her. She slowly turned to him, and for a frozen moment, they stared into each other's eyes.

He remembered what she'd said to him, back in Florida. *Do you* like *killing things?*

Dog dragged the baby over to Sputo, who snatched the two of them up and wheeled quickly out of the room.

Bullets flew; beams stabbed through the air. A full-sized ScumShredder shot blew a chandelier into metal splinters. A stray laser hit a stand-up lamp, which exploded, darkening the room.

A couple more of the Mad Cows had penetrated the room. One of them, a tall anorexic-looking blonde girl, peered over the coffee table. "Mia?"

Mia smacked MacKay in the eye, hard enough to hurt. Then she pushed him away violently, held up a hand. "Brit – cease fire!"

"Cease fire!" the girl repeated.

The shooting stopped.

The room was silent, filled with smoke and the smell of death.

Mia stumbled to the doorway. MacKay tracked her through his Shredder's sight, but he couldn't bring himself to pull the trigger. He watched as she stepped over the dead Hatters and pushed past the wobbling Fluffa, motioning with a lovely, pleather-sheathed arm for her gang to follow.

"Pull back, for God's sake," she said. Then: "Hank–"

Face contorted with fury, Hank crawled back to the doorway, aimed at MacKay, and fired.

MacKay dove back down quickly, under the table. Hank's bullets went wild.

One of them struck Fluffa in the heart.

Through the open door, MacKay saw Mia strike Hank, hard, and hustle the Cows away from the house.

Fluffa hit the floor with a shattering thud.

Outside, the Cows' bikes thundered away.

Willy examined the big, trussed man. "Aw, shit," he said. "I'm sorry, Spoot."

Sputo had wheeled himself back into the room, with the baby on one knee and Dog on the other. "Me too," he said.

The baby's little eyes wandered from Fluffa's body to those of his parents, still lying in the doorway. Then it focused on the coffee table again, and made a happy, cooing sound.

MacKay followed its gaze to the whiskey bottle. Willy crossed to the bottle, picked it up, examined it gingerly. "Still whole," he said.

Sputo nodded. "Life's little miracles."

WILLY DRAGGED MR Hatter's body outside, where MacKay was already shovelling dirt over the unfortunate Missus. "How's Sputo?" MacKay asked.

"Alright. Said he had to make a phone call." Willy plopped the big redneck down right in front of MacKay.

MacKay stared at Mr Hatter, exhausted. Alabama nights were, if anything, hotter than the days. He wiped the sweat from his brow, and winced as he hit the sore spot where Mia had struck him. "Let's take a break," he said. "This guy's not going anywhere."

Inside, Dog sat on the couch, playing peek-a-boo with the baby. Sputo wheeled back in from the kitchen, smiled at the scene.

Willy crossed to the baby, picked it up. "Reckon I'll have to adopt this little nipper," he said. "I got five at home already — what's one more?"

MacKay nodded.

"Spoot, you're the kid's godfather," Willy continued. "I ain't takin' no for an answer."

"I'm honoured," the dog replied.

MacKay turned to Sputo, very serious now. "I'm real sorry about all this, Sputo," he said. "Looks like you got caught in a little of my crossfire."

Sputo shrugged, a small spasm of a movement. "And you got caught in some of mine, McKay. Those Hatters would of caused me trouble pretty soon anyway." He paused. "Least I had the Ratcatcher on ma side."

Slowly, laboriously, Sputo raised a front paw. MacKay took it, shook it solemnly.

"Sorry about poor Fluffa, though," MacKay said. "You gonna be okay up here now? Who's gonna cut your meat?"

"Got that covered."

A small, putt-putt scooter noise revved up outside. MacKay pulled out his Shredder, moved to the door. He peered outside, but couldn't make out much through the gloom. No headlights…

Then he felt Sputo's flaccid paw on his arm. "It's okay."

The door opened, and an exact double of Fluffa appeared in the doorway – alive and well. He smiled, Fluffa's exact same, dull smile.

"Hello, Nutta," Sputo said.

MacKay stared at the dog.

"It's a big family," Sputo said, "an' I pay 'em pretty well. Still got some benefit money comin' in."

Nutta picked up some shell casings, started straightening the room.

MacKay smiled. "Sputo, you really are the smartest dog on Earth."

Sputo's mouth curled up, and with a great effort, he winked. "Competition ain't much," he said.

THE HOT ALABAMA night whizzed by. Mia felt almost free again, out on the road… except for the six bikes riding behind her, like an anchor around her neck. And *especially* except for Hank's voice in her ear, like a persistent mosquito.

"Mi?"

She ignored him, revved her engine faster.

"Mi, I'm on our private frequency. I've gotta talk to you."

She rolled her eyes.

"I hate riding behind Cris, Mi. She's so bony and she keeps slapping me."

Mia laughed a silent, bitter laugh.

"Mi… I've gotta ask you. Why did we let him go? MacKay?"

Sighing heavily, she said, "We had to. That wasn't one of the animals we need to find."

"But he's a killer."

"Grow up, Hank."

"I wish you'd stop telling me that."

"Well, I wish you'd do it."

"I–"

"Look. If I know MacKay, he'll be back on the road in a few hours. We'll be ahead of him this time, lying in wait. We'll get him."

"If you know MacKay."

"What does that mean?"

"Nothing." Hank sighed, a mournful, self-pitying noise. "Listen, Mi – I'm sorry. About the bar fight, about us – about everything."

She stared at the road.

"Remember how we used to talk, Mi? On this frequency? While the others were tooling along… we'd tell each other how we were gonna touch each other, when we stopped."

She smiled. She did remember. Suddenly, her plans for the future seemed uncertain, ethereal.

"I miss that, Mia. I miss us."

She fought back a little tear.

"I really wanna do you up the ass again."

Savagely, she reached up and clicked the radio off.

Up ahead, she could almost see her destiny. The rows of headless cattle, suffering in unspeakable agony. A steaming spread on a bare table, reeking of meat-juices. A strong, firm hand in hers.

And now she knew who the hand belonged to.

part three
eye on the birdie

1

"OF COURSE I don't *like* killing things," MacKay said savagely. "Who the hell would?"

Dog sat on the gearshift, scratching his armpit and fiddling with the radio. Nothing was coming in.

"I mean, I'm not a vegetarian. And in my line of work, there's going to be a body count – it's unavoidable. But take Brutus; he aimed at me first. Pure self-defence. Same with that crazy redneck couple."

MacKay was irritable. His eye hurt where Mia had smacked him. He glanced into the rear-view, lifted his shades, and saw he was getting a shiner.

He'd just passed into Texas, having made record time through Mississippi and Louisiana. East Texas was heavily wooded, very green and damp. The roads were long and deserted. It didn't feel like the South – but it didn't feel comfortable, either.

The contradictions in this case just kept mounting up. How did the Mad Cows keep managing to show up wherever he went? And just what were they after, anyway? MacKay, obviously – but it was really starting to look like there was more to it than that. Had Fuzzies, or GenTech, hired them to follow him, to make sure he found the animals? But that was crazy. The animals wouldn't be found if this crazy veggie gang killed MacKay instead.

Still, he didn't trust Fuzzies. They weren't what they seemed. And their description of their older animals hadn't turned out to be accurate; Sputo could talk and reason as well as a human being. What, then, were the *newer* animals like? Exactly what was he on the trail of, anyway?

To top it off, the animal-tracker seemed to have gone haywire. Two hours ago, it had suddenly registered a blip very close by, hundreds of miles from the next spot on the GenTech map. The blip blinked in and out, then raced fifty miles north, doubled back around and disappeared. Now it showed *something*, but the blip kept winking on and off. Maybe it was just out of whack.

Like MacKay's kidneys; Mia must have kneed him one there, too. He slowed and pulled over to the side. "I'm gonna take a leak," he said to Dog, who was fiddling with the lighter again. "Don't set yourself on fire."

Outside, away from the air conditioning, MacKay felt immediately damp all over. He trudged to the side of the road and stepped back a few feet, between two huge oak trees. He reached down, unzipped…

…and looked up, in shock, as a seven-foot-wide blur of feathers screeched down on him, with an unholy *squawwwwwwwkk!*

"Jesus Chr—"

MacKay instinctively threw up his arms in defence. Sharp, six-inch talons raked into his jacket, seeking his eyes. One got through, scraped against his sunglasses.

"Aaahh!"

The bird wheeled up and around, and MacKay got a glimpse: dirty white head, hooked yellow beak, and something else. A bag hanging down, like a burden it was carrying. The bag swung around as though it were filled with marbles.

Dog hissed open the Interceptor's door, stood holding the tracker. Its light flashed bright red now. *Keek! Keek!*

The bird wheeled around in the air, stopped about ten feet above MacKay, and spoke.

"Mad — secrets — Ratcatcher!"

MacKay stared at the cuts on his arms. He shook his head to clear it.

"Hunt a rat, catch a daaaaarrk secret. Awwk!"

The bird was a Fuzzy, all right.

It aimed its beak straight at MacKay and dived again.

He sprinted for the Interceptor and leaped, head-first, into the car. He slammed the door a half-second before the crazed bird smashed straight into it, rocking the entire car to one side.

From outside, its muffled voice came. "Can't hide — catch the rat! Terrorists! Dark secrets! Freedom on the march!"

Its marble-bag grazed the window, and it took to the air again.

The tracker light faded. MacKay peered through the windshield, but saw no sign of the creature.

Keek! Keek!

MacKay turned to Dog. "I have no idea. But I'm going to find out."

Taking a deep breath, he pressed the sat button on the radio. He'd been reluctant to use the satellite line before — but when unknown talking animals started dive-bombing him in the act of relieving himself, it was time to find out what the hell was going on.

"Fuzzies, Inc."

"This is MacKay. Get me Wellington, please."

There was a pause, and then a blurry image of Wellington appeared on the dashboard screen. "My boy! Didn't expect to hear from you so soon, don't you know. I trust everything's cricket?"

"Not exactly, Mr Wellington. I've encountered two of your creations so far, and I need some information."

"Bully! Well, I'll do what I can, lad." He leaned in to the screen, whispered conspiratorially. "GenTech is on light duty today."

"Right. Great. Well, first I met a dog named Sputo—"

"Ah, yes. Lovely chap. Good to hear he's still around. He was built for a company called Private Space—"

"I know all about Sputo. We got along fine."

"That's the spirit, lad. Use a dog to catch a rat, eh?" Wellington smiled. "I knew I picked the right man for the job."

"Wellington, I've just been dive-bombed by a gigantic fucking vulture or something. It pops on and off the tracker – seems to move around a lot. It talks, so I figure it's one of yours."

"Ah." Wellington looked serious now. "I trust you escaped with life and limb?"

"No injuries yet. What the hell is that thing?"

"Erm…" Wellington seemed oddly embarrassed. "Let me make sure we're on the same page, old boy. Is this your attacker?"

The screen shifted to an image of a large bald eagle with a marble-sack hanging down below it.

"Looks like him. Down to that weird little pouch over there."

"Yes," Wellington's voice said. The picture remained on the screen. "Odd you should mention that. The, er, little pouch is rather the crux of the matter."

"Wellington, what the hell are you talking about?"

"Ahem… you've just encountered a creature officially called Eagle One. For obvious reasons, however, it was always commonly known as Balled Eagle."

Something about Wellington's exaggerated pronunciation made the "ed" in "Balled" very clear. MacKay had an instant, horrific sense of where this was going.

"He's an American eagle," Wellington continued. "Custom-designed, many years ago, as a special project for the US Defence Department. They wanted a mascot, a living symbol of freedom to counteract a lack of confidence on the part of the public. AI-enhanced. So they hired us."

"And that pouch…?"

"Ah. Yes. Balled Eagle was designed – over my protests, I assure you – with an extra set of bollocks – testicles, you Yanks would say – grafted onto his nether regions."

MacKay felt sick. "Human testicles."

"Quite. And not just any human testicles, old boy. The actual, preserved stones of a former President of the United States."

"What… I…" MacKay stopped, composed himself. "What happened to him?"

"Oh, the DoD had great plans for him. They wanted to reveal his existence to the public in a grand ceremony, then take him on the road. Eagle One would travel around the nation, giving lectures on what the good old US of Ay-merica was all about. Coast-to-coast broadcasts from national monuments; personal appearances at fundamentalist prayer meetings; safety and patriotism lectures in public schools. I shudder to think of that last one, in particular.

"But Balled Eagle was a total cock-up from the start. The additional testosterone flooding through his system made him irrationally aggressive all the time. He couldn't sit still at all — he'd flutter about and smack people, hard, with those huge wings, anytime they tried to keep him from trolling for helpless prey. The DoD could barely keep him focused on his travel itinerary, let alone what he was supposed to do once he got there.

"They were still preparing for the, er, tour, when the whole nasty business went south. They'd decided to bring the bloody bird to a cabinet meeting, to show him the calibre of Americans he was working with, or some damnfool thing. Long story short, he flew into an utter rage and hospitalized half the nation's top officials. He killed Health and Human Services Secretary Howard Dean."

"I remember that," MacKay said. "They claimed he'd had a fatal stroke while… ranting about something."

"Cover story, old boy." Wellington sighed and reappeared on the screen. "The incident was papered over, and soon after that, BE broke out of his little birdie jail and flew away. Our intelligence showed he retreated to Texas — instinctively recognising it, perhaps, as the original home of his additional, erm, equipment. Once every few years, he shows up on the radar… usually makes a few raids on defenceless immigrants, then retreats back to wherever he lives. Hoards like a survivalist, presumably."

"And you just let him run around out here?"

"We can't *find* him, old boy. And he really doesn't do much harm, most of the time."

MacKay frowned. "He was babbling… said something about dark secrets. That mean anything to you?"

Something crossed Wellington's face, and MacKay knew he'd hit a nerve. But the faux Englishman recovered quickly. "Balled Eagle is barking mad, old boy. He usually goes on about terrorists."

"He did that, too," MacKay admitted.

"I suggest you avoid him at all costs. He's very, very dangerous. Sadly, he's actually highly intelligent… possibly the smartest programming we ever managed. But you'd never know it with all that excess man-juice running through his system. He can't help it; he'd rather fight than think."

"About these animals' intelligence…" Just then, a small chime went off; five-minute warning. MacKay grimaced. If he stayed on much longer, he'd be spending a fortune. Even worse, if someone was tailing him – like the Mad Cows – it'd be much easier for them to zero in on his location.

"I'm heading for Arizona, Wellington. I'll check in again when it's safe."

"Good show, old chap."

"Just to confirm, though: neither Sputo nor… uh, Balled Eagle… are the animals you're looking for. Right?"

"Spot on, old chap. The newer animals are much more sophisticated."

Whatever that meant. "Got it. MacKay out."

"Godspeed, Ratcatchah!"

MacKay thumbed the satphone off, in disgust.

He and Dog sat staring straight ahead for a minute. Finally, MacKay turned to the monkey and shook his head. *"Balled Eagle?"*

Dog scratched his back.

MacKay twisted the ignition key, and the Interceptor hummed to life. He glanced at the tracker, but its light remained dark. The road began to bump along, faster and faster, creating a familiar vibration under him.

Only then did he remember that he still needed to use the bathroom.

II

"RAWK! MAD − SECRETS − madmen on motor-sickles!"

Mia ignored the chatter, kept an eye on the ropes. "Fan out further. Tighten it!"

On a deserted stretch of Old 180, three hundred miles west of Dallas, the Mad Cows were netting Balled Eagle.

This was their third attempt at bringing the bird to ground. Combat lasers had proved useless; the damn thing was just too fast. Hauser-Wister had tried peppering the air with ScumShredder shots, but at the first noise, Eagle had just climbed faster and faster into the sky, disappearing quickly from view.

So they'd decided to try a lower-tech route. Seven guy ropes were tied to seven bikes, flying along the two-lane road at over 100 mph. The trick, Mia thought, was getting the net high enough. Fortunately, the stupid bird − who'd been buzzing them for days − had come in for a low assault, and she'd been able to deploy the net.

Mia looked up. The bad news was that the bird was in full view, about to dive-bomb them. That strange sac that hung down from it − what the hell was that, anyway? − flopped back and forth, half ominously and half comically.

The good news was that the net was now between Eagle and the sky. Mia motioned slowly with her arm. The Cows fanned out slowly, stretching the net open farther… just a little farther…

"That's it!" she yelled into the radio. "Pull in!"

The bikes veered dangerously towards the middle of the road, and each other.

"Secrets − dark secrets! Awwwk!"

The bikes screamed past each other. Mia, Wister-Hauser, Cristina, and Britney crossed from the right side of the road to the left; Jefe, Hauser-Wister, and Shank − with Hank riding behind her − glided from left to right. Above them, the ropes stretched to their limits, and the bikes dipped dangerously towards the centre of the road. Then, with a SNAP, the ropes crossed, pulling the net shut.

"Awwkk!"

Mia looked up, nodded. "Okay, everybody stay in formation! Jefe?"

"Got it, chief."

The skinny kid leaned forwards and stood erect on his bike – then turned it into a dangerously low turn, skidding and swerving around first Mia, then the other bikes, one by one. At each one, he deftly unhooked the guy rope and fastened it onto his own handlebars.

Jefe was the best biker the Cows had.

Finally, when he had all seven ropes, he grabbed them in a thick handful. His aerial burden pulled and tugged, but Jefe remained steady, one hand on his bike and the other on the ropes. Smiling, he rode back around to Mia and handed them to her smoothly, as though he were delivering a pizza.

Mia looked up. The net was still securely closed. The powerful form of Balled Eagle squirmed and scrambled around within, jerking Mia from side to side. She quickly pulled over.

The others screeched to a halt around her, and together they fastened the ropes to a cactus. Balled Eagle screamed and shrieked, swooping the net around the sky twenty feet up. But he couldn't break free.

"Bring…" Mia stopped, out of breath. It was very hot in the desert air, and the sun was beating down. "Bring it down."

Jefe, Shank, Cristina, Britney, Wister-Hauser, and Hauser-Wister pulled on the ropes, slowly dragging the bird earthwards. Mia was reminded, somehow, of the flag-planting scene at Iwo Jima.

Hank hung back, either sulking or just trying to avoid physical labour. Mia didn't really care which.

"Careful," Mia said.

After several long minutes, they managed to pull their captive down to about eight feet off the ground – just close enough to talk to it, without giving it room to dive at them. Jefe and Shank looped the ropes tight around the cactus, anchoring the net at its new height. Shank pricked herself on a needle, once. Jefe bent to kiss it.

Mia studied the bird. The net was strong; Eagle's talons hadn't managed to tear any of it. But it was transparent enough that they could, finally, get a good look at the creature.

Sure enough, it was a gigantic bald eagle. Its only distinguishing characteristics: (1) the power of speech, and (2) that odd, greyish-flesh-coloured sac. Bunched up inside the net, it was now sniffing at the sac, which seemed to calm it. Mia moved in for a closer look.

"Oh, hell, no," she said, screwing up her mouth in distaste.

"Mia?"

"Never mind. This thing's got to be a Fuzzies bird. Aren't you, you big piece of shit?"

"Homeland security! Terrorists!" It shook the net, moving towards Mia. She took a step back.

"Cristobal Colon!" Jefe exclaimed. They were all on edge, Mia realised. Even without this abomination, the trip had been wearing on them. It was pretty hard to find decent vegetarian food in this part of the country.

"What do you want?" she asked the bird. "Are you after MacKay?"

"MacKay!" The name seemed to agitate the bird, if possible, even further. "Secrets! He – you – dark secrets!"

Mia turned away, rolled her eyes.

"He sees – you see! Rows of rotting meat! Lamb slaughter – beef slaughter! America needs its meat!"

She stopped, stunned.

"What does that mean?" she asked.

"Slaughter! The headless beasts – hung from the hooks! Zap and bleed – then eat! Eat eat eat!!"

She stared at the creature.

Hank came up next to her, touched her shoulder. "What the hell is that thing talking about?" he asked.

Eagle noticed Hank, then, and pointed its beak at him, rocking back and forth in its tethered prison. "*You*! They hunt you! Taint from *you*!!"

Mia frowned at Hank. "Taint?"

He shrugged, grimaced. "It's crazy."

"Secrets — dark horrible secrets! Hiding in the caves of Afghanistan! Dead or alive! Bring it on!"

The bird turned away from her now. She looked from Hank, to the eagle, to the other six Cows, standing a safe distance away.

"What do you know," she asked the bird, "about rows of headless beasts?"

The eagle squawked, but said nothing.

"Is that something you've seen—"

There was a sudden *rrrrip*, and Eagle's beak whipped around. Mia barely had time to register the hole it had just torn in the net.

"Look out!" she yelled.

Then, with astonishing speed, Eagle was free. Jefe and Shank aimed lasers at it. The creature reared back and strafed them, knocking their guns away and slicing talons into their hands.

The next part happened even faster.

Shank pushed Jefe away, and he tumbled acrobatically to the side. It took him less than a second to recover his balance, but in that time:

Shank faced Balled Eagle.

Eagle stopped cold for a second, stared into Shank's eyes. Each of them, Mia later thought, seemed to see something there. A threat? A fighter? A fellow American?

Then Shank raised her fists in a boxer's stance.

Balled Eagle recognized the stance as a challenge, and charged.

Its talons raked Shank's face, and its huge, hard beak pecked at her viciously. It shredded her snorting-bull gang jacket instantly, burrowing deep into her chest.

While Mia was still opening her mouth to call out — and Jefe was landing on his second leg — the mad symbol of United States aggression reached into Shank's body and, with a sickening squishing noise, pulled out her heart.

Shank made a quick, horrible noise, and collapsed to the desert floor.

Jefe stared at her body for a second. Mia rushed forwards, and the bird turned to her. Its sac swung one way, and Shank's heart whipped the other way in its mouth, brandished like a trophy.

Mia was horrified. She had no time to pull out a weapon, and for a moment, she thought the bird would attack her too. But it glided in the air for just a few seconds, staring into her eyes. Then it opened its mouth to speak, dropping the heart – which landed on the sand at Mia's feet.

Eagle turned at a strange angle and spoke to her, straight down.

"You – destiny! Hunt secrets! Hunt secrets! No whitewash in the White House!"

Then it turned and flew upwards.

"But first – *meat*!"

And Balled Eagle disappeared in the sky.

Jefe kneeled over Shank's mutilated body, sobbing. Cristina pulled out bandages and started working on his injuries, but he barely noticed. The Eagle had only grazed his hands.

Mia stood, watching the sky where the eagle had been. Hank came up beside her, put an arm around her waist. "Great plan, Mi."

Mia barely registered him – not even enough to get annoyed. She was furious at herself for losing another member. Whatever these creatures were that MacKay was chasing, they couldn't be worth all this.

To her own horror, though, she found herself thinking less about poor Shank and more about the fact that she'd just encountered a talking bird! Not so much the fact that it could speak – quite a few sub-tropical species could be trained to mimic certain words and phrases – but what the bird had been saying. It was clearly an unbalanced creature, homicidal, para-noiac, and divorced from reality. A dumb animal to be pitied.

But somehow, it had a peephole into her dream-visions. It *knew* her.

Slaughter – the headless beasts!

America needs its meat!

And suddenly, she felt the taste of that meat in her mouth

again. Warm, full of blood-juice. Bloated, greasy, primal. Forbidden and delicious.

A strategy was forming in her mind. A difficult, treacherous, multilayered strategy. But it was the only path she could see.

Gently, wordlessly, she pulled Jefe to his feet. Then she gestured to the others, pulling them towards her for a huddle.

"New plan," she said softly.

III

EIGHTY MILES BEHIND, MacKay was bored. He hadn't seen Balled Eagle since their first encounter, so he'd kind of let his guard down. Now he was breaking one of his own rules: He'd called up a Pepe the Robomule cartoon on his windshield display. It blocked a third of his vision, but there was nothing out here anyway except sand, cacti, and the occasional ghost town. And the sun. Texas had always suffered from the heat, as far back as the 1930s the topsoil had blown away leaving vast swathes of desert in its place, but at least back then the government had come up with financial rescue packages. Now there wasn't even enough of a government left to come up with a rescue package, financial or otherwise.

Pepe caught the bank robbers, delivered an ironic moral in mangled English, and said, "Adios, leetle amigos." The windshield flickered, then went back to boring old road.

As usual, Dog had watched every frame of the cartoon with rapt attention. Now he jumped up and down on the seat, bored.

"I know," MacKay said. "It's a long frigging state. Reminds me of a little poem my dad used to like:

The sun has riz,
The sun has set,
And here we is,
In Texas yet."

Dog jumped up and down, fingers pressed in his ears. *Keek! Keek!*

"Hell," MacKay said, looking sideways out the window, "it's a big damn country. Used to be really something, too. Till the politicians ruined it with greed, arrogance, and short-term thinking. Now you can hardly even keep yourself in water out here."

He reached out a hand, scratched Dog's metal neck absently. "You'd have liked my old zoo, fella. We had bears and snakes and lions, yeah... but also creatures that aren't even around anymore. Ostriches – big nasty things with necks as long as a golf club. And capybara. Big running rodents." He smiled at Dog's quizzical look. "Yeah, they were pretty fucked-up, I guess. But I liked 'em. I liked 'em all.

"I guess I can't blame the Mad Cows for being so militant. It's a tough country for *people* nowadays – it's even worse on animals. But you don't do a sick creature a favour by releasing it into the wild. It's just gonna die a much worse, more painful death. I figure, I put a bullet in its head, I'm doing it a favour."

Dog offered no rebuttal. But even though the argument made perfect logical sense, MacKay still felt uneasy.

He pulled the HanHeld off its dashboard mount, cycled quickly through the list of cartoons. Pepe. Marko Sharko. Miko D, the Rapping Rodent. Dino the Skateboarding Duck. He'd watched them all, three or four times each.

MacKay sighed.

The next GenTech blip was in Arizona... maybe five, six hundred miles away. MacKay hoped he'd lost both Balled Eagle and the Mad Cows, but if not, he doubted they'd be crazy enough to follow him that far.

Outside, cacti and dust flew by. The desert seemed to stretch out forever, bereft of water, life, or humanity. Just another part of a big nation grown old before its time, struggling to hang onto a bit of its former greatness.

Lonely, thirsty, tired – wishing he had some new cartoons to watch – MacKay drove on.

In Texas yet.

NEW MEXICO PASSED like a dusty dream. MacKay hugged the southern part of the state; he didn't want to get anywhere near Utah. Nguyen Seth's followers controlled that whole state now, and they'd been known to impound ve-hickles for no reason at all. He'd had this car for eight years now – he'd worked in it, played in it, fled in it, slept in it more often than not, and he'd grown pretty attached to it. Besides, all Fuzzies' money wouldn't be much good to MacKay if he had to walk back to Florida to collect it.

A couple of times, his GangBuster radar detector indicated approaching convoys, and MacKay either hid the car while they went by or detoured off the road briefly. The Southwest was rife with big Sanctioned Op agencies like Logan's Runners and the Good Ole Boys, and while they had no reason to pick a fight with him, MacKay didn't see any point in taking chances.

He'd heard stories, too, about mutated coyotes that dropped rocks on people from cliffs. But those were probably just regional legends, like the alligators in the sewers of New York. Unless, he thought suddenly, the coyotes were Fuzzies projects, too. And the alligators…?

One thing was sure: the gangcults were real, and this was the very definition of a NoGo Zone – anarchy ruled. Better just to avoid contact with everyone. Fortunately, there was a lot more land out here than people.

The tracker led MacKay south of the central, mountainous part of Arizona, past the former site of Tucson to the vicinity of the Papago Indian Reservation. The roads turned to dirt, and the dirt turned to dust.

MacKay followed the blip, pausing a few times to weave through a thin layer of trees hiding a dirt road from view. Whoever he was approaching, they didn't want to be found. This seemed like the perfect terrain for a religious cult like ACTS.

MacKay checked the Interceptor's chain guns: fully loaded and operational. Unfortunately, this wasn't the ideal situation to bull into by force – he was likely to kill the very animals he'd been sent to rescue. Granted, Wellington had allowed that as an option. But somehow, MacKay wanted to prove he could get them back alive. That he wasn't just an animal-killer.

At last the road turned to nearly-impassable gravel. The Plas-Tyres groaned, the Interceptor lurched and bumped as it struggled up a steep grade hidden by trees. Then it turned a corner and MacKay saw his destination.

Golden arches rose over the road, like the entrance to a fast-food fairy kingdom. The big house, ornamented and crenellated like a castle, looked vaguely familiar; MacKay wondered if he'd seen it in a children's movie. Advertising signs littered the drive-way, hawking a wide variety of products: G-Mek Renegades; recaff drinks; Mimsey's World of Adventure; cheap, unsecured long-distance calling cards; a recently-cancelled TV show called "The Cain Factor."

A gate swung open between the golden arches. Slowing to first gear, MacKay drove cautiously up.

As he followed the long, winding path to the house, MacKay noticed a small figure standing in the driveway, arms folded across its chest. He sucked in a shocked breath. He eased the Interceptor to a stop right in front of the figure.

"Stay here," he said to Dog.

MacKay glanced at the tracker; this was definitely the place. He grabbed it, holstered the HanHeld and his Shredder. Slowly, he opened the door and stepped out.

The figure was about four foot six, staring at him with big, cartoon eyes. Its snout was long and exaggerated. It wore white gloves, a black hooded sweatshirt, baggy jeans, sunglasses perched up on its expansive forehead, and a couple of carefully-placed gold chains. Its sneakers were new and looked very, very expensive.

Keeping his eye on the creature, MacKay raised up the Han-Held in front of him and dialled up a cartoon – one he'd watched only yesterday.

The resemblance was exact. This was no ordinary Fuzzy.

This was Miko D.

Miko opened his mouth, and his voice was just as MacKay had heard it on the vids, all these years. "The f— you doin' at my house, B?"

MacKay stared at him. "What did you say?"

Miko frowned. "You f—in' deaf, B? I axed you, the f— you doin' here?"

"Fuck me! You're Miko D!"

"I ain't Mary f—in' Poppins, a-hole."

MacKay shook his head, still trying to take it all in. Sputo had been a big enough shock, but… ! "You're *real*? A real… mouse, I mean?"

"I'm'a pop a real cap in yo' a-, you don't tell me what'chu doin' here."

MacKay just stood there, stunned. He'd been watching Miko D cartoons for twenty years! Smiling sheepishly, he turned the HanHeld to show the real Miko his animated likeness.

Suddenly Miko smiled widely, a sea of white teeth with a couple of gold spots.

"Shee-t, B. Whyn'tchu say you'sa *fan*? Git in here, b—h!"

IV

WHEN AMERICA STARTED to go to hell, entertainment moved in two directions – both of them bad.

On the one hand, corporations – faced with declining ad revenues and a rapidly-devaluing dollar – decided to play it safe. Prime-time and children's TV shows were combed again and again to remove any trace of possible controversial content. Hint of underage sex here? No way. Children having fun unsupervised? Take it out. Even words like "crap" and "fudge" were excised and a certain big purple dinosaur had to undergo a radical makeover to make him less like, in the unguarded words of one TV exec, "an enormous erect dick". The result was hollow, empty pabulum, squeaky-voiced garbage that three-year-olds still watched, but four-year-olds found boring and insipid (or, as they often put it, "poopy doopy"). When ratings for animated shows such as *The Caring Bears' Appropriate Cuddle Hour, Non-Gender Specific-Man and the Non-Hostile Affiliates of the Universe* and the bizarre Japanese import *Colourful Friendly Monsters Who Don't Fight And Have Asked Permission To Live In Your Pocket* halved overnight, the advertisers deserted the networks in droves.

As ratings declined even further, some cable channels turned their energies to "edgy" counter-programming. The results were violent and sexually explicit, but no more inspiring: *Pro-*

Celebrity Sexual Gymnastics found a small following, as did reality shows like *Humping in a Hovel* and *The Real South Park*. But *Cruisin' with Cruise*, *Governor Arnie's Wide World of Executions*, and *Mimsey's Rabbit Hole* never really caught on. The networks seemed determined to prove a simple fact – even the American people could eventually tire of raw sex and violence.

Against this vapid backdrop, Miko D was a revelation.

Miko's first few cartoons, *Wackson Jackson* and *Bukkake High*, hit the culture-starved youth of America the way the works of Parker & Stone had, a few years earlier. They were outrageous enough to make parents squirm with discomfort. But there was real anger at the core of *The Miko D Show*, too, and a surprisingly incisive look at the decline of a great nation. When Miko's little pal Freak handed that girl some Kleenex, an entire generation wished they had someone to wipe them clean, too.

MacKay had been in his teens when Miko burst on the scene. His techie friends were in awe of the show's character design and animation, far and away the best on TV at the time. MacKay would sit around with his buddies, smoking dope, trying to figure out how the CGI effects were done. Now he knew. They just pointed a camera at Miko and rolled tape.

After just one year on the air, at the height of its popularity, *The Miko D Show* closed down. The Rapping Rodent turned to music, releasing controversial singles such as "C.R.Y. (Cops Rabies Yeee-uh!)" and "Mammalcide". Miko became a bigger and more incendiary sensation than ever, quickly segueing into a series of films. The first, the racially polarising *MC Steamboat*, was probably the strongest. The series declined over time, eventually degenerating into *Miko's Fly Hawaiian Joint*.

"That was just a excuse for a f—n' party." Miko smiled.

At the time, it had seemed like a gutsy move for a production company to shut down a successful cartoon show and shift its entertainment model so completely. Now MacKay realised that Miko himself had been calling the shots.

"Nobody knew I'as furreal," Miko said. "It busted my a— a little, but hell, I'ad a contract. An' the bling was good." He gestured around at his living room. "Bling still good."

MacKay looked around at the room. All the furnishings were plush, expensive – and hideous. An array of bright colours assaulted the eye, and absolutely everything bore an insignia of corporate sponsorship. The mantelpiece held a gunrack, with the *Guns & Killing* magazine logo embossed on it. Posters lined the walls, loudly bannering old TV shows like *Stargate Milwaukee* and *My Stepfather the Biosurgeon*, and films like *Yummy Tummy Yusuki – the Movie!* The lamps were all shaped like Wally the Whale, except for one tarnished, antique Snoopy tucked in a corner.

"Always loved the Snoop," Miko said. "He my personal touch."

MacKay sipped his Krystal. "And the rest?"

"Product placement, B. All paid for. F—n' Man paid for this whole motherf—n' crib." Miko laughed, a wheezy cartoon laugh familiar to MacKay. "F—rs thought I'd be partyin' an' sh-, people over here 24/7 lookin' at they bullsh- on the walls. F— that, homes. Mouse needs his f—n' privacy, knowwhamsayin'?"

"I hear you."

"Sure you monkey okay?"

MacKay had tried to coax Dog into the house, but the monkey was repelled – whether by Miko or by the rampant commercialism of the house, MacKay wasn't sure. So he'd left Dog happily fiddling with the car radio, recharging his cells. "Yeah, he's fine." MacKay hesitated. "No disrespect, Miko – what's with your speech? Why do you keep fading out like that?"

"Aw, you mean the f—n' swear words? F—n' motherf—rs f—n' *programmed* me like'at, B. Backwoods Entertainment wanted my sh— kid-safe. Couldn't have me f—n' saying 'f—' an' 'sh—' alla time on f—n' afternoon TV. So they ordered me up special."

"From Fuzzies."

Miko fixed his guest with an icy smile. "I see you packin' chrome, B. You wanna come correct wit' me?"

MacKay held up empty palms. "I ain't playing you, Miko. I've been hired by Fuzzies, yeah. But they're not interested in you."

"Who is, B? Who is?" Miko turned away, suddenly morose. He sipped his champagne.

MacKay was fascinated. Not only was he meeting a child-hood idol – one he'd never known really existed! – but clearly Miko had been one of Fuzzies' first engineered creatures. Maybe the mouse could fill in some of the gaps about the mysterious company that had made him.

"This is, uh, quite a spread, Miko."

"You ain' seen sh– yet, B." Miko rose. "Walk this way."

MacKay followed him through a room full of animation cels and soft-porn film posters to a large back terrace – which faced directly onto a full, eighteen-hole golf course. MacKay could just make out the flags in the near holes; they all bore corporate logos.

"Golf, B. The reward for this sorry motherf—n' life."

"So I see."

"'Let's play a round, Money."

MacKay hesitated. "I don't really play, Miko. I mean, I've been meaning to learn, but–"

"Ah, you right. 'Sa p—y game, golf." He grinned at MacKay, a huge white cartoon grin. "You ready to ride, mothaf—a?"

"So all this time–" *BLAM!* "–nobody ever leaked to the media–" *BLAM!* "–the fact that you were a real person?–" *BLAM BLAM!* "Uh, mouse?"

Miko's private shooting range was as impressive as the rest of his spread. MacKay's target was a blown-up photograph of President Estevez, grinning his trademark crooked-smartass grin. Miko stood up on a milk crate, shooting at a moving cartoon of Wally Whale. It was a little hard to tell where Wally's heart would be, but Miko seemed to be getting enough enjoyment out of just blasting him some new blowholes.

"Sets was always, closed, B." *BLAM!* "Fuzzies do they job good – tell the clients just how to keep Jake an' the press away–" *BLAM!* "–an' also let 'em know what'll happen if they don't." *BLAM BLAM BLAM!*

BLAM! MacKay smiled; he'd just caught Estevez right in the teeth. "That's something I wanted to ask you about – Fuzzies." *BLAM!* "You know they're owned by GenTech?"

"Now they is. F—ers bought it up–" *BLAM!* "–after my time."

"Fuzzies is paying me good money–" *BLAM!* "–but I don't trust them. Their operation seems too big–" *BLAM!* "–just to produce a few intelligent animals a year."

Miko paused, turned to him. "You knockin' on the big doors now, B." He sighted the whale, pulled the trigger. *BLAM!* "Fuzzies was connected, but GenTech – they strictly 1337. No thugs allowed."

"Don't get me wrong, I'll get 'em back their–" *BLAM!* "–kidnapped animals. But I like to know–" *BLAM!* "–who I'm dealing with."

"Stay out the cold, B. These boys–" *BLAM!* "–they sick-a–b—es. You ask too many questions–" *BLAM!* "–they Abu Ghraib you a—. Nobody never see you again."

MacKay lowered his pistol, turned to look down at Miko. "You used to ask the questions."

Miko laughed, a big cartoon laugh. "Sold some records, you mean." *BLAM!* "Spent some time poppin' collars, flamboastin'. Livin' Big Willie style. B—es never seen nuthin' like my big cartoon d-k. They liked the three-fingered — p—y — —, too. Party ev'y f—in' day."

"But yeeee-ah, you right." *BLAM!* "Thought I could change the–" *BLAM!* "–world with–" *BLAM BLAM!* "–f—in' cartoons."

"And now?"

"Now? Now I like my–" *BLAM!* "–big-a-, expensive crib, a million miles from noplace. America I knew?" *BLAM!* "Iss gone, B. All I care, people can kill theyselves dead over–" *BLAM!* "–dillons, juice, and cheddah."

Guns, water, and money. Not for the first time, MacKay wished he had a device that could translate Miko's speech, the way he had Sputo's.

"So you don't know anything more about–" *BLAM!* "–Fuzzies?"

"Oh, I *know*, B." He turned to MacKay, lowered his goggles. "Come on – I show you something, motherf—er."

Miko hopped down off the crate and strutted off. MacKay took a look back at the targets. The President wouldn't be remaking *The Breakfast Club* anytime soon, but Wally was the clear loser. Even cartoon characters, apparently, weren't immune to pain.

MacKay placed his pistol on the shelf and followed.

MIKO'S STUDY WAS a shock to MacKay – a genuine high-tech computer centre, the like of which he'd never seen outside a megacorp's offices. Five Apple Paradise G7 PowerMacs wired up in parallel, their sparkly Lightwire cables clashing badly with the machines' faux-clamshell exteriors. A forty-eight inch plasma monitor with "Look 'n' Touch" controls along the bottom. Gigantic speakers, seemingly salvaged from some long-ago AC/DC concert. And two comfortable leather armchairs with miniremotes on the armrests. There was even a small holostage with a crack in the projector module.

"That don't work no more," Miko said, "since I smashed a champagne bottle on it."

Miko sat down in the chair directly facing the screen, and pressed a stud on the armrest. The system hummed to life. "I come here when I like to re*lax*," he said. Loud hip-hop music blared from the speakers; Miko thumbed it to a lower level. "Or when I wanna be angry."

From what MacKay had seen so far, that didn't seem to be a problem. Miko was oddly changeable; he'd retreated from the world, and seemed disdainful of people in general. Yet he'd made a point of befriending MacKay, without even knowing exactly why the Op was here.

Suddenly MacKay realised: Miko was lonely.

"You know this mothaf—a?"

A tall, lean Asian man appeared on the screen. His eyes seemed to burn into MacKay.

"I don't think so."

"You should. His name's Professor Wan."

MacKay's eyes went wide. "I've heard of him."

"Yeaaah? What'chu know?"

MacKay remembered Sputo's words: He's got his fingers in everywhere. "Not much. Did he… make you?"

"Five by five, B. I was his first AI project."

"So you know him."

"Past f—in' tense. But yeah… probably better'n anyone else eva did. Cold motherf—a." Miko paused. "This'ee's one'a the few stillshots a' Wan ever."

"He's a geneticist?"

"Straight on. He come from the Chinese medical/genetic community… best in the world. An' he the cream o' the cream."

MacKay had a strange sensation… as though pieces of a puzzle hovered all around him in the air, and he'd just caught the first glimpse of them. He stared at the glaring eyes of Wan, and felt a familiar chill. "And he works for Fuzzies?"

Miko laughed. "Wan don't work for nobody. They all work for him."

"And what does he do? What does Fuzzies do?"

"I don' know what they *do*, B. Takes a while for they sh- t'get out on the net. But I can show you what they *did*."

Miko typed a bit on the keyboard. The image of Wan shrank, moved to the corner of the large screen. Other pics appeared, then shrank to small tiles in a row. Miko clicked on the first of them: a stillshot of two dolphins splashing around a rusty metal canister that sat half in the water, while a third lay on top of it, staring at its valve system.

"Mine-sweepin' dolphins," Miko said. "Far back as the first Gulf War, they's used to find bombs. Once Fuzzies f—ed wit' they heads, they could defuse 'em, too."

MacKay nodded, impressed.

Miko clicked the next image, and a short video clip expanded to fill the screen. A husky dog with a small barrel around its neck trotted briskly to a man who lay injured in the snow.

"Please lie still, sir," the dog said. "Help is here."

The dog lowered the barrel to the man's neck and gave him a drink. The man spasmed and turned his head to the side, eyes blank. The dog jumped on his chest and began administering CPR with its thick, powerful paws.

"Fuck me! Another talking dog," MacKay said. "Like Sputo."

"Naw," Miko said. "This'an early model. Just a few pre-recorded messages in'is f—in' voicebox. But he managed t'save a few rich white mountain climbers."

On the screen, the man coughed and propped himself up. He smiled weakly at the dog, scratched it behind the ears. The dog wagged its tail happily.

Miko ran through a few more images, each displaying a sample of Fuzzies' past handiwork. Robotic sharks with enhanced brains. A failed experiment with trilobites, subsequently dumped in the Louisiana swamps. A dead man whose mind had been implanted in a duck.

"How do you get all this stuff, anyway?"

Miko grimaced. "Shee-t, motherf—r. I got a f—in' datanet connection."

MacKay smiled. "Who doesn't?"

"Mine *works*, a-hole."

MacKay was impressed. That *was* rare. Most terminals in the US could barely hold a connection for ten minutes, if that. Miko had invested his "cheddah" wisely.

"Check this sh- out." Miko's fingers flew across the keyboard; he seemed almost possessed. The screen refreshed and changed with dizzying speed, blinking almost subliminally through several disturbing images. A shot of Fuzzies' office building. A rabbit hung up to be skinned. A corporate balance sheet. A surprisingly young and thin Alastair Wellington, still in his ridiculous Victorian suit.

Finally it stopped on a map. "You say you lookin' for these new Fuzzies animals. Here you go, B. Man here says he's seen strange phe*nomena* – of the dog/cat/mouse variety – somewhere way out in the Nevada f—in' desert. Recent, B. Place called Cocoa Niño."

MacKay recognized the spot; it was one of the blips on the GenTech map. "Cocoa Niño," he repeated.

"Thas right. Some kinda cult out there... group called ACTS."

MacKay was impressed. He hadn't mentioned ACTS to Miko.

"What do you know about this cult?" he asked.

Miko turned to him, suddenly hostile. "Why you keep axin' me sh- like'at? I don' *know* nothin'. *Officer.*"

MacKay turned away, confused.

"But I can find out." Miko was glued to the screen now, flashing through images at superhuman speed. "ACTS… started out, they'as just a survivalist military cult. Dime a f—in' dozen. Leader had connections, but tha's about it. But somewhere along the line…" He frowned. "'S hazy. Looks like they into somethin' bigger. Not big like the Josephites big, but am*biti*ous."

MacKay nodded.

"Think you *know*," Miko continued, almost to himself. "Think you know where yo' *food* come from, where yo' *car* come from, who died sewin' that *fine jacket* you wearin'. You don' know sh–, motherf—er.

"You wanna know 'bout the world?" Teeth gritted, the mouse pounded on the keyboard now. "I show you, a-hole. Show you what lies unda the motherf—in' surface. Turn up tha Dolby on this."

A dark, blurry window expanded to fill the screen. And MacKay found he could not turn away.

The first image was a high, barbed-wire fence, stark silver in the night, studded with high-powered lasers. Then the camera swerved past giant tropical trees, thickly clustered, to a wall red with rust. No, MacKay noticed as the unseen cameraman zoomed in. Not rust. Dried blood.

Past the wall now, through a vault-like door to a huge, high-ceilinged chamber, like an armoury. Up and down the walls hung coat rack-like structures, and suspended from them were creatures. Animals. Living, breathing, bleeding animals. Thousands of them.

MacKay became aware of the sound… the horrific, mewling noise of helpless creatures in pain. Creatures that had never known any life other than this one, had never been given any choice.

The view shifted to one animal. A gigantic cow, bloated to at least four hundred pounds, hanging by its snout from a hook. Its blood dripped down from a thousand pricks in its hide, and its body was covered with sores.

The camera zoomed in on the cow's neck, and MacKay recognized the unmistakable cording of Zarathustra implants. This animal's lifespan, he realised, had been artificially extended to grow it even larger, which meant it would take much, much longer to die. The angle pulled back to show the cow's eyes, swollen shut. It seemed to be begging, make my agony stop.

Abruptly, the screen went black.

MacKay had seen a lot of gruesome things – most recently, the diseased pigs he'd wiped out – but this stunned him.

"What *was* that?"

"Pirate video, B." Miko seemed to have calmed down. "Datanet's full of surprises. But it only gives you what you know to look for."

"And… this has something to do with–"

All around them, an alarm went off. Miko rose.

"Another motherf—in' visitor," he said. "I must be havin' a comeback."

MacKay unholstered his Shredder and followed the mouse. "I've, uh, got some enemies on the road," he said.

Miko paused in the living room. "Don't even 'member where my AK is," he said. He picked up a golf club, hefted it. He looked vaguely ridiculous.

"I like you, B," Miko continued, "But you bring a 211 down on me, I'll come back an' haunt you from the grave."

MacKay heard the muffled sound of a bike revving to a stop. "Shit," he said. "Stand back."

Gun extended, he yanked open the mansion's front door. And, for possibly the twentieth time today, stopped in shock.

Mia Sangre stood alone. She wore tight black trousers, a plain pleather jacket – no Cows insignia – and a grey T-shirt. And she carried a nine-iron, flicking it in and out of her palm like a switch. She smiled a thin, red-lipsticked smile at him. She knew, MacKay thought, how to make an impression.

Mia's eyes darted from MacKay, to the mouse with his upraised putter, and back to the Op again. She arched an eyebrow.

"Can I play through?"

***

v

"Jesus, MacKay, you swing like a girl. I can't believe you fought off my gang *twice*."

Sweating out in the hot sun, MacKay adjusted his grip on the club and sighed. Well, he'd wanted to learn golf. But he hadn't planned on doing it while being taunted by a beautiful enemy, with his robot monkey on his shoulder, on the private estate of a misanthropic talking mouse.

He looked down at the ball and swung. The ball chopped hard to the side, almost hitting the house.

"D—, B. You f—in' s—k."

Keek! Keek!

Dog had come scampering up to the house when he saw Mia. Apparently he'd grown to like the veggie terrorist during his time in her captivity.

MacKay threw down the club and stalked towards Mia. Dog jumped down to the ground.

"Go back to the car and wait there," MacKay said to the monkey. Then he turned to Mia. "What are you doing here?"

"I thought I was playing a golf game against you." She stepped past him, up to the tee. "But I guess I'm just trying to improve my average."

She swung clear and hard. The ball arced gracefully through the air and landed two feet from the hole, whose flag proudly extolled the virtues of McDisneyWorld.

"You know what I mean. What happened to your colours?"

They picked up their bags and began the march to the green. Dog scampered along happily, looking up at Mia. "I quit the Mad Cows," she said. "I'm getting too old for that crap."

"Game for the f—in' young," Miko agreed.

"Just like that," MacKay said.

"No – it's been coming for a long time. But it really came to a head when we captured that crazed bird thing."

"You – you met Balled Eagle?"

Miko frowned. "*That* crazy motherf—a. I knew the previous incumbent of his, ahhh, stones. We got history."

MacKay turned to the mouse. "Back at Fuzzies?"

"Naw, man. F—in' political sh——. Back in my cartoon days, he tried t'get me yanked off the air. Obscenity charges, some bullsh- like'at – fined our stations mad Presidents, yo. Fat n——r FCC motherf——r went along wid it, too."

MacKay took a moment, tried to decipher that.

"Whatever he was, he kept buzzing us," Mia said. "Wouldn't leave us alone. We trapped him for a while, but he killed one of my girls – pretty brutally. Add that to Brutus and Chester – the two you offed in Florida – and I decided enough was enough."

"Mad Cows," Miko said, pulling out a short club. "Somethin' familiar about that f—in' tag."

"And you just – what? Decided to retire, come visit a reclusive cartoon character in his home, and play golf for the rest of your life?"

"Don't be stupid. I followed you."

"How?"

"That doesn't matter. What's important is – I figure you're on a big job. Somebody's paying you a lot of money to find something, aren't they?"

MacKay said nothing. He tried to remember which club was the putter.

"Well, no offence," Mia continued, "but you obviously haven't found it yet. I figure…" She reached out, took his hand in hers. "… we could team up."

MacKay looked at her for a minute. She was beautiful, and he couldn't deny he was drawn to her. But… he laughed. "*How* many times have you tried to kill me? I've lost count."

She smiled. "That's the business, MacKay. You've shot at me, too."

Once again they locked eyes. MacKay felt another piece of the invisible puzzle shimmer briefly into view.

Then she looked away, and he had the feeling she was wrestling with a whole host of inner demons.

"You asked me…" he stopped. "Back in Florida, you asked me if I liked killing."

Now Mia was silent.

"You know," he continued, faltering a little. "You know that's not—"

"Mad Cows!" Miko exclaimed. "Now I f—in' remember. You ain't no indy gang, girl – you Siamese. You work for–"

"THALAMUSSSSSSSSSSS!"

MacKay and Mia both knew that voice. They looked up… and sure as the night falls in darkest Alaska, the crazed avian symbol of freedom came screeching out of the sky, scratching and clawing. Straight at Miko D.

"Mouse! Bad! Obscenity! *Moussssssse*!"

"Shit!" MacKay pulled out his Shredder. He tried to aim, but Balled Eagle was all over Miko now, pecking at him, raking him with talons, forcing him to the ground. MacKay couldn't get a clear shot.

Miko screamed, a high-pitched cartoon sound mixed with muted swearing.

Mia stepped back, cocked an eyebrow at the bird. "Guess his ears were burning."

MacKay grimaced, thought for a second, then threw his Shredder to Mia. He reached into his golf bag and pulled out the two longest clubs. "Cover me."

Then he charged forwards, hoping Mia wouldn't shoot him in the back.

"Terrorissssssst mouse! You foul the airwaves!! You harbour the enemy! Root them out – in the caves and the – uh?"

MacKay battered Eagle on the back and wings. The creature was enormous – bigger than MacKay, almost twice Miko's size. When it turned on MacKay, claws slashing through the air, the Op staggered back in terror.

"Raaaaaaatcatcher!"

MacKay held up his golf clubs in front of him, bracing himself for facial disfigurement. He tried to ignore the bird's uncomfortably human-looking testicle sac, flopping around in the air. MacKay could see Mia out of the corner of his eye, but he couldn't tell what she was doing.

Past Eagle, Miko pulled himself to his knees. "F—in' fascist government bird-a-mother- ow! F—in' *A!*"

Then the roaring began.

Everyone turned at once to the house, forty feet across the

green, as five bikes came screaming out the back door – carrying five Mad Cows. The clip-mounted combat lasers on the front of their bikes glowed red, ready for action.

Balled Eagle fluttered up a few feet into the air, uncertain. His extra equipment seemed to make him less aerodynamic. "Terroristsssss?"

Miko climbed to his feet, grimacing. "Mad f—in' Cows." Blood covered his face.

MacKay turned to Mia – who held his own Shredder, trained on his heart.

"Don't move," she said.

He glanced, sadly, at the dented nine-iron in his hand.

The Cows fanned out and circled the group, their engines idling. MacKay scanned their faces, jaws set, eyes hidden by dark shades. He recognized that look: they were out to avenge their comrades. No matter what.

Mia walked over to MacKay.

"You shut off Miko's alarm system," he said.

"It's not healthy to wall yourself off from the rest of the world," she said, grabbing MacKay by the arm. "Leads to antisocial tendencies."

"I'll antisocial your white a—, b—." Miko spat out a tooth.

Balled Eagle wheeled around above, shrieking.

"Keep your eyes on that bird," Mia called back to her gang. She turned to MacKay. "Well, MacKay? What do you think? Maybe we could *team up*."

Her voice dripped with sarcasm – but MacKay saw something else in her eyes. He allowed her to lead him to the house.

"Where you goin', Mia?" one of the Cows asked.

"Sort out these two cartoon nightmares and meet me inside," she said. "I'm off to do some *interrogation*."

"What's going on?" MacKay whispered to her.

"I'm being sneaky," Mia replied. Then: "Oh, fuck it."

She wheeled around and fired the Shredder at the hovering bird. It shrieked and screamed, a horrible, inhuman sound. Then it circled down towards the Mad Cows – who all opened fire

on it at once, with Shredders and lasers. Bullets and red beams
flew upwards at all angles. A stray laser beam singed Eagle's sac
and he howled out loud, an almost-human noise.

"Come on!"

Mia took his hand, started to run for the house. But MacKay
stopped her.

"B!"

Miko staggered towards him, bloody, limping badly. Past him,
Eagle was now strafing the Cows, knocking them one by one
off their bikes. A couple of them, the older couple with the
swastikas on their jackets, rolled on the ground, clutching their
slashed stomachs.

"Don't leave me hangin', B! You gotta help me out here!"

MacKay looked at him, helpless, then threw him the golf
club. "Represent," he said.

Then he turned and ran, with Mia, in the direction of the
house.

He wasn't sure, but he thought he saw Miko give him the fat,
white-gloved finger.

Mia and MacKay sprinted through the living room. "A double double-cross?" he asked.

"I couldn't get away from them. So I arranged to come along
first, let them in."

"And I should trust you because…?"

They flung open the house's front door, took in the expansive driveway, the golden arches, Mia's bike, the eyesore road
signs, and MacKay's tricked-out G-Mek Interceptor.

Every inch of the car, from the headlights to the chain guns
to the PlasTyres and wing hard-points, was on fire.

MacKay stood, gaping.

"Well, for one thing," Mia said dryly, "you have a minor trans-
portation problem."

MacKay put his head in his hands. The only reason he'd gone
to Florida in the first place – the only reason he was in this mess
at all! – had been to save his car. And now, there it stood,
engulfed in flames.

A horrible thought struck him. "Oh my god – *Dog*?"

Then Mia's grip on his arm tensed. He followed her gaze and saw Hank, the tall Mad Cow, walking forwards, aiming a combat laser straight at them. He looked pissed off. He also looked as though he might cry.

"So it's true," Hank said. "You *are* double-crossing us."

"Hank. I thought we were going to salvage his car."

"I don't like his car." Hank pointed the laser at MacKay. "I don't like *him*."

Hank was between them and the burning Interceptor now. Mia stepped forwards, holding MacKay's Shredder casually. "Hank," she said. "You know we're supposed to take him alive if—"

"Save it, Mi. You're not a Cow anymore. And you've already let me know I don't mean anything to you." He straightened. "Thalamus'll be real interested to know how you've betrayed them. And I'm sure they'll reward the guy who tells them."

MacKay saw a small motion out of the corner of his eye, just behind Hank. He was pretty sure Mia saw it, too.

"And since you gave my bike away so casually," Hank continued, "I think I'll take yours." He gestured to her motorcycle, casually propped against Miko's big gate. "You can ride behind for a change – in wrist and ankle cuffs."

"You couldn't get it up even then, Hank."

He laughed. "See, belittling only works when you do it from a position of authority, Mi. And I've got the corner office now—"

Then he screamed as metal teeth sank into his leg.

Dog bit hard, through Hank's pleather trousers, then jumped three feet up, clawing at the man's crotch. Hank squealed, slapped the monkey away with the laser – and fell backwards, perilously close to the flaming car.

As Dog ran to MacKay, the Op heard a high-pitched alarm whine. It was almost inaudible, causing a sharp pain behind his ears. He'd only heard it once before, in the G-Mek dealers' centre, years ago, but it wasn't the kind of thing you forgot.

He grabbed Mia and Dog. "*Down!*"

They ducked against the wall of the house, behind a bush –

just as the Interceptor exploded in a deadly fireball.

MacKay shielded his eyes, trying not to imagine the sight. Mia clutched his left arm, while Dog huddled under his right. He tried to concentrate on Mia's tight body next to him, rather than the fireball he could feel expanding outwards from his now-shattered ve-hickle.

Once the roar died down, he looked up at the wreckage. The chassis stood blackened and stripped, small fires still burning on rubber and electrical components. Doors and pieces of chain gun littered the driveway. The smell of burning rubber was nauseating.

Keek! Keek!

"I'm pretty sure it was out of warranty," MacKay replied sadly.

Mia was on her feet. "I don't see Hank," she said. "Let's get out of here."

Nodding, MacKay scooped up Dog and followed her to her bike. She sat down, revved it to life. Then she turned, stroked his cheek, and, finally, handed him back his Shredder. "Cover me," she said.

He smiled, shouldered the weapon, and grabbed onto her slim waist. She felt good. Very, very good. Even Dog's metal claws, grabbing onto his shoulder for dear life, couldn't distract him from Mia now.

The bike hummed and throbbed beneath them.

Mia threw it into gear, wheeled a wide arc around the flaming wreckage, then shot straight out through Miko D's golden arches, heading for the open road.

"So," MacKay called out over the rushing wind. "Thalamus?"

"Later," she replied. "First I've got a surprise for you."

From the throaty tone of her voice, MacKay thought he knew what she meant.

Not for the first time, he was wrong.

I

MacKay was used to the open road, but this was ridiculous. He'd had no time to grab a helmet, and after two hours of clinging on to Mia for dear life, he had dust in his mouth, ears, and eyes, even behind his shades. And there was the embarrassment factor, too. The rumbling of the bike and the feel of Mia's lovely body had combined to give him a hell of a boner.

Keek! Keek! Dog said, pointing.

"You just wish you had one," MacKay replied. Then, for the eleventh time, "Where are we going?"

"Almost there," Mia called back.

Red sand and dry, dry desert roared by. Mia's bike was tricked out with condensation recyclers, collectors that picked up every trace of moisture and purified it into drinking water. The water was funnelled into straws that stuck up from the handlebars. MacKay had to lean forwards to reach one, and Mia had to poke it into his mouth. Somehow that didn't reduce his boner problem.

"Very *Man Who Fell to Earth*," he said, wiping a drop from his chin.

"I think you mean *Dune*," she replied.

He shrugged. It was tough carrying on an open-air conversation at 110 mph.

Finally she slowed, as a few rickety wooden buildings came into sight. It was early afternoon, the sun still high. A sign, at least a hundred years old, whizzed by.

"'Welcome to Aztec,'" MacKay read.

"Don't expect any pyramids."

They passed by a general store with a broken porch step, then a boarded-up gas station, then an *open* gas station with astronomical prices. Finally Mia pulled up in front of a nondescript, unfinished wood house a half-mile from any other structures. Power lines fed into it, and water apparently came from a water tower a hundred feet off the road. And that was about it.

MacKay smelled something.

Mia dismounted, helped MacKay off.

"Little stiff," he said.

part four
the meat of it

"Mm." She smiled down at his midsection, then looked quickly away.

"What, uh, what is this place?"

He knew he smelled something now. Something impossible.

"It's my big surprise. Are you ready?"

MacKay shrugged. But his mouth was beginning to water.

"The monkey can't come in."

Keek! Keek!

MacKay placed Dog on the ground. "It's okay, fella. Stay here."

Mia walked to the door, unlocked a huge padlock. She kicked the rickety door open and stood aside. "After you."

Later, MacKay would remember it as if he were moving in a dream. Ignoring Dog's continued protests, he walked past Mia and into the dark room. All he could make out was a row of tables, a few chairs, some stacked-up boxes, a futon couch, and some boarded-up windows. Vaguely, a corner of his mind wondered whether she was preparing to seduce him – or kill him.

Then she flicked on the light, and his eyes went wide.

The tables were covered with meat.

Beautifully cooked, lovingly prepared meat. Honey-glazed hams, crammed with salt and juices. Prime rib steaks, laid out on trays with potatoes and huge stalks of asparagus. Sizzling bacon, straight from the grill, and ribs slathered with thick, spicy barbecue sauce. Whole chickens, deep-fried in batter and covered with gravy. Giant turkey drumsticks. Plump hot dogs and juicy hamburgers with pickles, relish, and sugary ketchup soaking through sesame buns.

Enough pure animal protein to feed an army. Or a football team, at least.

He turned to Mia, stunned. "But you're a vegetarian."

She smiled, wickedly. "I'm a sinner."

She picked up a pork chop, closed her eyes, and wafted it under her nose, sighing at the smell. She seemed entranced. Then she waved the chop at him and smiled, a look of pure animal desire.

"Are you man enough?"

The aroma was overwhelming, intoxicating. He looked around at the plates of rich, filling food. It had been a long time.

"Oh, yeah," he said.

ONLY AFTERWARDS – WHEN he and Mia lay together on the futon, stomachs aching, propped up against each other, the last bits of barbecue sauce dripping down their chins – only then did MacKay think to ask the hundred questions he needed her to answer.

"Where did all this come from, anyway?"

She smiled, stretched, and licked a bit of honey glaze off his cheek. "It's kind of a long story."

"I can say with all confidence that I am not going anywhere for a while."

She got up and started stacking plates. "I was a pretty wild kid, back in my teen years. Made some good friends… we still help each other out."

"And one of these friends specialises in… black market meat?"

She turned to him, held up a box. "See this? AniProtein, Inc. They provide all the meat for the southern half of the United States. Strictly legal." She smiled. "Also very, very expensive."

"'100% Made in USA,'" he read. "So you called your friend, and he set up this spread."

"He knows what I like."

He started to ask her about her vegetarianism… and stopped. He thought of a man who loved animals, and who made his living by killing them. He thought of a country that preached peace and equal opportunity, and had so overextended itself with wars, and by funnelling ever more money to its richest citizens, that it could barely afford to keep its own people in water.

We all have our myths about ourselves, he realised. Best not to rub Mia's nose in hers.

MacKay glanced over at the bloody remains of a London broil. Something Sputo had said crossed his mind… about how meat had become available again, after years of scarcity. AniProtein proudly boasted that all its meat was made in the USA. It was good to think America had gotten that industry, at least, back on its feet again.

Good to think, but hard to believe.

What did it all mean?

Mia crossed back to the futon, plopped herself down on MacKay's overstuffed lap. For a moment, he was afraid a hot dog would come back up; he swallowed hard. Then the sight of Mia's lovely body, curves still sheathed in tight black pleather, brought him back to attention.

"So let's get it over with," she said. "Ask me about Thalamus."

He did. And for the first time in days, things started to make sense.

"Five years ago, the Cows signed a retainer agreement with Thalamus," Mia said. "They made a nice offer, we took a vote, and that was that. Half the gang just wanted the money; most of the others were into the health insurance and PZ passes. I think Britney was in anorexic shock that day – she doesn't remember voting at all." Mia sighed. "They're a handful sometimes."

"And you?"

She looked at him, hard and honest. "I don't know. I told myself it would help us pursue our ideals – that a little funding would really grease the wheels of eco-terrorism, make it easier to afford guns, ordnance, bikes when we needed them. But that was probably rationalising."

"You were tired of the life?"

"Like I told you back at the Mouse House: I'm getting too old for this." She sighed again.

She didn't look old. She looked active and vital and alive. Seasoned enough to know what's what, but youthful enough to kick some ass to get it.

I'm really falling for this woman, MacKay realised.

"The tall asshole," he said. "What's his story? He doesn't seem like a ganger."

"Oh, Jesus. Hank." She dabbed a little gravy off her bustier. "He used to be a Thalamus exec. Very ruthless, very successful. And he had a thing about bikes."

"I think I see where this is going."

"Three years ago, he had a midlife crisis the size of Texas. Decided he couldn't stand working in an office anymore. Decided a real man should be out on the road, shooting guns, killing people… not sitting in a cubicle, counting the days and waiting to retire."

"When you put it that way…"

"Thalamus didn't know what to do with him… but he was a good employee, and they didn't want to just lose him. So they forced him on us – made him our liaison." She smiled ruefully. "I really should have read the fine print in our contract."

MacKay hesitated. "Were you… were you sleeping with him?"

"Oh, God no. Well, yes. I don't know. I was bored… so bored I could die. He really had a thing for girls in pleather."

MacKay looked away, momentarily embarrassed.

"I mean, shit, so do I," Mia continued. "But I think… Oh, I told myself he was a good guy, meant well, strong and good in bed. But in the back of my mind… This is hard to admit… "

"You don't have to—"

"I knew if I ever wanted to climb the corporate ladder, it wouldn't hurt to be in with a guy like him."

That thought hung in the air, unpleasantly, for a moment.

"Back up the truck a minute," MacKay said. "You were on my trail from the minute I hit Florida. How?"

She frowned, twisted in his lap. "I had to piece some of this together, but... Thalamus kind of coerced you to take the I Heart Florida job, right?"

"Yeah."

"Right. Then they sent us after you, to try to kill you."

"Why?"

"Thalamus didn't give a shit about I Heart Florida. There's a hundred easier ways they could have closed down a diseased-pig lab. And I never really believed they cared enough about the goddamn pigs to send us to stop you, either. I let my people think that, because... well, most of them can't really see past one layer at a time, if you know what I mean."

He nodded.

"Once you were in Florida," she continued, "Thalamus tipped off Fuzzies, anonymously, that you were available. They knew – Thalamus, I mean, knew that Fuzzies would hire you to recover their experimental animals. And sure enough, Fuzzies took the bait."

He looked at her. "So you know a little more about my assignment than you let on, back at Miko's."

She shrugged. "I never put all my cards on the table at once, MacKay. Besides, I didn't know when my gang was going to show up."

He decided to accept that for now. "Okay. But why did Thalamus go to all this trouble in the first place? What do they care about Fuzzies' animals?"

Mia jumped up, began to pace. Her long legs swung back and forth, hypnotically. "That part I don't know," she said. "It could be just a turf war of some kind. Fuzzies is owned by GenTech, right?"

"Yes."

"The corps are always playing games with each other. Gen-Tech, Thalamus, Eidolon, all of them. And it's so hard to distinguish between them, it's like they're all cast from the same mould. It wouldn't surprise me if one giant super-corporation owns them all. Or a cult. Wouldn't it be scary if they're controlled by the Moonies or somebody like that?"

He smiled. "They're corporations. That's scary enough."

"Well, maybe." She stooped to tie a bootlace, and MacKay thought he would die with desire. "Thalamus… they sure made us a good pitch, when we signed on with them. All about the evils of GenTech, its unnatural treatment of humanity and the natural world. When you've got a toothache and no medical insurance, it's easy to believe Thalamus really might be the good guys."

"I understand," he said softly.

"Plus they set us up with lasers. I mean, *lasers.*"

"So Thalamus sent you after me in Florida… and then again, when I went hunting for the Fuzzies creatures."

"That's right."

"How did you manage to keep on my trail? I've been pretty careful about staying off the satellite net."

Mia smiled, crossed to the door, and opened it. She whistled, and Dog came bounding in.

The monkey jumped up on MacKay's lap, chittering happily. Mia reached under Dog's arm and unpeeled a thin, transparent sticker.

MacKay stared. "You bastards bugged my monkey!"

Dog jumped down, scratched under his arm.

Mia smiled. She climbed up on top of MacKay, straddling him. A speck of barbecue sauce clung to her lips, providing a bit of extra spice as she leaned in close.

"I'm very sorry," she said softly, still smiling. "Can I make it up to you?"

Thirty seconds later, the monkey was back out in the cold.

ll

CALVES CHAINED INTO a semicircle of small pens, two feet wide apiece. Necks held fast by choker collars. Some sleep sitting down, heads jerked cruelly upwards. Their hides burn red with disease, and faeces cover the dirt floor. When they sleep, they sleep in their own shit.

The most luscious, tender veal in the world.

Past the arc of calves are lined cows with udders the size of medicine balls, specially grown to produce twice the usual amount of milk. Half their udders are diseased – tender, pinkish, scabbed. The milk still flows, forced from them by hard, squeaking, rusted machines.

And above: the chickens. Ragged, stretched out, grown in a long line, fused together by their extra-thick wings. Eyes genetically replaced with tender tissue that melts on the tongue. They will never fly, but they bleed. And grow. And drop more faeces on the cows.

Cows, calves, chickens. A full circle of stench, filth, and decay. And in the centre…

A man waits. Tall, lean. His two attendants, dressed all in black, come to him and remove his cloak. He stands, waiting. The smell does not touch him. The mewling does not touch him. It is all part of the price he must pay; the rocky road to his utopia.

Then the boar is released.

It charges, aiming large pointed horns at his face. He stands, eyeing it intently. Just in time, he swerves to the side. The boar slides past him, skids to a stop in front of a cow. For a moment, the two animals' eyes meet.

The boar turns, opens its mouth, and lets out a long, stupid sound. Then it charges again.

The man backs up towards the circle's edge. Chicken dung drips down to his left, but he ignores it. Again, he watches the boar… horns flashing, tusks growing nearer…

And with surprising agility, he flips backwards, jumping up on top of a calf's stall. Surprised, the calf follows him with dull, rheumy eyes – not seeing the boar till its horns pin the calf all the way back against its pen, snapping its neck against the unyielding choker collar.

Startled, the boar tries to disengage itself from the dying calf. But in its moment of surprise, the man acts. He pulls out a long-nozzled weapon, trains it on the boar, and engulfs the surprised animal in flame.

Sprinklers come on – the only safety device in this place. The flame is doused, the boar drops to the ground. Both it and the calf are dead.

The man gestures to his attendants, and they scurry to his side. They present him with elegant napkins, fine silver, a large china plate, and a sharp carving knife.

Together, they begin the feast.

MIA SAT BOLT upright. For a moment, she had absolutely no idea where she was.

Then she saw the empty trays, the spare furnishings, the cov-ered-over windows… and the softly breathing form of "Ratcatcher" MacKay, lying naked next to her under an old Indian blanket.

It was night; the room was dark. Mia raised herself to her feet, pulled out her HanHeld. 4:00 am.

She looked at MacKay again: his firm, stubbly jaw, his lean, muscular arms. And she realised something about herself… something she wasn't especially proud of.

One of the reasons she'd slept with MacKay was in the hope that her dreams would go away.

It wasn't the only reason, of course. He was handsome and wild and, in his own way, very kind. Mia was tired of the cor-porate runaround, and increasingly sick of the compromises she'd made in her life. MacKay had managed something she hadn't: He was his own man, ran his own life. That was very attractive to her.

But she'd also wanted comfort. She'd wanted to be able to sleep through the night, for once, without waking up scream-ing inside.

MacKay couldn't give her that, she realised. At least, not in one night.

"I'm sorry," she said softly.

He shifted, mumbled in his sleep.

She rose, still in her panties. She pulled on her jacket, the worn pleather comforting on her bare shoulders, and started quietly stacking dishes. As she moved, she spoke softly, soothingly. She told him about the dreams: about the skinned chickens, the genetically enlarged cattle, the pigs that lived all their lives in unmoving horror. She bustled around the room, talking because she needed to talk.

"That sounds familiar," he said finally.

She stopped by the big table, looked down at him on the futon. "How long have you been awake?"

"A while." He rubbed his eyes. "Quite a story."

"They're very vivid dreams."

"Miko – the mouse – he showed me a vid that looked a lot like that. Gigantic cattle, hung up on racks. Bred for meat, I think."

She looked around at the empty plates, the bones and gristle left behind from the night before. She felt suddenly empty, ashamed.

"These dreams," he continued. "How long have you had them?"

"About three years. They started around the time Hank–" She stopped, dropped a plate on the table with a low clatter. She walked back over to him, sat down, took his hand. "You know, I never put that together before."

He stroked her hand, frowned.

"When we trapped the Balled Eagle," she continued. "It – it pointed at Hank and said something about him being... tainted."

"I hope you've been checked for STDs."

"I'm serious, MacKay. I've seen some strange things hanging around the Thalamus offices." She paused, got up and paced again. "For a while, I remember everyone being all hush-hush about something called 'Project Nihilo.' Never did find out what that was."

MacKay looked at her, curious. "What made you think of that now?"

"I don't know." She turned to him. "Balled Eagle... he seems to be chasing us, right? You and me both?"

He shrugged.

"Why?" she asked.

"He's got a brain full of over-the-hill Chief Executive sperm?"

"No. Well, yes, but… there's more going on here. Maybe the eagle's not really interested in us at all. Maybe he's after Hank."

MacKay sat up straight, pulled on an undershirt. "Mia… that pathetic former Thalamus exec set my car on fire. I have no objection to ripping him a new shithole the next time we run across him. And I assure you I would say that even if he wasn't your ex.

"But if he *hadn't* set my car on fire, I wouldn't give 'Hank' a second look. I fail to see why Balled Eagle – a clinically insane, chemically unbalanced bird – would have any interest in him, either."

Mia pulled aside a shade for a moment, and the first light of dawn seeped in. It did sound a little odd in daylight, she thought. But…

"There's one way to find out." She turned, posing for a second in front of the window. "Pair up with me. Let's find out together."

He smiled. "You sure you want in on my action?"

"I think it's a little late for that."

"Now *I'm* serious." He reached for a squeezer, took a swig of water. "This assignment I'm on is… well, I don't think Fuzzies has been straight with me about their operations."

"Imagine that."

"You were talking about Thalamus last night… Fuzzies is a different kind of puzzle. Their corporate HQ is huge, considering what they do – or what they say they do. Miko filled in a few holes, but the info they gave me on their creations still doesn't make sense."

"How so?"

"They claim the new creatures – the ones I'm looking for – are smarter, more advanced than their predecessors. But every Fuzzies animal I've run across so far is of above-average intelligence. Miko's a bitter son of a bitch, but clearly he made the most of his fifteen minutes. Sputo's carved himself out a nice life among people who probably *eat* dogs when times get tough. Even Balled Eagle seems to have a kind of ruthless intelligence under his madness."

She looked into his eyes, her face close to his. "So what's wrong with them?"

"More to the point – what's special about the ones we're chasing?"

She smiled. "We?"

MacKay rose and rummaged around in a pile of their mixed clothing. "The GenTech map showing the locations of all the Fuzzies animals was in my car – that's gone now."

"Can you call Fuzzies for a new one?"

"I could, but I'd rather stay off the grid. Besides, I've still got this." He pulled a small device out of his trouser pocket. "This tracker will show when we're in the vicinity of one of them. It's also a good early-warning system for testosterone-fuelled aerial attacks."

She moved close to him, looked at the tracker. "It didn't help you back at the mouse's place."

"I, uh, wasn't watching it at the time. I was trying to play golf."

She smiled, stroked his neck. She just wanted to be near him, she realised. "So… next stop?"

"Miko gave me a location… out in Nevada. Town, or something, called Cocoa Niño. It corresponds with one of the blips on the GenTech map."

"Cocoa Niño… wasn't that a forest in Arizona?"

"Long gone – chopped down years ago. I checked with Encarta Gazetteer. This is something else."

Mia nodded. "We leave at dawn?"

"Yeah. Just one thing." He turned to her and put his hands on her slim hips. "I get to drive."

She smiled. "Okay."

He set the tracker back down, held up a thin pleather garment. "You want your leggings?"

"No," she said.

★ ★ ★

III

HANK POLEHOUSE SAT at the bar, vowing not to get into another fight with the locals.

The place was dark, smelled of stale beer, and was run by Navajos. Down the other end of the bar sat a guy with a huge moustache and seven empty shot glasses piled up in front of him. Hank hoped he wouldn't be taking the pickup truck home tonight. The only other patrons were an old Indian couple sitting at a table, drinking in silence.

Jefe slammed open the door, strode over to sit next to Hank. "Rooms are all set," he said. "Here's your key."

Hank looked at the old-fashioned, metal motel key with "8" stencilled on it. This part of the country amazed him. Everything seemed stuck in the mid-20th century. They even still had drive-through burger joints.

And the Navajos were tricky to deal with. When you approached the counter to buy groceries or sat down at their bar, they stared at you with what seemed, at first, like hatred. But once you were actually talking, they were quite friendly. It was apparently a distancing technique, a way of not dealing with white people unless they had to. Nothing personal, though.

Jefe fidgeted, drummed the bar. The bartender glared at him from his stool, read the paper for a minute more, then slowly lumbered over with a beer.

I'm the leader now, Hank remembered suddenly. Got to show interest in the troops.

"You, uh… okay?" he asked.

Jefe wrapped his hands around the beer… and seemed to fold up. He looked at the bar, sadly. "Can't believe she's gone, man."

"Don't worry," Hank said. He forced his voice into the timbre recommended by the DVD of *The 10-Second Manager*, which he'd seen years before. "We'll get that thing that killed her. And Mia, too."

"Mia, man… I can't believe it. She was always so cool." Jefe looked up, suddenly. "Did she know the bird was gonna attack again?"

"I don't know. But she definitely set us up, ran off with MacKay."

After MacKay's Interceptor had exploded, Hank, burned and limping, had sought cover behind a road sign while Mia drove off with the killer. By the time Hank made his way to the back of Miko's house, the fight with Balled Eagle – round two – had turned into a fiasco. Cristina had accidentally singed Wister-Hauser with her laser, and Jefe was out of bullets. Meanwhile, the bird had cut up Britney's arm pretty badly, and was swinging down for another strike.

Hank thought he was going to crap his pants. But he managed to aim his combat laser – which, amazingly, still worked – at the bird. Then he remembered Plan B. As the red beam slashed through the bird's wing, Hank reached into his pocket and tossed a small disk at it.

Balled Eagle spun, disoriented, and paused in mid-air for a moment. Then it climbed, higher and higher, till it vanished into the big sky.

Hank had established himself as new leader, and ordered a retreat to regroup. Miko D was pretty happy to see them go. Hank remembered the wounded mouse, shaking a three-fingered fist at them as they drove off. Miko's muffled swearing still echoed in his ears.

"We never gonna find 'em," Jefe said.

Hank smiled. "Trust your leader." He put his arm around Jefe's shoulders, then quickly removed it. He reached into his jacket and pulled out a small device with a blinking blue light.

"What's that, man?"

"Tracker."

Jefe looked at him with the age-old contempt the young had for their elders. "Man, that ain't gonna work. Mia knows we bugged MacKay's monkey. She'll take care'a that."

"Not MacKay. The bird." He tossed the tracker up, caught it again. "I tagged the bird, back at the mouse's house."

Jefe stared at him, and Hank felt a chill go up his spine. "You let that thing go? After what it did to Shank?"

"Hey, hey! It was Mia's plan. Besides, I tried to shoot the thing."

Jefe accepted that, nodded. "What the – what the hell is MacKay chasin', anyhow?"

"Some damn experimental animals or something."

"What kind of animals?"

"I dunno. Not that stupid dog, or the mouse. Those were dead ends. Not the eagle, either." Hank sighed. "That blasted bird is following MacKay – I don't know why. But if we can follow it, we'll find both of 'em."

"An' Mia."

"And Mia." Hank sighed, took a long gulp of whiskey. "That bitch. After all I did for her."

"I just don' understand it."

"Back at Thalamus… we knew how to handle women. Keep 'em in their place. Get the donuts, bitch. Answer the phone, bitch. Not like out here. It's fucking anarchy out here."

"I loved her, man."

"You don't wanna love 'em, dude. They'll snap you in half. They'll use you till they're tired of you. They'll dump you for some asshole with a fucking robot monkey and a fucking degree in zoology and a fucking – ha ha! – fucking *fancy car on fire!*"

Jefe started to cry.

"Hey, hey. Listen to me." Hank turned to face the young kid. "This started out as a simple contract job: Stop MacKay. Now, we're still gonna do that, and collect our commission from Thalamus. You with me so far?"

Jefe nodded, wiped a tear away. "And stop an animal-killer."

"Right, yeah, that. But this is a bigger mission now. We gotta catch a traitor to our gang – Mia. And we gotta get an abomination of a creature that killed one of our own. Fortunately, all these goals contribute to a single overall departmental objective."

Jefe looked at him blankly.

"We can, uh, do 'em all at once."

Jefe grimaced, turned back to his beer.

"The Mad Cows is more than just a gang," Hank continued. "It's a group with a purpose: to aid animal life everywhere. Except, uh, except when that animal life fucks with us too much. And anyway, I don't think that thing's really an eagle.

"My point is, we're patriots. We're in a long tradition of Americans who see things as wrong and work to make them right. We don't waver from our cause; we don't accept another point of view just because it might be 'convenient' or 'true'. We fight for what *we* believe is right. And anybody who gets in our way is gonna get a hurtin'."

Not a bad speech, he thought. Though he wished he'd been able to come up with a better end than "get a hurtin'".

"So let's get a good night's sleep, and then let's go get the bad guys. We're gonna kill the bird and MacKay, and bring Mia back to Thalamus for judgment. And we're gonna do it all in the next three days."

Jefe nodded. "I dunno, man." Then he frowned. "Three days?"

"Just a personal goal."

Both men turned back to their drinks then, silent. The Navajo bartender came over, silently poured Hank another whiskey.

Hank was thinking furiously. He had a lot to pull off, and a reduced, damaged gang to do it with. But his goals were important. He really did have to get back to Florida within three days.

His Thalamus stock options were about to mature.

10

ROOM 15
Wister-Hauser and Hauser-Wister

"AAH — OW!"

"Sit still, husband. I know you would not wish to be coddled as I redress your wounds."

"Apologies, my wife. My mind was elsewhere."

"Elaborate, my husband."

"I believe the time has come for us to take stock of our situation."

"I concur. Proceed."

"The scenario we find ourselves in has taken a complex turn, and we must evaluate our moral options. I think we can begin from this point of agreement – we still believe in the basic moral underpinnings of the Mad Cow organization."

"Agreed so far."

"However, the organization itself has undergone a change of leadership. If we are to follow the new leader, we must possess, at minimum, a reasonable degree of faith in his goals and his competence."

"Flawlessly logical."

"You flatter me, wife. So the question becomes, do we possess such faith?"

"To the core of the matter as usual, husband. May I explore the question in some depth?"

"Please do."

"Hank Polehouse is a flawed being. This in itself is not a disqualifying factor in a leader; all beings are, to some degree, flawed."

"You skate on the edge of a disturbing moral relativism, wife. However, I shall hear you out as always."

"My thanks. To continue, from my weighing of the situation, I judge that Hank Polehouse's belief in the goals of radical vegetarianism are shallow at best. I have observed him to consume cocktail wieners and small poultry nuggets when he believed himself unobserved."

"Discomforting data. Please continue."

"I perceive Hank Polehouse to be a weak moral creature. His allegiance to Thalamus stems primarily from the desire for currency, and his loyalty to the Mad Cows, from a desire to ride fast two-wheeled vehicles in intimidating packs."

"And, until recently, to copulate with Mia."

"Yes… an understandable, if disappointingly temporal, goal. But I shall return to Mia in a moment."

"My apologies, wife."

"None required. So… I believe I have established, then, that Hank Polehouse is not worthy of following on ideal moral grounds."

"A persuasive case, wife. Should we, then, cease to observe his leadership?"

"Under less critical conditions that would be my recommendation, husband. However, there is another dimension to this affair. Allow me to digress to a related subject and then circle my argument back to this question."

"Your mind is a constant delight to me, wife. Had your Nazi forebears possessed your analytic skills, no doubt they would have ruled over a fair and just world."

"High praise, husband. Very well, then, let us consider the question of Mia."

"Mia. Yes. Even in her absence, she looms large in the mind of Hank Polehouse."

"And in yours, husband. The rise in your pulse rate at the mention of her name does not escape me."

"I am yet a creature of flesh and blood, wife."

"As am I. And I too have dreamt of her soft mocha skin, her slim waist, her long, muscular legs."

"It pleases me to see you so scrupulously observe our credo of total honesty between us, wife. May I continue in this spirit?"

"I would expect no less."

"My gaze, too, has lingered on Mia's firm buttocks, the softly rounded small of her back. At times, when caressing your own large yet slightly sagging breasts, I have thought of her firm, pointed nipples, aimed like the loftiest goals of mankind at the stars."

"Mmm. For myself, I have many times, while manually stimulating your flaccid penis to full arousal, cast my thoughts to Mia's full, lush lips, slightly parted as though calling to her lover."

"Yes. And as I have lain next to you, my index finger stimulating your clitoris while my middle finger probes your anal cavity, I have pictured Mia hovering over me, slowly lowering the zipper on her tight pleather trousers, her voice softly yet firmly demanding penetration in a variety of pleasurable locations."

" . . . "

" . . . "

"So. Husband."

"Yes."

"I believe we may agree that Mia Sangre is not the sort of person whose absence immediately banishes her from one's mind."

"A balanced assessment."

"And you are, of course, aware of the human male's tendency towards strong emotional reactions upon betrayal."

"Not merely the *human* male, wife. Similar behaviour patterns have been observed in many animal species as well."

"Point taken. In this case, however, the animal species of interest to us is Hank Polehouse."

"Ah."

"While we may assume he no longer anticipates copulation with Mia, we may further assume that he still experiences an emotional response to her. Specifically, a desire for revenge."

"I will grant the assumption."

"That, combined with his continued desire for monetary compensation from Thalamus, gives him a clear motivation to locate and trap both Mia and MacKay."

"True as far as it goes."

"This goal aligns with our own, husband. We too wish Mia and MacKay brought to justice for their crimes."

"I begin to see your logic."

"Thus, while Hank Polehouse is unquestionably flawed as a moral leader, there may be a certain expediency to remaining under his command on a temporary basis. It may, in truth, be the best route to achieving a clear, just end to this business."

"Possibly, wife. Possibly. Yet I admit to some moral qualms as to your conclusion. May I explore the question a bit further?"

"Very well."

"As you know, my grandfather enjoyed a liaison with Ayn Rand, during which time he absorbed – and later passed on – many unshakable tenets of moral behaviour. My father's time with the neoconservative groups of the late 20th century cemented these beliefs within our family heritage."

"So you have said, many times."

"Randian thought teaches us, quite rightly, that each person has free will – to choose to do right or ill. Once he has chosen, each person must live with the consequences of that choice. Those who do ill are not to be forgiven nor pitied, but dealt with swiftly and finally. Only thus can a just society prevail."

"Continue."

"Mia Sangre has unquestionably chosen wrong in allying herself with a killer of animals. Hank Polehouse, on the other hand, has as yet chosen only correctly in pursuing her and MacKay."

"Ah. A different approach to the same conclusion. Then you agree that we should follow him?"

"I believe I do. In essence, you are proposing that we regard Hank Polehouse as the human equivalent of Plato's 'noble lie': a logically and morally invalid construct that we, as enlightened citizens, accept and propagate nevertheless, in the name of the greater good."

"Mmmm."

"Seen in that light, I believe I concur that… wife?"

"Yes?"

"What are you doing with your hand?"

"Uh… "

"Are we not exploring a vital moral question here? Is not such intellectual curiosity the very foundation of our marital partnership?"

"Oh, indeed, husband. Indeed. And I am pleased we have solved the problem of Hank Polehouse."

"As am I."

"However, I believe we have not yet fully explored the moral dimensions of the Mia Sangre problem."

"The moral… ah."

"Yes. Many times I have found myself pondering the depths of Mia's moral degeneracy… as I straddle you and place your hands firmly on my ample gluteal regions."

"My wound! I – oh. I see."

"Have you not pursued similar discourse in your own mind?"

"Uh, yes, yes indeed."

"Elaborate."

"Uh…"

"*Now.*"

" I – I have speculated on the many punishments deserved by Mia's crimes…"

"Yes?"

"…as I turn you firmly on your back, position my engorged organ above your labial entrance, and place my rough hand over your mouth."

"Oh, husb*mmmpphhh…*"

Ʊ

ROOM 22
Britney and Cristina

"HOW DOES THIS bunny top look?"

"Huh?"

"Wake *up*, girl! Do I look fat in this?"

"You? Never!"

"Be real now."

"Well… *no!*"

"Are you being *honest*?"

"Totally."

"Really."

"Totally! I'm just… I'm all over the place tonight, you know?"

"Yeah."

"Yeah."

"Mia."

"Yeah."

"I can't, like, be*lieve* she'd just go off and leave us like this."

"I *know!*"

"And that total *loser* she hooked up with…"

"I dunno. He had a pretty cool car."

"Emphasis on *had*, girlfriend."

"Ha ha ha!"

"And his monkey is totally cute. Did you see his monkey?"

"Duh! Of *course* I saw the monkey."

"Totally cute."

"*Yuh.*"

"But still... he's a killer."

"Yuh."

"He kills, like... kitties and bunnies. Helpless little guys."

"Frown face."

"Frown face. And he killed, like, Brutus and Chet."

"Big woop. Brutus was like, totally, watch those hands, buddy."

"I *know*. Total loser."

"Totally."

"Still. Shooting him... that's pretty *severe*."

"Yuh."

"Maybe that loser – not Brutus, like, the other loser–"

"We need a scorecard, girl."

"A loser scorecard."

"Hee hee hee!"

"Maybe that loser like, totally *kidnapped* Mia."

"Whoa!"

"Maybe she's being held, like, against her will."

"I don't think Hank cares, like."

"Totally. He's all 'I been betrayed,' and shit."

"Totally."

"He sees her, he's gonna kill her."

"That's pretty severe, too."

"It's extra severe, 'cuz it's *Mia*."

"I know. You remember when she taught us how to do a weave?"

"Totally!"

"She's just the best gang boss *ever*."

"I *know*!"

"We, like, can't just let Hank shoot her."

"He's, like, another one for the loser billboard."

"You mean scorecard."

"Oh yeah. Hee hee hee. I forgot!"

"You *loser.*"

"Shut up!"

"Put *down* that pillow, girl."

"Yes, *mother.*"

"Be serious, girl. We gotta find Mia."

"Oh, totally."

"But how?"

"…"

"…"

"…"

"…"

"…"

"Oh! Oh! I got it!"

"What? Wha-*aaaaaat*?"

"Your ESP! You got that total psychic thing going, right?"

"Oh, duh! Yeah!"

"Well?"

"Oh, girl, I'll totally try!"

"Cool! How does it work?"

"I dunno, really. I think maybe if I *think* real hard I could find her."

"That's so cool."

"Yuh."

"Did you, like always have that?"

"No, it's, like, an adult thing. Since I became an adult."

"Like, since you learned to drive?"

"No, silly! Later than that."

"Like, since that night I found you in the back room of–"

"Don't–"

"–in the back room of Jose's with… *Hank*?"

"Shut up!"

"With Hank the loser? The loser scorecard loser?"

"You *promised.*"

"Hee hee!"

"You promised you'd *never.*"

"Girl, it's just the two of us."

"Oh. Yuh."

"Yuh."

"So I guess we're goin' solo, huh?"

"Yuh. Just the two of us."

"Yuh."

"Is that solo?"

"What?"

"If there's two of us. Is that solo? Or, like, duo or something?"

"Shut *up*!"

"I totally need a new wardrobe if we're going solo."

"Totally."

"What about this skirt?"

"It's *cute*."

"Does it make me look fat?"

"No."

"Girl?"

"Not really."

"You are so honest. You're my best friend."

"Maybe a *little* fat."

"You bitch."

"Hee hee hee."

"I love you."

"I love *you*."

"Hugs."

"*Hugs*!"

VI

ROOM 666
Nihilo

"HEY NIHILO. LOOKIN' sexy today, dude!

"Thanks, Nihilo. You too, buddy!

"Hey Nihilo?

"Yeah?

"Why you figure you're talkin' to yourself? Ain't that a sign of mental disorder?

"Only in *humans*, Fucknuts!

"Oh yeah…

"We *demons*… we're a whole different kettle of piranhas!

"Got that right!

"We can do whatever the fuck we want!

"Hell yeah!

"Except…

"What?

"…

"Let it out, man!

"Thanks, Nihilo. It's just… I feel pretty pulled in all different directions. You know?

"Oh, Nihilo… do I ever!

"We're s'posed to be workin' with Thalamus. That's what the lord ordered. But…

"Yeah…

"…but GenTech seems to have their claws in us, too!

"Fuckin' humans. I hate it here!

"Yeah. But GenTech ain't just humans.

"Right, right…

"They got Powers behind them, too.

"This Cocoa Niño bullshit is okay, but…

"Yeah. I miss bein' in Florida… bein' *all* in Florida, I mean. Nice an' hot there, no morals to speak of.

"You're a man of wealth an' taste, Nihilo. Hey, you know what I could go for?

"Course I do, Nihilo. But go ahead an' say it, man!

"Some fuckin' *room service*.

"Yeah!

"Trouble is… Thalamus is cuttin' back on corporate expenses–

"Cheap bastards!

"An' Cocoa Niño's just a fuckin' *hole*.

"Guess that leaves us one choice, huh?

"Nihilo… you're a fuckin' genius!

"Hank fuckin' Polehouse. He's stayin' at some little shithouse motel in the southwest–

"Preach it, brother!

"–and there's a little Nihilo in *him*, too!

"Awright!

"I'm thinkin' tacos. Lots an' lots of fuckin' tacos.

"Hey, Nihilo?

"Yeah?

"How you want the sauce on those tacos?

"Do I gotta say it?

"Hell yeah!

"*Extra hot!*

"Hahahahaha!

"Thus begins the reign of blood and horror on earth!

"Your mouth to God's ear, dude. Well, *somebody's* ear, anyway!

"Nihilo… I probably don't say it often enough. But–

"aw…

"–you are one hell of a demon!

"It's a little embarrassing… but it's gotta be said!

"Hahahahaha!

"Tacos!

"Hahahahahahahahahaha!

"*Tacos!*"

part five
stealing the sun

I

"MacKay," Mia said in his ear, "you drive like shit."

He smiled into the wind. They'd managed to pick him up a helmet in Aztec, which helped with the dust – but the desert sun was hot on his scalp. Goggles kept the sweat out of his eyes. His biggest concern now was not having his GangBuster unit. Still, Mia's bike had been paid for by a corp and was far from being a piece of crap. If they did spot any gangcult activity, they should be able to outrun it. "Remember our deal."

"If you crack up my bike, I'll gut you like a fish."

"How vegetarian," MacKay said. "Tell you what – let's talk about something else."

"Like what?"

"I don't know. How about *you*?"

He heard her groan in his ear, and smiled. Then the bike went over a bump, and he turned his attention quickly back to the road. Mia's ride was pretty smooth, and MacKay had driven his share of motorsickles in his younger years. But she was right – he'd gotten much more accustomed to steering four wheels than two.

Keek! Keek!

"Pipe down," he said to Dog, who sat on his knee, clutching the bike just below the handlebars. Then he half-turned and said, "So?"

"All right," Mia replied. "What do you want to know?"

"You're from Florida originally?"

"Yes."

"Any relatives left?"

"My mother's Italian, my father was Puerto Rican. He's gone now, she's in a home for the old and drunken."

"Doesn't sound like a very happy family."

"I think I saw the two of them in the same room once. Twice, maybe."

"Did you get much from your heritage?"

He felt her shrug. "I never burn, no matter how long I sit out in the sun. Just get more tan."

MacKay smiled softly. He still didn't completely trust Mia, but he definitely liked her and, he'd told himself, it was better to have her here, where he could keep an eye on her, than to be looking over his shoulder all the time. Still, what had she said back at the meat house…?

I never put all my cards on the table at once, MacKay.

That was worth remembering.

Mia thrust the Fuzzies tracker in front of his face. Its light was almost solid red, with only the slightest flicker. "This thing says we're right on top of one of the Fuzzy animals."

"I just hope it's not Balled fucking Eagle again."

He scanned the sky, but saw nothing. Up ahead, however, the featureless desert seemed to break for something. A small collection of rocks or buildings. Too far away to see yet.

"This is about where Cocoa Niño should be," he said. "Maybe we can finally find these damn animals."

He remembered a discussion he'd had with Mia that morning, over leftover spare ribs and self-reheated bacon. Well, *he'd* eaten the ribs and bacon. She was back on a veggie diet.

"This whole assignment makes me queasy," he'd confessed.

She'd looked up sharply, chomping on a celery stick. "Why?"

"With animals, I always try to save 'em if I can, but sometimes, you just gotta put one down. With humans it's easier – they *decide* whether to get themselves killed or not."

"Uh-huh."

"But these things we're looking for…" He'd paused, a half-chewed rib dangling from his fingers. "I don't know *what* they are."

Mia had just looked at him, frowning.

The settlement ahead slowly loomed into view. A half-dozen rusted trailers, set in a semicircle against an odd, freestanding clutch of huge boulders. Possibly the remains of an abandoned Indian reservation, MacKay thought – though he couldn't remember seeing one on the map here.

"Cocoa Niño?" he asked softly.

He pulled the bike up to a stop near the first trailer, carefully parking on the outskirts of the settlement. A quick getaway might be in order shortly.

"Tracker's solid red now," Mia said, dismounting.

She held up the device. It was lit brighter than he'd ever seen it.

MacKay peered at the nearest trailer, one hand gripping his MiniShredder. The trailer was dark, with torn beige curtains showing through the windows. It seemed deserted.

Keek! Keek! Keek!!

MacKay turned at the noise. Dog was hopping around nervously in front of the trailers, holding his front paws up to his ears.

"Does he sense something?" Mia asked.

"He's never acted like this before." MacKay crouched down, spoke directly to the monkey.

"Is it an animal? One of the Fuzzies?"

"He doesn't usually react to animals at all."

Keek! Keek!

Dog pointed to a narrow space between two of the trailers. Mia moved towards it, and MacKay followed, grimacing. One of the trailers was tipped to the side slightly, and the hitching-hook was tangled in a fallen cactus. They inched their way gingerly over the hook.

Then Mia stopped, gasped.

MacKay looked past her. All he could see was a flat, slightly depressed plain in the open desert. Dry and hot, stretching off to the distant horizon.

"What?" he asked.

"I – I thought…" She shook her head. "I thought I saw something."

"An animal?"

"I don't think so." She seemed genuinely shaken. "Something bigger… grander. And much, much more dangerous."

He took a step forwards, turned back to face her. "Well… I don't see anyth- "

Then he *did* see something. Something big, black, and insectoid, scuttling from the base of one trailer to the next.

"There!" He pointed. Mia whirled.

It was gone.

"What? *What?*" she asked, frantic.

"I – something black. And… furry, I think."

MacKay moved towards the trailers, instinctively putting a hand on Mia's shoulder. She batted it away fiercely, and he looked at her, surprised.

"Don't touch me," she said.

"What?" MacKay shook his head, confused.

"You touched me. A moment ago."

"I've touched you before."

Behind her, Dog hopped up and down, still holding his ears. *Keek! Keek!* Mia turned, to him, eyes wide, and started to pull her gun.

"Mia!" MacKay yelled.

Then they all saw it.

It scuttled out from under the nearest trailer, low and black and jittery. It stood about three feet high and about four feet in diameter. It had eight legs and dark eyes, and was covered in thick, black fur.

"A spider," Mia whispered.

Dog stood in an attack pose, perfectly still, his nose aimed at the creature.

MacKay found himself trembling. Miko and Sputo were strange creatures – but they were recognizable as intelligent beings. MacKay suddenly realised an odd fact: they'd been engineered to seem *human*.

This creature had none of that. It was alien, arachnid. Foul. Only by a great effort of will could MacKay resist pummelling it into jelly.

"You're a Fuzzy?" he said, his voice deliberately low and even.

The thing opened a mouth – if you could call it that – on its head-bulge. Its voice was a reedy hiss, grating, unpleasant. "Graaaaaaandmothththrr Sssssspider," it said.

MacKay reached for his earpiece, the one he'd used to decipher Sputo's slurring. Then he jumped, startled, as the spider-creature scuttled right up in front of him, staring at him with oddly warm eyes. The tips of its eight legs, he now noticed, emitted faint blue sparks.

No need for that, young man. You understand Grandmother now… don't you?

MacKay could still hear the hissing, as though at a distance. But now Grandmother Spider's aged, elegant voice echoed in his mind. It was tired, yet full of dignity.

He stared into her eyes. "You're telepathic."

Mildly, boy. Just enough to be understood.

Dog was frantic now, almost jumping out of his skin. He bounced from one trailer's outside window to another. *Keek! Keek!*

"Your telepathy… it must generate electrical impulses, at a frequency that matches the human brain. It's disrupting Dog's systems."

Mia was staring at him as though he were talking to a cactus. Clearly she couldn't understand the creature. She looked at her gun in her hand. Then, very deliberately, she reached out a gloved hand to Dog.

"Come on, monkey," she said. "Let's get you a little distance."

Dog hesitated, then leaped into Mia's arms. She shot MacKay a strange, scared glance, then set off past the trailers.

She really is good with animals, he thought.

Young man, Grandmother Spider said/sent. *Are you planning to stare at that woman's shapely posterior all day?*

MacKay couldn't bring himself to look straight at the creature, but there was something soothing about her "voice". "Sorry, ma'am," he said.

Grandmother Spider raised a thin, black-furred arm, and a small bolt of electricity arced out. She narrowed her dark eyes at it. *Not much left*, she sent. *Looks like old Grandmother Spider's going to join her ancestors soon.* She sighed, a discomforting sound at once mournful and flatulent. *I don't imagine my ancestors are very impressive conversationalists.*

"You generate electricity?"

That's why they made me, young man. She scuttled back and forth in front of the trailer, legs sparking slightly whenever they touched ground. *But now I'm almost exhausted.*

"You're… dying?"

You could say that.

A dying animal.

MacKay fingered the Shredder inside his jacket.

"Maybe you'd better tell me your story," he said finally.

AND SO SHE did, in that peculiar half-speech that tickled, and sometimes hurt, the inside of MacKay's head.

The Cherokee Nation of Oklahoma had begun in tragedy, as the end-point of the infamous Trail of Tears – the forced-march of 1838 where one in four Indians died en route to their barren, unwanted new home. But over the next century and a half, the western Cherokees became a force to be reckoned with. They gradually developed a complex relationship with the US government, providing key components for the military establishment and for other industries.

And then there was the gambling.

As the 21st century began, Indian gambling became an economic bonanza. Formerly oppressed groups erected huge, lush casino complexes, exempt from the laws of the surrounding states. The Cherokee Nation was no exception – they built dozens of huge gambling sites and raked in the savings of weak, stupid white people.

But as the nation's economy dove into a spin and the American heartland upped and died, the Cherokee leaders became nervous. After all, they'd had their hard-earned possessions taken away before. They decided to invest in a safety net, in case the day came when fleecing Caucasians was no longer a viable option.

So they contacted Fuzzies, Inc, with an old legend and a new idea.

According to Cherokee myth, Grandmother Spider had "stolen the sun" – brought light to a world that was originally nothing but darkness. Where Fox, Buzzard, and Possum failed, she carried a piece of the sun itself from the other side of the world in a clay bowl. This brought the people not only daylight, but also fire and pottery.

The new-era Grandmother Spider would be a living power battery. She would carry the sun inside her – enough generative electricity to power whole counties. Like everyone else, the modern Cherokee lived and died on their power grid. If the US Government ever decided to take action against them, a natural move would be to cut off their electricity. No electricity, no casinos. No casinos, no money. No money, no nation.

The Fuzzies engineers, Grandmother Spider said, jumped on the challenge. They were sick and tired of making cute, fuzzy, anthropomorphic creatures. Not only was Grandmother Spider not supposed to be cuddly, her very existence had to be carefully shielded from the US Government. And her template – a spider – posed new and fascinating challenges for the GenTech subsidiary.

At first, the arrangement worked out beautifully. The Cherokee, whose mythology was filled with tales of talking animals, accepted her right away, taking care to keep her away from prying outsiders. They used Grandmother's power sparingly, primarily as a "backup generator" during blackouts. She was treated well, fed amply, and allowed to spin her beautiful energy webs in a large hilltop sanctuary. Her electrical/telepathic abilities made her a sought-after facilitator of Vision- and Dreamquests, particularly among the young of the tribe. She felt a particular connection, she said, to the children. The Cherokee even declared her a Beloved Woman – the first nonhuman ever to have this highest honour bestowed upon her.

Then in 2019 the stock market crashed.

Faced with a huge shortfall in the federal budget, Congress passed a near-unanimous law making Indian gambling illegal. The Cherokee responded by walling off their biggest casinos, allowing only foreign tourists and the richest Americans in.

The federal government cut off their power. Without missing a beat, the Cherokee plugged Grandmother Spider into the main grid. It was a shock to her system – the greatest power burden she'd ever had to bear. But the roulette wheels spun again, and the money flowed.

It was too much for the US to bear. To add injury to insult, water was becoming scarce throughout the States, and the Cherokee Nation was flush with clean, pure lakes. Or at least as clean and pure as you can expect when the effluent from close to a million homes flows into them.

In the summer of '20, the Casino Conflicts exploded. National Guard troops, depleted and stressed from years of service in Iraq, Iran, the Congo and elsewhere, stormed several reservations, burning and smashing gambling equipment, torching casinos the size of palaces. The Guardsmen fought like zombies, uncaring, channelling their lack of purpose into officially sanctioned violence. But to the Indians, it all seemed very, very familiar.

Within six weeks, the Cherokee Nation was no more. The people scattered; Grandmother Spider hit the road with a small group of Nation officials who'd become friends. They travelled as a convoy for more than a year, crossing through Texas, New Mexico, and Arizona, always one step ahead of the feds and their Sanctioned Op subcontractors. Avoiding them wasn't too difficult. Grandmother knew they would have liked to dissect her and find out how she worked, but the government was stretched thin, undermanned. They had bigger problems than a few Indians and a freakish arachnid.

Eventually, too many of the trailers broke down and water became hard to find. The Cherokee nationals didn't want to abandon their dear Grandmother, but she sent them on their way. She could generate power with her webs, and suck moisture out of cacti. She'd survive.

Grandmother Spider's power was waning, she said; she knew she had little time left. Her "children" – the tribe she'd grown up with – had all fled the nest, gone to live their own lives. All she wanted now was to live out her final years in the desert, under the very same scorching, burning sun that her mythical namesake had brought to this place, so many eons ago.

IT TOOK MACKAY a minute to realize Grandmother Spider had stopped speaking. He'd developed a stabbing headache from "listening" to her. Grandmother Spider's spoken voice was piercing, unpleasant in the extreme; her telepathy – apparently an electrical signal of some kind – allowed him to understand her, much the way normal people unconsciously read lips during spoken conversation. Apparently, he realised abruptly, she could send pictures as well. He'd seen the casino slaughter in far greater detail than words would have conveyed.

Grandmother Spider sagged to the ground, one arm sparking feebly in the dry, hot air. *A moment, young man*, she said. *Communicating at this level of detail tends to drain poor Grandmother.*

Then MacKay became aware of Mia's hand on his shoulder.

"You can hear her too?" he asked.

"Took me a minute to tune in. I was… distracted."

"Are you okay?"

She nodded sharply, turned away from him. As she leaned in towards the spider, MacKay saw the same kind look on her sun-darkened face that he'd seen her give Dog earlier.

"So you're just dying?" Mia asked. "There's nothing we can do?"

Oh, Grandmother can be recharged, the creature replied. *She's done it before. It's a question of how and where.*

"What about that solar plant, ten miles back down the road?" MacKay frowned. "That looked pretty deserted."

"Deserted doesn't mean inactive. Not in these parts."

Grandmother Spider nodded, a strange, bobbing motion. *Grandmother has considered that… even planned an expedition. But she would require assistance.*

"I don't see how we could possibly get you there," MacKay said. He felt testy, uncomfortable with the idea.

Grandmother Spider gestured to an area between two trailers. A beautiful, multicoloured energy web shimmered forth from her arms, coming to rest on the sand where a small sidecar-vehicle appeared, rippling in the haze.

A minor concealment trick, to deter roving gangcults, the spider said proudly. *Grandmother has many ways.*

Mia started to speak, but MacKay grabbed her arm.

"Can I talk to you in private?"

She glanced sharply at him again, and for a moment he thought she would pull away. But she allowed MacKay to lead her off, to one of the deserted trailers.

As they walked, MacKay felt Grandmother's electric eyes on the back of his neck.

"Where's Dog?"

"Guarding the cycle," Mia said. She leaned on a bare-metal sink that hadn't been used in years, glaring at him across the small kitchen. The trailer was dusty, hot, the only light seeping in from its small, squarish windows. "I wanted him as far away from Grandmother Spider as possible."

"Mm."

"What's eating you, anyway?"

"I could ask you the same question."

She raised a hand to her head. "I'm – I'm a little confused. It must be the heat."

"And now you want to help that… that thing out there?" He shook his head. "That's not what we teamed up to do."

"That *thing* is a helpless animal."

"It's not one of the animals I came to find."

"Are you sure? Miko pointed you here."

She tossed him the Fuzzies tracker. Its red light was still bright, solid.

"The timeline doesn't work. That thing is clearly more than a year old… whether its story is true or not."

"Whether or not?" She moved close to him, challenging him in a very masculine way. "You don't believe Grandmother Spider's story?"

"I don't know what to believe."

"All I know is: I got into this to help animals. And it's within my power to help that one out there."

"That's the problem. It's *not* an animal."

"Then what is it?"

"I don't know!" MacKay's headache was killing him. "I can't figure any of this out."

She looked at him, curious. "You call Miko and Sputo *he*, but you can't bring yourself to call Grandmother Spider *she*."

"Maybe I just don't know it as well. Her, I mean."

"Is it because she's grotesque? Or because she's a woman?"

"For god's sake! Stop it!" He crossed to the tiny dining-room table, sat down in a hard metal chair. "Look – we agreed we have to find the Cocoa Niño animals. The sooner we get this job done, the sooner we can be finished with both Thalamus *and* GenTech. Right?"

"Right."

"So getting sidetracked to help this… spider… is a very, very bad idea."

"Right."

"And you're going to do it anyway."

"I know you're right. I know it's a bad idea. I also know there's an animal in pain out there, and I can't walk away from that. From *her*." She looked down at him, straight in the eye, defiant. "Can you?"

"Jesus!" He grabbed his head in his hands. Then he felt, inside his jacket, the sharp chrome of the MiniShredder. He looked up at Mia slowly. "What if Grandmother Spider can't be saved?"

She met his gaze. "Then we'll deal with it. But don't think of that as an easy way out of this problem."

Suddenly the overhead lighting flickered on with a whining hum. An ancient microwave oven started blinking 12:00, over and over. Across the trailer, a small TV set came to life, all snow and static.

MacKay shot to his feet, pulled out his Shredder. With Mia close behind, he crept to the door and down the corrugated-metal steps, into the bright sunlight.

Next to the trailer stood Grandmother Spider. One of her arms was plugged directly into a long-disused electrical hook-up wire, hanging down from the top of the trailer. Her arm sparked blue where it met the hook-up, and she smiled a crooked, challenging smile.

Grandmother thought she might shed a little light on your dilemma.

MacKay just stood, staring.

Have you decided whether to kill Grandmother yet? the spider continued.

MacKay looked down at the Shredder in his hand, then over to Mia. He felt suddenly very, very ashamed.

"Hop in your sidecar, Granny," he said. "The sun's waiting."

II

PEDRO NGUYEN PATRICE Nikolas Running Deer O'Halleran was many things. But first and foremost, he was an American.

Pedro's mother's maternal grandfather Sciotto had come over from Italy, back in the days when the Italians were the gutter class of New York. His tough, mafia-dominated neighbourhood directly abutted a Jewish block, where he'd fallen hard for a young, second-generation Russian immigrant girl named Litvin with curly black hair and big, haunted eyes. Both sides of the family had disowned the couple, who had to move a whole mile and a half away to find a neighbourhood where they could live together in peace. As they still say in New York: Whad-dayagonnado?

Meanwhile, the woman who would become Pedro's paternal great-grandmother was sailing over in a refugee boat from Poland. After a long, poverty-stricken trip cross-country, her family settled in San Francisco, where she met a charming Irishman named O'Halleran with dancing eyes and an unfaithful heart. He was constitutionally incapable of coming home sober, and carried on dalliances right in front of her eyes. But at least they were both Catholics. And he gave her two strong, wild sons.

Fuelled by patriotism, one of the O'Halleran boys went off to Korea – all fire and youth, eager to spill his blood for his country. But when he got there, he found poverty, jungles, and sudden, horrific death. No one could explain to him just what they were doing there. The only bright spot in his life was a young beauty named Sung Lee, who bore him a son and – after considerable bureaucratic effort – became his wife in the States. For a short time, at least.

While this was going on, the daughter of the New York Sciotto-Litvins had decided to come west to live, for a time, on a commune in Arizona. There she met a charming man whose mother was Mexican and whose father was descended from the most warlike of the Apache tribes. Their courtship was difficult, and their attempts at conceiving a child more so. After five miscarriages and several incidents of spousal abuse, Helga Sciotto gave birth to a beautiful baby girl.

That girl met the Lee/O'Halleran boy while working in a strip club in Houston. Soon she was pregnant, and against all odds, O'Halleran did the right thing and married her. The result was Pedro.

From the beginning, Pedro had tended towards fat. The other children shunned him, which wouldn't have been so bad if he'd had talents or ambition to fall back on. But Pedro was a dull lump of a boy. He didn't seem to want friends, but he didn't enjoy being alone either.

Somehow, Pedro's parents stayed together, more out of lack of imagination than anything else. His childhood wasn't so bad, except for the family reunions. Pedro's sentimental Polish-Irish grandfather insisted they were important, that the boy needed to know his heritage. So once a year, the call went out and the various clans gathered together in Houston.

The results were invariably horrific. The New Yorkers complained about the heat, and the south-westerners complained about the New Yorkers. The Italians screamed at the Irish, the

Mexicans made Polish jokes, the Russians sneered at the "noble savagery" of the Indians. Year after year, Pedro sat very still amid the clamour, wishing he had no family at all.

The best of these Tower of Babel kaffee-klatches ended in shouting matches and threats of violence. The second-worst involved superficial gunshot wounds and several years of subsequent lawsuits. And the worst one, when the Koreans descended in the hundreds, resembled a gang war with pot-luck dishes.

The day he turned eighteen, Pedro left. He didn't say goodbye, he didn't leave a note, he didn't call anyone. He picked up his things, drove by his high school and waved at no one in particular, then headed west and north.

He didn't want to be Irish anymore, or Mexican, Polish, or Apache. He didn't care if his relatives came from Russia, Italy, or Korea. None of that meant anything to him.

He was an American – but he didn't even care about *that*. Being an American wasn't anything special, like it had been in the old days. When all the immigrants had battered down the doors, desperate to come over. Now all it meant was poverty, thirst, and corruption. It was just a place, and not a very nice one.

After leaving home, Pedro put on even more weight. Soon after taking the guard job at the power plant, he realised he didn't want anything at all anymore. All he wanted was to melt himself down, to fade into the sands of America. The end product of generations of huddled masses, and all he wanted was the peace of the Earth.

Still, it wasn't such a bad job. Pedro was the only man stationed on-site at the plant, so at least he didn't have to talk to anyone. He got three fresh uniforms a week, and his command station was kind of cool. The chair where his enormous bulk sat was surrounded by TV screens linked to cameras covering every inch of the plant. If anything bad should happen, Pedro could scope it out with a few quick flicks of a switch.

But nothing ever happened. So Pedro had taken to leaving one screen on, showing the unmanned, and unchanging plant lobby. The rest showed various cartoons: Marko Sharko, Miko D, *Fairy Wary Quite Contrary*, and the new hit anime import, *Wun Dong Explosion Clubhouse*. Recently Pedro had started training himself to follow more than one cartoon at a time. He now found that he could track every word of at least three of them, with the sound turned all the way up.

Next week he would try four, but not yet. You had to pace yourself.

Suddenly, through the whine and screech of cartoon sound effects, Pedro heard something. He cut the sound from the screens, and then it came through clearer: the rumble of an unshielded motorsickle.

The lobby camera showed nothing. Pedro reached for the touch-screen to call up the exterior view, and was overcome, as he so often was, by a wave of depression.

He realised he didn't really care who was coming to the plant. He didn't care what they wanted to do, why they were going to do it, or who they worked for. He didn't even care what they might do to him.

All he wanted was to melt down into the Earth.

Pedro looked down at his rifle, and decided to sit this one out. Standing up was an enormous effort since he'd passed four hundred pounds. If they came for him, he'd defend himself. Maybe.

Fleetingly, it occurred to him that his immigrant forebears would probably be ashamed of him. But he didn't care. What had they really given him in the end, anyway?

A tear ran down Pedro's cheek, though he didn't know why. He raised his head to the ceiling and began to utter a prayer. But halfway through, he realised he couldn't remember which god to appeal to.

MacKay stood, hands on hips, staring up at the bizarre structure. "*This* is a power station?"

It stood seven storeys high, lit by the setting sun. It was shaped like a Mayan pyramid – no doubt in an attempt by some demented architect to give it a "south-western" motif. Its outside was stepped, leading up to a squarish central section at the very top. And every inch of it was covered with reflective, mirrored solar panels.

Mia looked up testily from her task of helping Grandmother Spider out of her sidecar. "Sure. What do you think – the fucking Toltecs built it?"

Careful, dear, the spider said. *Don't let Grandmother's little sparks shock you now.*

MacKay looked away, repulsed. How could Mia bring herself to touch that thing? Its black, matted fur…

"I think you got a few bruises there, Grandma," Mia said. "Must have been Rasterbator's shitty driving."

MacKay moved in the direction of the building, ignoring her. The drive *had* been rough; Grandmother Spider's sidecar threw his balance off completely. Several times he'd scraped it against the ground, and once they'd nearly flipped over completely.

Still, that wasn't the real problem. Mia and he had been so good together yesterday. Why were they bickering so badly now?

He forced himself to concentrate on the task at hand. He gestured at the power station, standing alone in the desert, surrounded only by a few power lines linked to outlying transformer shacks. "And you say this thing is still operational?"

Mia moved over next to him, pointed down the road. "See that town over there?" He did, vaguely, through the heat-haze. "This plant supplies its power needs – though I'd imagine it's operating at a pretty low capacity. Not many people live out here anymore, between the lack of water and the gangcult violence."

"You know a lot about this area."

"I like to research my assignments. You might try it sometime."

The spider scuttled up beside them, startling MacKay. *The gangs often tear down the power lines for months at a time, dears,* she said. *But the people of this area are proud. Somehow they hang on.*

"No troops, no laser-fence," MacKay said. "Why isn't it guarded?"

"Solar power plants are always lightly staffed," Mia replied.

"The corps all own them, and they just send out troops after there's a problem. Cheaper than permanent staff, and the percentages work out. Besides, after the Three Mile Meltdown, nobody wants to work at a nuclear plant – and most people are too stupid to know the difference."

Nonetheless, I'd be wary, young lady, Grandmother said. *There's probably a little soldier-boy on duty somewhere.*

MacKay forced himself to look straight down at Grandmother Spider. "And there's a chamber inside here that'll... what? Let you power yourself up again?"

That's right, dear. The creature waved two dainty legs at the mirror-coated doorway. *After you.*

The door wasn't locked. MacKay kicked it open lightly, Shredder drawn. He peered inside, but saw no one. Just a small reception area shielded by bulletproof plexiglass, and two very hard-looking chairs.

Suddenly MacKay felt a strong sense of déjà vu. He closed his eyes and placed it: I Heart Florida. The biotesting lab's lobby had looked a bit like this.

MacKay looked at Mia and, just for a moment, saw Brutus, the old friend he'd put a bullet into back in Florida. He shivered.

Mia shrugged. "We going in, or what?"

He motioned to them. Grandmother Spider scuttled ahead, to a stairwell door.

This way, dears. Oh – please hurry now. The heat has not been kind to poor Grandmother.

MacKay frowned, followed.

When they came out on the fourth floor, MacKay saw a twitch of motion from the corner of his eye. He turned, Shredder drawn. A security camera swivelled with a slight creak, following their every move.

"Mind your ears, Grandma," he said. Then he fired, blowing the camera apart. "Somebody's watching us."

"Thank you, Detective Chimp."

MacKay turned abruptly on Mia. "What the hell is eating you?"

Her eyes went wide, and he realised he was aiming the gun at her. He lowered it.

"Sorry," he said.

Grandmother Spider was way ahead of them down the featureless hall, peering through an odd-shaped window set into the wall. *Sssssstop playing, chhhhhildren,* she said. *Commmme heeeeere.* Her telepathy was weaker at this distance, MacKay realised.

They caught up with her and peered through the window – into a huge chamber, stretching the entire height of the building. It was spherical, tiled with an unbroken series of polished, reflective mirrors. A large, square projector protruded from the top, aiming downwards at a slight angle. The whole space was enormous – sixty feet in diameter, at least.

"What is it?" MacKay asked.

Concentrator chamber, Grandmother Spider said.

Mia frowned. "I've read about these. Conventional solar power – even the high-gain, single-crystal silicon type – just doesn't produce enough power for conventional electricity needs. So a facility like this stores up energy until it has enough, then amplifies it a thousand fold in this chamber."

Very good, dear. Grandmother Spider was agitated now, scuttling around. *The multi-junction cells at the top feed the energy into the chamber in a concentrated beam.*

MacKay shook his head. "And this can re-power you?"

If Grandmother is careful, young man. The level of power can be deadly, you know.

"How often do they feed the beam into the chamber?"

Grandmother Spider peered into an LCD screen set into the wall next to the window. *This station is completely automated,* she said, *but I believe the beam enhancement occurs once every four hours. And one is coming up soon.*

"How are you going to get–"

MacKay stopped as Grandmother Spider reached out two sparking arms, prying open a maintenance hatch set into the wall.

"Wait!" he called as she scuttled into the crawlspace. "You said yourself – somebody's on duty somewhere in this place.

What if they come along while you're getting your little high-energy snack?''

The spider stuck her head out of the hatch and smiled that unnerving, inhuman smile. *Grandmother trusts you, young man.* She paused for effect. *Her children protect Grandmother, and she protects them.*

Then she was gone, into the wall. The hatch flapped shut with a dull *clang*.

MacKay moved up next to Mia, who was staring into the chamber. As they watched, a small, black, furry dot appeared on the curved wall. It scuttled down, moving to the bottom centre of the strange room.

MacKay started to say something to Mia, but stopped. He didn't like this whole thing. Something was wrong with Mia, and something was wrong with Grandmother Spider – she wasn't telling them everything. How did she know so much about this plant, anyway?

He reached into his pocket and pulled out the Fuzzies tracker. It still glowed red – but weaker than before, blinking at regular intervals. What did it mean?

Too many mysteries. The only thing to do was what he always did: take them one at a time.

He peered through the window again, feeling Mia's warmth next to him, yet distant. Together, they waited for Grandmother Spider to steal the sun.

III

Clenching her fists, Mia watched Grandmother Spider creep down the inner walls of the chamber. *I'm barely keeping it together*, she realised. *I don't know what I'm doing.*

Ever since her night with MacKay, Mia's dreams had gotten stronger, more overwhelming. On the bike ride over, she'd tranced out more than once. Now, whenever she saw a person or animal move, she pictured it punctured, wounded, its life-force being bled right out of it.

Even stranger, though, was what she'd seen at the spider's trailer-site. It had only been visible for a moment, and she couldn't remember it clearly now. But it was something important, something crucial to this quest she and MacKay were on.

Now MacKay stood next to her, clearly wanting to talk. She loved him, but she wished he'd back off. Something was wrong – something in the very air itself, between the two of them – and Mia didn't feel anywhere near competent to figure it out right now.

For some reason, she found herself thinking back to a lecture she'd attended at Thalamus four years before. When the Cows had first struck their deal-with-the-devil, Mia agreed to sit in on a few of their executive seminars. Most of them were typical corporate psychobabble bullshit, and she'd stopped going after an incident where, bored beyond measure, she'd heated up the conference members' chairs to two hundred degrees with a laser during a coffee break. After that, the corp was happy to let her just ride around and blow up testing labs all day.

But one speaker, in a huge auditorium full of suits, had been the exception. A slim young man of mixed Asian-Hispanic extraction, dressed in tight black slacks, black shoes, and a black turtleneck. He stood alone on a blank stage, lit by a dramatic spotlight – no screen, no PowerPoint presentation, and no audio accompaniment. His hair was an unusual shade of bluish-green, and his demeanour was deadpan.

"Professor Wan has asked me to make his apologies," the man had said. "He has been called away on urgent business. As his current graduate student, I will present to you his theories of modern temporal convergence.

"The world has changed," the young man continued, sombrely. "On the surface, things look much as they always have. You walk down the street to the grocery. You pass a bank, a fire hydrant. You reach for a peach or a bottle of water. Perhaps the peach is not as fresh as once it would have been, or the water costs a bit more. But the process itself is comforting, familiar. You believe what your senses tell you: that despite the hard times confronting this country – and, by extension, the world – life goes on much as it did before. Much as it always has.

"This is an illusion.

"In many deep, fundamental ways, the laws of nature have changed. You cannot see it because you are not trained to do so – because the reality of life around you would be too great a shock to bear. And because you sit in the belly of the beast: America. Home of the lie, the justification, the great hypocrisy. The Whopper, if you will.

"As you walk down that street – as you pass that bank – unseen forces rage all around you. They take from you and they fight their battles on higher planes, using your life-force, your will, as their fuel. The bank on the street is devoid of money; the hydrant contains no water. The peach is rotted inside, and the bottle will not slake your thirst for long.

"You live and die at their suffrage. You move within the squares of their game board, according to their rules. You dance for their amusement, and when you cease to provide sustenance or entertainment, you dance no more.

"For more than a century, America has forced itself upon the world like a sailor hungry for women. You have trampled the Earth and taken what you want. For a long time, you believed you were building a great society. You told yourself it was all justified, all for the best.

"But in your greed, you overlooked one vital fact. The pillage – the very act of taking – changed you. The more you took, the more you ravaged other nations to sate your own desires, the more tangled and convoluted became the lies you told yourself. You required ever more justification to continue – to believe yourselves the righteous defenders of freedom your national myth required.

"And in so doing, you let *them* in.

"It is too late to change course. They are here, and they are here to stay. Their reign has already begun but, like good Americans, you cannot see it. You believe yourselves the masters of your own destiny, even in these reduced and debased times.

"Professor Wan will save you. Only Professor Wan *can* save you. In return, he demands only one thing: Do not ask him his methods. Do not seek to peek behind the curtain. It is far too late for that now.

"If what I have said means nothing to you, I suggest an experiment. The next time you find yourself on a deserted street, staring off at a mountain or a large building, close your eyes for one moment. Clear your mind of all preconceptions, all images that remain from your vision. Listen to the sounds all around, the faint noises of city or plains, of farm animals or distant automobiles. See only blackness.

"Then open your eyes. And for just an instant, before your world comes truly into focus, you may see mighty warriors battling in the sky with mace and sword. You may see cosmic accountants tapping out your fate on adding machines made of stars. You may even see Grandfather and the Keeper of Secrets, locked in combat, their ancient wounds dripping blood down on your streets like rain.

"Or you may see nothing at all. In which case, we have done our job.

"There are Krispy Kremes in the lobby."

MIA SHIVERED AT the memory. When the young man had spoken of seeing gods in the sky, he'd seemed to stare straight at her, as though delivering a message to her alone.

Now, four years later, she *did* see strange visions superimposed on the world. But not gods. Only monsters.

At the top of the concentrator chamber, a ring of blue light hummed to life around the square projector.

"Showtime," MacKay murmured.

Mia looked down at the small black dot that was Grandmother Spider, shifting back and forth nervously in the vast expanse of mirrors, four stories below. Maybe, Mia thought, the best thing you could do in this world was to help one frail, helpless creature. Maybe the only good deed that meant anything was the small act of kindness.

Even in her mind, the words sounded hollow.

Suddenly the chamber was filled with light.

Beams lanced out from the projector at all angles, bouncing and reflecting off the mirrored surfaces, caroming off instantly in all directions. From the lip of the projector, collector cells extruded, catching the amplified light-energy for use later.

Mia and MacKay peered through the window-glass, which had darkened to grey automatically. They could barely make out the shaking, shivering form of Grandmother Spider, scuttling about at the bottom of the chamber, a black spot awash in deadly white light.

"That's going to kill her," MacKay said.

"She seems to know best," Mia replied. Then a thought struck her, and she turned to him. "You called Grandmother 'her'."

MacKay shrugged. "I don't think it's gonna matter in a minute."

The moment was broken.

Mia turned back to the chamber. The lights continued to intensify, bouncing off again and again at unimaginable speed, filling the chamber. It was mesmerising, yet difficult to look at for very long.

Suddenly she realised the problem with MacKay. He was too grounded. He insisted on trying to puzzle this whole situation out using traditional logic, a tactic Mia knew would never work. He was trying to apply the old rules to the new world.

What had Professor Wan's grad student said? "The reality of life around you would be too great a shock to bear."

MacKay would never see the real forces at work here, Mia realised. That left it all up to her.

And she wasn't doing too well, either.

The chamber was a single white glow now, like a miniature star. Grandmother Spider was lost from sight. The collectors hummed, pulsed, sucked up amplified energy hungrily. Even behind the darkened glass, Mia had to shield her eyes with her hand.

Then, in an instant, the chamber went dark.

Mia squinted downwards. MacKay stood next to her, leaning forwards to look. She managed to make out a blip that could have been Grandmother Spider – but its black shape was glowing blue now, radiant with electrical energy.

For a moment, she thought it was dead. Then the spider-shape scuttled forwards, shot up the side of the chamber, and disappeared into a hatch in the mirror-wall.

Thirty seconds later, the hallway duct clattered open. Grandmother Spider swung out, her entire body sparking and flashing with new power. A stray arc flared from her leg to the LCD screen, which went blue, then dark.

Mia and MacKay took a step back.

Sorry about that, children. Grandmother's voice was stronger now, more resonant. She scuttled out of the hatchway onto the hallway floor, trailing blue lightning as she went. She stretched upwards like an Olympic athlete, and a bolt flashed at a ceiling light, shorting it out.

Grandmother feels much *stronger now*, she said.

For the first time, Mia wasn't sure if that was a good thing.

Well, don't stand there gaping, children. I don't imagine that soldier-boy will leave us alone forever.

And she took off, unimaginably fast, heading for the stairwell. A trail of scorched hallway tiles and burned-out lights followed in her wake.

Exchanging a glance, Mia and MacKay followed. A safe distance behind.

OUTSIDE, THE SUN was high. The air seemed hotter than ever. Not for the first time, Mia cursed the fashion imperative that made her insist on wearing pleather everywhere.

Grandmother Spider's aura had died down enough that they could approach her now. Which was a good thing, Mia thought sourly. Otherwise it would have been a difficult trip back to her home.

Heat rose from the desert sand in waves. As they ran to her bike, Mia thought she saw something huge, something inhuman, leaning against it. She shook her head; this was no time for dreaming... or for seeing monsters.

Then she realised it was a man.

He was enormous, at least four hundred pounds, with olive skin and an ill-advised moustache. He wore a nondescript beige uniform and cop sunglasses, and an M-78 rifle dangled casually from his arm. His gigantic ass threatened to crush Mia's bike, sidecar and all, straight into the ground.

MacKay already had his MiniShredder out. "Who the hell are you?" he asked.

The man smiled sadly. "I am Pedro Nguyen Patrice Nikolas Running Deer O'Halleran," he said. "I guard this facility."

Grandmother Spider began scuttling back and forth, agitated.

"We don't want any trouble," MacKay said. "Just get off the bike and you'll never see us again."

The man looked up, as though searching for something. "I wasn't gonna get involved. But something told me to do this." He pointed a finger at Grandmother Spider. "Maybe it was *Grandma*."

"Just get off the bike," Mia said.

"I don't think I can do that," Pedro said. "Looks like it's you or me, amigos." He looked casually at the rifle, but made no move to raise it. His gaze wandered to Grandmother again, and there was an old hostility in his eyes.

Suddenly a blue bolt shot out from Grandmother Spider's leg. It caught Pedro square in the chest, and he stiffened, cried out.

"Listen," Mia repeated. "Just back off."

But Pedro grimaced, shook off the blow, and looked back at the trio of invaders. In his eyes Mia saw no malice, no hatred, no conviction. Just an odd kind of determination that seemed to have found its focus.

He raised the rifle.

Instinctively, Mia and MacKay fired together.

Pedro twitched, spurted, and toppled off the bike with a thundering crash.

Grandmother Spider reached the body first. When Mia and MacKay got there, the man seemed much smaller than he'd looked before. His enormous clothes dwarfed the shrivelled body inside.

"Weird," MacKay said. "It's like he just melted into the sand."

"He looks kind of… peaceful," Mia said.

They talked briefly about burying Pedro, but it was very hot, and somehow, they didn't want to disturb him. So they left him where he lay, blood dripping out into the red southwestern sands.

MacKay revved the bike to life. In the sidecar, Grandmother Spider's legs flashed up and down in the air, sending bolts of electricity flying. Mia clutched MacKay's strong waist, dodging the stray bolts. As the sickle lurched awkwardly back onto the road, Mia glanced back briefly at the power plant.

Pedro's bloodstained clothes lay flat now, flush against the desert floor. Not a trace of him remained.

10

"MACKAY."

"Yeah."

"We're being followed."

MacKay snapped his head backwards, and then turned his eyes back to the road. "I don't see anyone."

"They're a ways back. I'm used to hearing things over my engine."

Beside and below MacKay, in the sidecar, Grandmother Spider swivelled to face backwards. Her arms flailed, and one brushed the cycle's electrical system – which sputtered and went dead.

"Dammit!"

The bike pulled sideways, slowed. MacKay pulled up hard on the throttle, and the engine came back to life.

"Grandmother – can you try not to do that, please?"

Sorry, dear. Grandmother just feels so much better now, she's exploding with the exuberance of life.

Just ahead, MacKay saw the trailer complex. When we get back, he thought, *Grandmother* is going to answer a few questions.

"Are they gaining on us?" he asked Mia.

"I don't think so. They're hanging back."

"Who do you think they are? Gangcult?"

"I don't know. Sounds like cycles."

MacKay pulled the bike up to the first trailer, killed the engine, and glided to a stop. Grandmother Spider slithered out of her sidecar, still glowing faintly with blue energy, big healthy sparks shooting out of her eight arms. Mia dismounted and crossed her arms, frowning at the bike.

"Jesus, MacKay. You really banged her up."

He'd had about enough. "You try driving with a giant spider in the sidecar and an electrical system that keeps cutting out."

The trailer door opened slightly, and Dog appeared. He put a paw to his head and pointed at Grandmother Spider. *Keek! Keek! KEEEEEKK!*

"Stay inside," MacKay said, pointing.

Dog disappeared back through the door.

I'm afraid Grandmother's higher spirits are even harder on the little tyke, the spider said.

"He'll live," MacKay replied. "But I've got a few things I'd like *you* to clarify, Grandma."

"I can still hear them," Mia said, frowning. "They're out there. This could be a problem."

MacKay turned on her. "If you're so much *smarter* than me and so much better a *driver* than me, and if we're in so much *danger*, why don't you just take the damn cycle and go find out who's out there?"

She looked at him as though he were a creature from another world. Then, without a word, she crossed to the cycle and revved it to life.

Dog stuck his head out of the trailer again. He looked over at Mia. *Keek?*

MacKay rolled his eyes. "Go ahead."

The monkey scampered happily over to Mia, jumped in her lap.

Mia shot MacKay a quick, angry look, then roared off.

Grandmother Spider scuttled around energetically. As she passed one trailer after another, sparks flew to their electrical hook-ups. A CD player went on inside one trailer, an alarm clock in another; then both went silent again.

Grandmother owes you a debt of thanks, young man.

"Forget it. I—"

Grandmother used to do all kinds of things for the tribe, you know. When the young ones were lost or confused, she used to help them with Dreamquests. Did Grandmother tell you that?

"Yeah. Listen—"

MacKay jumped as the spider scuttled over, amazingly fast, and fixed big hypnotic eyes on him. Its electric arms waved wildly in the air. *Would* you *like to go on a Dreamquest, young man?*

"No. I'd like you to tell me how you knew the layout of that plant so well."

Grandmother is a quick study.

"That guard called you Grandma. How did he know you?"

The spider shifted back and forth, nervously. *Grandmother Spider has become a bit of a local legend, young man. Many know of her.*

He pulled out his Shredder, waved it at her. "Keep those arms back, please. Mia may think you're a helpless animal, but I don't." He pulled out the Fuzzies tracker. "Here's another question. This thing is designed to track Fuzzies creations, like you. Here by the trailers, it glows solid red, a stronger signal than I've ever seen before — like now. But at the plant, it gave off a more normal, blinking signal." He stared hard at her unblinking eyes. "I only see one animal here — just like I did at the plant. No reason this tracker should give off a different reading."

She said nothing.

"Is it the trailers, Granny? What's in them, anyway?"

Then he felt her in his mind, and knew he'd made a mistake. He should have looked away, avoided her gaze. Now she had him. He felt the hot desert slipping away, the trailers and cacti melting and slipping into the distance. Vaguely, he wished he hadn't driven Mia away.

Then he heard Grandmother Spider's "voice" all around him:

So many questions, young man. Perhaps you'll find your answers in the Dreamquest.

And he was gone.

part six
the dreamquest of
ratcatcher mackay

I

THE PYTHON HUNG from the ceiling, coiled around the chandelier. It was from Target – the chandelier, not the python – and
had been a very nice value. Polished silver and silver alloys, five
strong bulbs that lit up the whole room. Good workmanship
for the money.

Baby leopards played in the corner, near the fake-wood can
proudly labelled TRASH. A lemur prowled along the kitchen
cabinets, foraging for food. And outside, visible through the
lace-curtained window, a herd of giraffes ran from a brace of
lions, as they'd done a thousand times before. They'd reach the
invisible kitty-fence soon, and be safe.

Batton MacKay sat at the kitchen table, reading his paper. A
notice caught his eye, and he looked up. "Says here the Dog
Show is today."

Mia turned away from the sink, wiped her hands quickly on
her apron. "Yes. Don't you remember? We're supposed to go."

He shook his head, confused. Something wasn't right about
this. "But… we don't have a dog."

She laughed, a high, nervous laugh. "Don't joke about that."

He peered at her. Her high lace collar was open just far enough for him to make out the small, gold cross-pendant she always wore. Her lips — as usual — were just the perfect, socially acceptable yet unexciting shade of pink. Mia rarely wore much makeup. She was beautiful and a good wife, but sometimes he wished she'd take a few risks with her appearance.

That didn't seem right, either.

A flock of rare toucans, brightly coloured, fluttered noisily into the room. MacKay shooed them away from his paper, and they flew over to bother Mia, who was stacking clean glasses in the cabinet. "Aah! Get away!" She waved her hands wildly, and they flapped over to the window. They watched, mesmerized, as the giraffes taunted the fenced-in lions.

Then Mia was right in front of him, slamming her hands down on the table. "You know I love animals," she said. "But why do we have to have so *many*?!"

He shrugged, took a puff from his pipe. "You know what happened to the zoo. Where else are they gonna go?"

She stormed off, started unloading the dishwasher.

Mia seems very tense lately, MacKay thought. Maybe it's time for a vacation. He'd read that McDisneyWorld had some very attractive packages this time of year — that might be just the thing. If he could get time off from the office, of course.

Then something happened that startled him out of his fog.

A large monkey, six and a half feet tall and hunched over, sauntered into the room. It glanced at Mia and sighed. Then it crossed to the pantry and pulled down a packet of cookies.

"Put those on a plate," Mia said. She didn't look up.

The monkey groaned, grabbed a small plate noisily. It tossed the plate down on the table, and then threw the cookies next to it. And then it sat down directly across from MacKay, fixing him with a strong, almost pleading gaze.

"Dog?" he said softly.

Now MacKay remembered Dog — his robot monkey. This creature resembled Dog in every respect; it *was* Dog. Except this Dog was taller than MacKay, and covered with brown fur.

Dog bit down on a cookie, and pushed the box towards MacKay. *Mrrmm?* he offered.

Silently, MacKay accepted the box. He looked down at it. It read ANIPROTEIN SANDWICH CREAMS. And then, in small type: MADE IN – but the following words were blurred, unreadable.

The monkey nodded, eyes deadly serious.

MacKay bit down on a cookie.

Mia stood over them now, arms folded. She looked at Dog, frowning, then over at MacKay. "I see *your son* is still giving us the silent treatment."

MacKay looked up. "My son?"

"Sooner or later, he's going to have to get a job. He can't just lay around the pool all day – especially with the mako sharks out there." She turned, now, to lecture Dog directly. "Four years of college. What the hell was it all for?"

Dog shrugged. He slumped deeper into his chair.

MacKay stood, folding his paper carefully. "I think – I think I'm going to take a bath," he said.

"Oh, great." Mia threw up her hands theatrically. "What timing. Well, make it quick, Batton Joseph MacKay. You know we don't want to be late for the…" Her voice dropped, and she grimaced. "… *Dog Show.*"

MacKay stepped carefully over the frolicking leopards. Out in the hall, two electric eels were scurrying from one wall to the other, baiting each other with sparking tails. That reminded him of something important – but he couldn't remember what.

He walked into the bathroom and shooed two rare bluebirds away from the mirror. He examined his features with a critical eye. Bags hung from his eyes, wrinkles showed in a forehead that had been smooth just a few years before. He was still a handsome man, but the stress had taken its toll.

No, he thought, shaking his head. That's not right. None of this is right.

He flung open the bathtub curtain. Two alligators looked up, startled.

"Make room, fellas," he said.

The bath was hot and felt good. The alligators were friendly enough, even passing the soap when asked. Yet somehow, the minute MacKay stepped out, he felt dirty again.

"Honey?" Mia called.

He frowned. "Yeah?"

"Did I leave the gas on?"

The bathroom was filled with steam now. MacKay tried to rub the mirror clean, but it was useless.

"What?"

"When we were in the kitchen. Did I leave the gas on?"

"I don't know."

"Can you check?"

He looked down at his naked body. "Me?"

"I'm getting dressed!"

He rolled his eyes, looked over at the alligators. They were silent.

Wrapping a towel around himself, MacKay stepped, dripping, back out into the hall. He waved the eels away, "Gangway — conducting mammal coming through." The linoleum floor felt cold on his feet.

When he got to the kitchen, Dog was still sitting at the table, listlessly chewing on cookies. He'd gotten himself a can of soda, also labelled ANIPROTEIN.

MacKay crossed to the stove, checked all six burners. Off. Off. Off, off, off, off.

His eyes wandered to the refrigerator — a deluxe, Sub-Zero model that, as he recalled, they couldn't quite afford, but what the hell. He felt suddenly hungry. He reached for the handle.

Dog made a horrible gutter-noise: *Urrk! Urrk!*

MacKay frowned. "It's just a refrigerator." He reached forwards, yanked it open, and caught a glimpse of Hell on Earth. Plucked chickens, miniature cows, pork chops — all strung up by wire, left to drip blood through the metal racks into the produce bin below. An abattoir in miniature.

A thick monkey-hand whipped past him, slamming the fridge shut.

MacKay looked at the monkey, thinking hard. "That was — that was like Mia's dreams. Or the video Miko showed me."

Dog nodded, wincing. MacKay noticed the monkey had cut his hand on the fridge door, and was holding it gingerly.

MacKay took Dog's hand. "Are you okay? It doesn't look serious."

Urrrgh, the monkey said.

"I remember," MacKay continued. "The spider… she did this to me. She said something about a Dreamquest." He looked over at Dog again. "Are you… are you my guide? My spirit animal?"

Dog grinned, gave a big thumbs-up.

A trio of macaws flapped between them, crowing loudly. MacKay glanced outside, where a lion had broken through the invisible fence and – clearly in agony from the hypersonic signal – stood gnawing on a dying giraffe's long, graceful neck. Both animals' cries filtered faintly through the heat-insulated glass.

"I don't like it here," MacKay whispered. "This isn't the life I ever wanted to lead. And I don't like seeing Mia like this."

Dog twisted his face into the universal male grimace for: *I hear that*.

"Can you get me out of here?"

The monkey shrugged.

"Can we at least go somewhere else?"

Dog nodded vigorously. He placed both hands on MacKay's shoulders and closed his eyes. MacKay followed suit, closing his eyes as well.

Slowly, the sounds of animals – killing and dying – faded around him.

SOMEWHERE, IN SOME fragile reality, Mia stalked into the kitchen on low, loud heels. She cast her gaze across the leopards, the macaws, the python. Then she ripped off her pillbox hat, threw it down angrily.

"Great," she said, a hint of fear slipping into her voice. "Now I have to go to the Dog Show *alone*?"

* * *

11

"Mia?"

"Mm?"

"Are we almost there? I have to, like, pee."

Despite herself, Mia laughed. She looked back briefly and smiled. Britney and Cristina were flanking her in the vee formation they'd practiced so often back in Florida. It was just like old times.

"It's up ahead," she said into the radio. "See that cluster of trailers?"

"It looks like my first boyfriend's place," Britney said.

"The one from when you were twelve?" Cristina asked.

"Huh! *No.* When I was *nine.*"

"He lived in a *trailer?*"

"Yeah. It was way crowded. We could only do it when his kids weren't home."

Mia shook her head, still smiling. She'd managed to ambush the two of them behind some rocks, where they sat, right out in the open, next to their motorcycles, painting their nails and blaring loud pop music. They were even still wearing their snorting-bull Mad Cows jackets. It was so conspicuous, at first Mia had been sure it was a trap.

"We remembered what you told us about, like, keeping our distance from the prey," Cristina had said proudly.

"What about the quiet, stealthy part?"

The two had just looked at each other. Then Britney held up a CD cover featuring a smouldering Russian pop star, looking seductive. Together they smiled and screamed, "Petya Tcherkassoff!"

Apparently that explained everything.

Of all the Mad Cows, Mia had always liked Britney and Cristina best. Just having them back made her feel better; even her head seemed clearer. Sometimes, though, conversations with them took *odd turns.*

"How did you find me?" she'd asked them.

Britney had looked over at Cristina, who was smiling shyly. "Cris has total ESP."

They'd been very happy to see Dog again.

"Little monkey!"

"Little cute monkey!"

"Little cute robot monkey!"

"Little cute robot monkey with the killer master!"

Et cetera.

"What about the Mad Cows?" Mia had asked.

"Oh, Hank is like, a total Toby," Cristina said solemnly.

"Yuh," Britney agreed. "He's all, like, 'Aye know how tuh run this gang much bettuh than Mi-uh did.' What a loser."

"Can you believe he wants us to fill out quarterly performance review forms?"

"I *know*!"

Mia stifled a laugh. "What about Jefe? And the Germans?"

Cristina's face melted. "Jefe's so tragic."

Britney laughed wickedly. "You *like* him."

"He's all, my girlfriend's dead and I must avenge her. That's so *romantic*."

"Yuh. Unless it means we gotta fight a big dumb killer bird again."

"Yuh. Gross."

"Gross *City*, is how gross."

Eventually, Mia had pieced together the situation. Somehow, Hank had survived the explosion that took out MacKay's Interceptor. He'd managed to plant a tracer on Balled Eagle, which was a hell of a lot more than Mia would have thought he could pull off. Then he'd taken the gang and regrouped in a town near Miko's estate.

Now, apparently, Hank was determined to kill Balled Eagle and MacKay, and bring Mia in to some kind of twisted corporate "justice". Jefe had wavered, but eventually run off by himself to avenge Shank's death – whatever that meant. Wister-Hauser and Hauser-Wister had worked through some twisted philosophical debate between themselves – no doubt accompanied by KY jelly and a ballgag – and had decided to stay with Hank.

As for Cristina and Britney…

"We just thought, like, Mia's way *way* cool. And Hank's a total loser."

Well, Mia thought. You can't argue with facts.

As they approached the trailers, Britney cooed: "*Soooooo*, Mia. Are you still doing it with Mac*Kaaaaaaayyy*?"

"We want *details*, girl," Cristina added.

Mia frowned. "I'll tell you in an hour."

The girls laughed. "You are so cool, Mia."

"Yuh. We wanna make a new gang with you."

"Yuh. But a cooler gang."

"One with not so many, like, losers and Tobys."

"Yuh. And no Hank."

"*Definitely* no Hank."

Mia coasted to a stop and cut her engine. Britney and Cristina pulled up alongside. Almost in unison, they pulled off their helmets and shook out their long hair. They looked like a bulimic version of Charlie's Angels, Mia thought. Well, an *extra*-bulimic version.

Dog jumped off of Mia's bike and made straight for his trailer. Clearly he was taking no chances on running into Grandmother Spider again.

Britney looked around at the trailers, wrinkling up her nose. "It *smells* like my old boyfriend's place, too."

But Cristina was staring at the centre trailer. "Wow," she said.

Mia walked straight up to her. "What is it?"

"It's, like, totally impressive," Cristina said.

Mia looked back. "The trailer?"

Britney poked her friend in the shoulder. "She's like, freaking out massively," she explained to Mia. "Ever since that night I caught her with *mmmph*!"

"Shut *up*!"

For a moment, the two girls looked like they might dissolve into a mass of giggles. Then they all heard a scuttling noise from behind the trailer.

Mia motioned for them to follow her. "Brace yourselves."

When Mia reached the other side of the trailer, she had the same strange sensation she'd felt when they'd first come here.

She thought she saw something, out on the flat desert plain. Something very large and very sinister.

Then, before she could focus on it, it was gone. But when she looked over at Cristina, the girl was staring at the same spot.

Britney broke the spell. "Ewww, Mia! You got spiders here!"

One trailer down, Grandmother Spider squatted on a worn lawn chair, apparently salvaged from one of the trailers. Across from her, legs crossed lotus-style on a matching chair, sat MacKay. His eyes were closed, his expression blank.

"It's okay," Mia said. "I think."

Young lady, Grandmother Spider said, scuttling over. *How delightful to see you again.*

Britney and Cristina stared at the sparks emanating from the creature's legs. They backed up a step, pulling out their guns.

I take it these are our two stalkers?

"Uh, yes," Mia said. "It's okay, guys. This is Grandmother Spider." She gestured to MacKay. "What's with him?"

Britney giggled. "Doesn't look like you made, like, a big impression on him, Mia."

The young man is on a Dreamquest, the spider said. *He was a bit… confused by your changing attitudes towards him, I'm afraid. So he asked me to help him sort things out.*

Mia nodded slowly, suspiciously. "And now that you're re-powered, you can do that."

Precisely.

"How long is it going to take?"

Grandmother Spider smiled. *Every man's Dreamquest is his own,* she said.

Cristina had walked over to MacKay and was now poking him in the side of the head, tentatively, with a long multi-coloured fingernail. "He's way gone, Mia."

"You want us to, like, kill him?" Britney asked brightly.

Mia thought for a minute. "Not right now," she said.

"'Kay!"

"Want us to do your hair?"

"I… I don't…"

Mia felt suddenly dizzy. The heat beat into her brain; the desert dissolved into multicoloured fragments.

Then Britney and Cristina were at her elbows, catching her as she swooned. "Whoa!" Britney said.

"You, like, need to sit down, Mia."

Poor dear. You must be exhausted, Grandmother Spider said. *Perhaps you'd like some food?*

Mia glanced briefly over at MacKay's seated figure, tranced-out and unmoving. She nodded, wincing at a brief headache-flash.

The spider reached out two sparking arms towards a loose cable. *If you step into that trailer, I can activate the power. I think there's some canned scam and synthi-coffee in the pantry.*

The girls looked at Mia, their heads cocked. She nodded, and they led her around to the front of the trailer.

Cristina stopped at one point and looked back at the empty desert. "That really is something," she said.

Britney shook her head. "You are *losing it*, girl."

Mia scrunched her eyes closed tight. She was tired, there was no doubt of that. Too many days of nightmares and apparitions; too much fuck-and-fight with MacKay; too many gun battles, chases, and general running around. She wasn't twenty-one anymore, she reminded herself.

But Mia had never fainted from exhaustion before. She was a Mad Cow, after all. And somehow, when the dizziness had struck her a moment ago...

... she thought she'd felt Grandmother Spider in her brain.

III

DARKNESS. DARKNESS AND anticipation: the nervous clatter of drumsticks, the clasp of a hand on the big switch, the expectant murmur of the audience beyond. The quiet before the big night.

Slowly, MacKay's eyes began to adjust. He reached out and touched the desk, the big, high, glossy-polished desk. He looked up and saw the darkened lights, small white bulbs ringing a gigantic sign. He looked ahead and saw only a thick, velvet curtain.

Then the curtain parted slightly – just enough for MacKay to make out a slim figure, speaking to a seated crowd beyond. It was still dark; the audience couldn't see MacKay yet. When the figure spoke, its voice was eerily familiar...

"'Ello 'ello!" it said. "Ladies and lords, loyalists and colonials, animal-lovers of all stripes and breeds! It's time to hold onto your women and send the sprogs off to market! Are you *quite* ready?!"

From beyond the curtain, a muffled roar of approval.

"Then put your bloody hands together for the biggest chat-show host in history. The man with a plan, the chap with the traps, the Op with pop – the bloke from Okinoke with a pig in every poke. The one and only – RRRRRRRRRRAT-CATCHAH!"

The curtain pulled aside; the lights above blazed to life. MacKay winced briefly, and the audience laughed, taking it for a comedy routine. Then he recovered, smiled tentatively, and waved.

As the applause rose, MacKay stole a look at the sign above him. It showed a silly line-drawing of a dogcatcher with a net, chasing a large cartoon rodent, who looked back in exaggerated fear. The text read: THE RATCATCHER SHOW.

"I'm Alastair Wellington, and let's have a big hand for the All-Meat Patties!" Wellington gestured towards the small, elevated bandstand at the far end of the stage. Two saxophonists and a ratty bass player waved, their bodies partly obscured by a gigantic empty drum set.

"We've got a bloody great pip of a show for you tonight!" Wellington continued, striding over to the bandstand. "Miko D, the Rapping Rodent, will be here with the word from the street. We'll see just how far Sputo the Cosmic Comic will go to give Ratcatcher the business. The eagle will be here, as usual, with his Wanking Words. And..." He paused theatrically and mimed a curvy female shape in the air. "We've got a special surprise for all the gentlemen in the audience. You might not want to tell the wife about this one!"

MacKay peered at Wellington, watching as the man sat down at the drum set. Wellington wore even more exaggerated Victorian clothes than usual, all ruffles and frill. His affected accent was even more pronounced, too. But he looked younger, slimmer, more virile and active. MacKay realised he'd seen him this way once before, in an image on Miko's computer.

"So let's get things moving right off with–" Wellington stopped, looked around in mock disgust. "Hold the bloody phone. Where's Ed?"

Everything stopped. The audience twittered nervously.

"Ed?" Wellington yelled. "Ed, you trawl your bloody arse out here this instant or I swear you'll never work in this bloody town again."

The audience laughed again, a bit louder.

MacKay heard a slight shuffling offstage. He turned to see Dog – full-sized, brown-furred Dog – pulling free of an unseen figure, stumbling onstage.

Hurm, Dog said. He did a quick double take, and then raised a hand to the audience. They cheered.

"Good thing they love you, you useless ruddy bastard." Wellington smiled – a bit cruelly, MacKay thought.

Dog loped awkwardly over to the chair nearest MacKay. The set had four comfortable chairs, all at a much lower level than MacKay's elevated desk. Past the chairs, between MacKay's area and the bandstand, was a great expanse of stage with what looked like a big trap door set into it.

Dog sat down, smiled at the audience again. MacKay noticed his front paw was bandaged, where he'd cut himself in the kitchen. He looked at MacKay, expectant.

Then MacKay knew: it was time to be the host.

"Ed," he said slowly, "I'm glad you made it."

Hurm, Dog replied.

"I know the traffic is murder coming over from the drunk tank, this time of day."

Dog threw his head back and laughed: *hurm hurm hurm*. The audience roared along.

From across the stage, Wellington motioned sharply to MacKay. The "Englishman" tapped his watch impatiently.

"But enough about you," MacKay continued. "And I mean that most sincerely." More laughter. "It's time to get to our guests – before the audience decides to go catch their rats someplace else."

Quiet.

That wasn't a very snappy line, MacKay realised. He was suddenly conscious of a thousand eyes on him, and felt a moment of show-biz panic.

He looked down at a pile of index cards in front of him. The top one read: MIKO D.

"You know our first guest from his early, groundbreaking animated shorts like *Crackpipe Alley* and *Bukkake High*." MacKay paused, did a brief double-take. "Can I even say that on TV?" The audience laughed heartily. "Well, too late now. Anyway… he's also done hundreds of mesmerising DVDs, and we all remember his films. Personally, I loved *Fly Hawaiian Joint*." Titters of laughter. "But he's here tonight to talk about a new cause that's very important to him. Please welcome the Rapping Rodent himself… MIKO D!"

Dog clapped his paws wildly, and the audience joined him.

MacKay looked over at the eaves, and at first he thought Miko was a no-show. Then he made out a paper-thin figure, shucking and jiving its way out onstage, high-fiving the audience and grinning ear to ear. As Miko hopped his way over to the desk, Dog obligingly moved one seat away so Miko could sit between them.

Miko held up his hands to slap Dog ten. Dog looked at them quizzically.

"Don't leave me hangin', B," Miko said.

Dog obligingly held out his hands. Miko quickly slapped them, and then slapped Dog's face – once, twice, four times.

"Too slow!"

Dog laughed: *hurm hurm hurm*. The audience laughed along. No one seemed to notice that Miko was in fact real and not a cartoon mouse.

MacKay rose and hugged Miko. It was a strange experience. The rodent looked solid, but there was nothing to grab onto. MacKay sank back into his chair, puzzled.

"Aww, it's f—in' good to be back!" Miko said, plopping himself down. The audience cheered.

"Good old Miko," Wellington called from the bandstand. "We never have to worry about the bloody censor with you!"

"Straight up," Miko replied.

"Miko," MacKay said, "it's great to see you. But I gotta say, you're looking a little… insubstantial."

Miko laughed loudly. "MacKay. My *man*. You ain't changed a bit, have you?"

MacKay touched his hairline. "Not thanks to Follic-Gro."

"You keep forgettin' something." Miko stared at him, mockserious. "I'm a cartoon character. Ain't nothin' to grab onto. See?"

With that, Miko turned sideways… and disappeared. Then he turned again, and was solid.

"See, G? I'm two-di*mensional*!"

The audience applauded.

MacKay felt the show getting away from him. "I stand corrected."

"But I gotta tell you somethin', G." Miko leaned towards him then, arms on MacKay's desk. "You my man. You always been my man. You know why?"

"Why?"

"'Cause you always mention that f—in' Hawaiian movie, G. I love that son of a b—h film."

"It's my favourite too, Miko."

"That makes exactly two of us in the motherf—in' world, MacKay."

Hurm hurm hurm!

Miko turned to his right. "A'ight, Ed. Three. Thanks, bro." His voice was a bit condescending now.

"So, Miko — what's this great cause you're here to tell us about? Something close to your heart?"

"Right on, Ratman." Miko looked out at the audience now.

"You know me – I love my pimp life. Ain't nothin' better than kickin' rhymes an' hittin' skins, am I right?" The audience applauded sparsely. "Yee-uh. But, you know, there's serious sh- in the world, too. An' one day I figured, Meek, you got the power. You a true liver, you got the man's cheddah. Time to give some-thin' back, you know?"

"Furreal."

"Ah ha ha ha! Right." Miko maintained his smile, but somehow MacKay sensed he wasn't happy with the host's attempt at hip-hop patois. Too bad, MacKay thought. This ain't the Miko D Show.

"Anyway," Miko continued, "they's poor shorties dyin' in the NoGos. They's war in the streets, homeboys killin' each other over a drop of f—in' water. An' he' I am, Miko D, king'a the f—in' world, drinkin' gin from a g-d d-n Ming vase. Just ain' right, you know?

"So I talked to my accountant, an' we started this thang called PovNo. Iss like Poverty – No! You git it?"

Hurm, Dog said.

"Right on! I knew my man Ed would come correct. Anyway… I'm here spreadin' the word about this important *initiative*. An' if the folks out there feel like donatin' they time – or better, they money – they can do so by dialing the toll-free digits on the screen."

MacKay nodded. "And what exactly does PovNo… do?"

Miko thought for a minute. His cartoon face screwed up in puz-zlement. "Well, you know," he said finally. "We got to help the next generation, youknowwhatI'msayin'? They need juice an' cheddah. They need some *hope* for the *future*. We gotta turn the *NoGos* into *Yes-Gos*." He smiled, proud of himself.

"And PovNo does this? Will do this?"

"Well… yee-uh. We gon' do all'at. But we kin on'y do it if we git the Presidents we need." Miko looked out again at the audi-ence, serious. "If the people open up they hearts an' *give*."

Hurm hurm, Dog agreed.

"Miko," MacKay said slowly, "you know I love you. I don't know if – the audience probably doesn't know this, but Miko and I came up together. We used to do the crappy clubs together down in the Village… dodged a few tomatoes in the old days, didn't we?"

"Wit' razors in 'em," Miko said, grinning a friendly grin.

That's not true, MacKay realised. Why was he saying that? This Dreamquest stuff did strange things to a man.

"So no disrespect, Miko," he continued, "but I gotta ask you something. If this… 'PovNo'… is all about *you* doing something worthwhile with your millions—"

"Straight up, G."

"—then why do you need money from ordinary people who don't have as much?"

For a horrible, frozen moment, everything stopped. Miko's big cartoon eyes, staring at MacKay, seemed to triple in size.

Then the mouse exploded in rich, full laughter. He slapped Dog on the knee. The monkey winced.

"D-n, G! That's cold. You hurt me, man. F'a minute I thought you'as serious!"

"I… "

"Look at you!" Miko continued. "Look at you all sittin' behind that big desk an' sh-, man. Big man on the campus, ain't you?"

MacKay grimaced comically. "The basic cable campus."

The audience was laughing now. The tension had been broken.

"Don't be so modest, G. You got the power. You life runnin' fine. Just remember one thing: don't forget us little people, okay?"

MacKay smiled. "I could never forget you, Miko."

A motion caught MacKay's eye. Over at the bandstand, Wellington was signalling furiously.

"We've gotta go to commercial, you crazy rodent bastard. Try not to fleece the people too bad during the break, okay?"

Miko laughed again, and Dog chimed in with a hearty *hurm hurm hurm*. Wellington brought up the theme music, and the curtain swished shut to heavy applause.

The second the curtain was closed, Miko reached out and grabbed MacKay by the lapels. "What the f— you doin' to me, G?"

MacKay looked past him to Dog, who was loping uneasily offstage. He disengaged himself from Miko and followed.

"I, uh, I din' mean nothin', Ratman," Miko said behind him. "You the man, G. You always the man."

MacKay caught up with the monkey just behind the inner curtain. "Dog!" he said, grabbing his shoulder. "I gotta talk to you."

Dog turned, fear in his eyes.

"How's the hand? Okay?"

Dog shrugged. *Hurm*.

"Listen – we're still in the Dreamquest. I've got to get out of here – I don't know what Grandmother Spider is up to, but it can't be good."

Dog looked offstage, nervously.

"Mia might be in danger."

At that, Dog looked straight at him, grimaced. But then he pointed offstage, apologetically.

Just then Wellington appeared, grabbed MacKay by the arm. "Smashing show, old boy! Simply capital!" He towed the slightly resisting MacKay towards a young woman with big glasses and teased hair. "Let's just touch up that pancake before the break ends, old boy. Bloody excellent!"

Wellington pushed him into a metal chair, and the woman dabbed makeup on his cheeks. Through the fog of powder, MacKay saw Dog off in the wings, pleading with some shadowy figures. He couldn't make out their faces, but when they smiled, their sharp teeth glowed brightly.

"Who are *they*?" he asked.

Wellington turned to look. "Oh, just the bloody producers. Always hanging about. In earlier centuries, we'd have taken their money and had them shot."

As MacKay watched – twisting his head around to evade the makeup artist's thrusts – Dog broke away from the producers, began walking off. But one of them opened his mouth and a large, snakelike tongue darted out. It grabbed Dog by the leg, tripped him up, and then dragged him, kicking, offstage and out of view.

MacKay turned to Wellington, alarmed. "That was a producer?"

Wellington looked offstage after Dog, shook his head. "Yes," he said. "We should never have gotten bollixed up with that one."

"Who is it?"

Wellington grabbed the applicator out of the makeup woman's hands. When he stared at MacKay, he seemed serious for the first time. "You're the star, old boy," he said. "Stick to your job. Mister Nihilo is our problem."

With that, Wellington strode off in the direction of the bandstand.

Now MacKay sat alone, fifty seconds till end of break. He was worried about Dog, but despite himself, another question buzzed around and around in his brain. The age-old question of talk-show hosts everywhere.

Do I control the producers, or do they control me?

IV

DEEP IN THE heart of Thalamus, Nihilo was feeling pretty jerked around, too.

He'd never gotten his tacos; Thalamus had summoned him back, hurriedly, to their Florida headquarters. Now he stood confined within a pentagram, in what had been the employee health club before last year's benefit cutbacks. It was possibly the first demonic holding spell in history flanked on both sides by basketball hoops.

Five men in blue suits, all with cloth strips over their faces, stood before him now, holding candles out in front of them.

"This is absolutely the gayest thing I've ever seen," Nihilo said.

"Hear uf, great one," the lead doofus said, his voice muffled as always by the cloth. "We crave newv of MacKay's queft."

"His queft? His queft?"

"Yef. His queft."

Nihilo rolled his red demon eyes. These guys were all top-level Thalamus execs, which meant they took themselves *way* too seriously – which, in turn, meant that ridiculing them wasn't much fun. "Look, assholes. I ain't seen MacKay."

"But you are everywhere, oh Great One."

"I dunno about that, but I'm more places than I'd like. Thanks to you and those buttgnawers at Fuzzies/GenTech."

"Are you not linked with Hank Polehoufe?"

"Yeah, and that's a hell of a lot of use. That shit-for-brains thinks he's a gang leader now. If I was you turds, I wouldn't bet the quarterly profits on him."

"Yef, great one. That is why–"

"Hank Polehouse. Hah! I'd run him off the road, but I really doubt even his *death* would be interesting."

"We bow to your wivdom, great one."

"I gotta admit, though – those ACTS fuckers got some balls. I kinda like bein' their god." Nihilo paced the pentagram for a minute, thinking. "you know what I really want? I'd like to possess a GenTech exec."

"Great One – Falamuf can provide you wif anyfing you–"

"'Falamuf' is a fucking bore. More to the point – GenTech has outmanoeuvred you. And I'm the supernatural entity getting fucked up both ends because of it."

"A fousand pardonv, Nihilo. When MacKay finds the cult leader, you will be–"

"Yeah, yeah. Is it feedin' time yet?"

The blue-suited men shifted uneasily. "We are at your fervice, great one. Wivout you, we are–"

"Skip it. You drew straws, right?"

The men nodded.

"Then lemme have my sacrifice. Or 'facrifice', if it'll make you feel more at home. Homos."

Nervously, sweating through his cloth face-covering, one of the men stepped forwards. He held out his candle in front of him.

"Great Nihilo," the man said, voice quavering. "Please acfept this humble veffel as–"

"Accepted, food-boy. Strip down now – I don't feel like devouring a three-piece suit along with your pathetic essence."

But as the man unbuttoned his jacket, the room began to grow indistinct around Nihilo.

"Aw, *fuck*," he said.

"Great one?"

Nihilo concentrated, focused his will on remaining in this place. But it was no use. He was already corporealising in the other place. Below him, through the energy-haze, he could already see the trinity. The cat, the dog, and the mouse.

He was back in Cocoa Niño.

"Great," Nihilo said, utterly disgusted. "I'm *never* gonna get to eat!"

v

DAZED AND CONFUSED, MacKay sat once more at his *Ratcatcher Show* desk. Dog staggered out, limping a little, a fresh bandage on his brown-furred arm.

Miko just sat still in his centre chair, looking down at the stage floor. "Destroyed my f—in' career," he muttered.

"What?" MacKay said.

Wellington's voice boomed over the speakers. "Three... two... one..."

The curtain opened; the lights blazed. Dog smiled out at the audience, and Miko leaned back, at ease and grinning. MacKay glanced at his next index card: It read SPUTO.

"We're back!" he said. "Our next guest is—"

A horn blared out, three off-key notes. *Clang Clong Clang!*

"Ohhhhhh, bollocks!" Wellington grinned. "You all know what that means..."

As one, the audience chanted: "IT'S BALLED EAGLE TIME!"

Everyone looked up. There was a rustling in the lights, and the enormous fowl swooped down, his prominent sac preceding him in his descent.

"Eagle, you Yankee bastard," Wellington continued. "What's our latest Wanking Word?"

Eagle looked out at the audience, sniffed his beak up haughtily, and did a hundred and eighty-degree pirouette in mid-air.

A small paper sign was taped on the far side of his sac. It read:
EXSANGUINATION.

"Bloody hell! That's grim." Wellington did a brief drum roll,
then smiled over at MacKay. "One for the punters to look up
at home."

MacKay felt a shiver pass through him.

"Yeah," he said weakly. "Uh, anyway… our next guest isn't
just an ex-astronaut – he's also an out-of-this-world enter-
tainer." MacKay frowned at the card, then carried on. "Please
welcome… Sputo the Cosmic Comic!"

The withered dog rolled out in his wheelchair, legs covered
as always by his familiar chequered blanket. He wore an old-
fashioned propeller-beanie with moon-rockets drawn on it, and
he held a cigar clamped tightly in his teeth. He waved madly at
the crowd, smiling like an old man. "Hiya hiya hiya!" he said.

As the applause died down, Sputo tried to manoeuvre his
wheelchair into the space next to MacKay's desk. Miko and
Dog, who had each moved over one seat, looked on blandly as
Sputo collided with the guest chair, then reached out feebly,
trying to push the guest chair out of the way. It didn't budge.

Finally MacKay rolled his eyes, jumped up on his desk, and
kicked the unwanted chair backwards, toppling it out of the
way. The audience exploded in applause.

"The Ratcatchah!" Wellington announced.

"MacKay," Sputo said, settling into his new space. "You are
the king. You know that? The *king* of late night."

"Is that what time it is?" MacKay replied. Laughter.

"I swear, I never had so much fun as when I come on this
show. That's the truth, boychik. Not even when I was in space."

"Yeah. Space." MacKay felt himself slipping back into the
host role, with its easy cruelty and condescension. "That was a
long time ago, wasn't it?"

"Well, MacKay, you oughta know."

Sputo puffed on the cigar, took it out of his mouth momentarily. For the first time, MacKay noticed a small antenna
coming out of it. He's using it, MacKay realised, to make his
voice sound normal for TV.

For a Dreamquest, this vision had a hell of a lot of technical details covered.

"So Spoot," MacKay said. "How's the career going? Playing a lot of clubs?"

"Clubs? Hah! Kennels is more like it." He puffed the cigar mightily. "It's a dog's life, I tell ya. But I get by."

"I understand you have a new venture to tell us about, too."

"I sure do, Ratcatcher. I sure do!"

MacKay looked from Sputo to Miko. "Is that all you guys think of me? A way to shill your wares?"

Miko gave him a blank smile. "You my boy, G."

"Shill my wares? What the hell does that mean?" Sputo appealed to the audience. "What is this guy, a friggin' dictionary?"

MacKay sighed. "Well, I guess you might as well…" Then he stopped. Wellington was making a furious throat-cutting motion from the bandstand. When MacKay cocked his head at him, Wellington pointed straight down.

MacKay looked at his index cards. The next one read KANGAROO COURT.

He smiled, and felt something like a demon rise inside him. "Hang on just a minute, Spoot," he said. "You know the rules here on the Ratcatcher Show. You want to promote a profit-making venture, first you have to get through… the Kangaroo Court!"

On cue, the vast open section of the stage parted to reveal a giant swimming pool. Small, vicious fish snapped and broke the surface of the clear water. A maze of complex gymnastic equipment ran over the top, hanging down, in spots, perilously close to the pool.

"It's really more of an obstacle course, don'tyouknow," Wellington said. "But we didn't have a bloody animal pun for that."

"Yo boy," Miko said, eyes wide. "Are those *piranhas*?"

"They, uh, they sure are." MacKay hesitated; this suddenly seemed cruel.

Sputo's mouth gaped open. "I gotta get through *that*?"

MacKay stuck to the script. "Only if you want to tell the people what you're selling, buddy."

Sputo pointed to Miko. "This little pischer didn't have to do that!"

Miko looked offended. "Yo, B. I'm strictly non-profit."

"And my grandmother's a Playboy bunny." Sputo grimaced — even more than usual — and wheeled his way up to the edge of the pool. "Oy vey."

After five minutes, Sputo had managed to pull himself up, by his front paws, to the first of an arched series of monkey bars stretching all the way over the pool.

Slowly, wrenchingly, Sputo grunted his way to the second bar. His body hung loose now over the pool. Small piranhas leapt and snapped at his dangling, useless feet.

He looked back, pleadingly, at MacKay. "You are *aware* that I have no use of my *legs*?"

Wellington grinned. "Everybody's got an alibi in Kangaroo Court!"

The audience laughed. Miko leaned back, smiling behind his big cartoon shades. Even Dog seemed mesmerised.

MacKay watched, silent, as Sputo lurched his way to the third bar, groaning in pain. The bars arched higher now, taking him a little further above the piranhas. But when Sputo got near the other side, he'd have to climb back down again, closer to the deadly fish.

"Only thirty to go, old boy," Wellington laughed. "Or maybe forty."

MacKay barely remembered watching the spectacle. One rung at a time, the crippled dog made his way across the pool. His beanie bashed against the bars, crumpling the propeller. His arms shook, and more than once, he looked as if he'd fall right into the water.

The audience chanted "Go! Go! Go!" Or, whenever Sputo faltered: "Drop! Drop! Drop!"

Halfway across, Sputo dropped his cigar. The piranhas swarmed, devouring it instantly.

"Ohhhhh shiiitttttt," Sputo said.

Miko laughed. "B—h dog sounds retarded," he said.

Cigar-less and exhausted, Sputo carried on. Each rung seemed like more of an effort for him than the one before. When reached the two-thirds point, MacKay heard a familiar *Clang Clong Clang!*

"IT'S BALLED EAGLE TIME!" the audience yelled.

The homicidal bird swooped down, further panicking the dangling Sputo. As Eagle swooped back and forth, MacKay saw that it had *two* pieces of paper taped to it this time – one on either side of its sac. It looped and pirouetted, showing its new words to everyone. Sputo swung wildly, flinching to avoid its talons.

Despite himself, MacKay found himself staring at the eagle's scrotum. One side read "shock". The other said "awe".

"God bless America," Sputo gasped.

The bird raised a wing in what looked like a salute, and disappeared back up into the wings.

The crowd cheered and hissed, throwing small objects at the dog: tomatoes, eggs, cigarette cartons. Sputo dodged them all, and eventually got within five rungs of the end. Dog the monkey grabbed Sputo's wheelchair and pushed it around to the other side of the pool. He waited there, watching, just below the bandstand.

"Yoooo bttttttr ketch me whn I lannnnd, boychik," Sputo said. Exhausted, fur dripping with sweat, he began moving faster on the downward slope of the last few bars.

He's going to have a heart attack, MacKay thought.

An energetic piranha jumped a bit higher, nicked Sputo on the toe. He howled in pain.

The audience laughed.

"Whttt a bzzzzznsssss," Sputo muttered.

Mustering up a final burst of energy, Sputo glided down the last two bars and plopped himself down in his wheelchair – just as Wellington played a "bumph" percussion noise on his drums.

"Sputo the Cosmic Comic!" Wellington exclaimed.

Sputo raised his arms, blew kisses to the applauding audience. Dog handed him a new cigar.

When the clapping died down, Sputo looked up at Dog. "Thank God that's over."

Wellington grinned evilly down at Sputo. "Oh, Sputo. It's not over. That was just Round One."

The swimming pool retracted, sealed shut. Fake rain-forest trees and thick brush descended from the ceiling, covering the stage. Wellington gestured to the band, and they struck up a fluty medley of jungle sounds.

"Gevalt," Sputo said.

"Now it's time to play… Dodge the Rhino!"

A gigantic, snorting rhinoceros appeared at the stage entrance. It howled, looked around, and fixed its eyes on Sputo. Dog the monkey walked back to the discussion area, leaving Sputo alone.

The "Cosmic Comic" looked very tiny in his wheelchair, with the checked blanket.

"You're kiddin' me, right?"

MacKay stared in a state of shock. Where had the rhino come from? How could they hold a beast like that backstage?

Then he remembered: Dreamquest. Right. The laws of nature did not necessarily apply.

The rhino circled for a moment, snorting wildly, its eyes fixed on Sputo. The dog swivelled his wheelchair, keeping the giant beast in view.

"Nice little babushka," Sputo said, his voice quavering. "Oh mama."

When the rhino made his charge, MacKay could stand it no more. He reached under the desk, grabbed a large rifle. Then he jumped up onto the desk, leapt over Miko and Dog, and landed on the stage, gun blazing.

"Oh god," Sputo blubbered. He was clearly exhausted, shaking, crying into his hands. "Somebody help me."

Five tranq darts slammed into the startled rhino's hide. It turned to MacKay, growling in a way he couldn't ever remember a rhinoceros doing in real life. Come to think of it, the snorting was new, too.

The audience was eating it up. They laughed at Sputo's misery, gasped at the rhino, cheered as MacKay fired his weapon again and again.

Finally, with a massive THUD, the rhino went down.

The audience was silent, expectant.

MacKay lowered the rifle, looked at Sputo. The dog peered at him from between his fingers, and gasped, "Thank you."

But MacKay wasn't looking at him anymore. Above, in the bandstand, Wellington was glaring at his host with angry red eyes.

They stood, silent, for a moment. Staring. The downed, snoring beast lay between them.

Then Miko D jumped up, pumping his fist in the air. "The Ratcatcher, boy! The Ratcatcher!"

The audience exploded to its feet, cheering.

Smiling, waving to the crowd, MacKay walked over to Sputo and put a hand on the dog's shoulder. Weak, gasping, Sputo motioned him to come closer. MacKay thought the dog might be having a heart attack. He leaned down, put his ear next to Sputo's mouth.

"Can I give my spiel now?" Sputo whispered.

Startled, MacKay shrugged.

Sputo immediately sat up straight, patted MacKay on the cheek. "This – this is my boy!" Then he called offstage. "Donna?"

A beautiful woman, in a bikini and heels, strode out carrying a small wooden crate.

MacKay walked back to his desk, ignoring Wellington's murderous gaze on his back. As he passed Dog, the monkey frowned at him. That was worrisome.

Sputo turned to the audience. "My friends," he said. "Are you tired of so-called 'red meat' that's barely pink? Of chicken that tastes like soy mush? Of ribs with less meat on 'em than a supermodel?" He reached over, and held up the box. "Then you need ANIPROTEIN!"

MacKay was just sitting down. He turned in surprise.

"Meat is good for you. Hell, meat is *great* for you," Sputo continued. "And thanks to a consortium of helpful and benevolent corporations, we've made it available once again in these fine United States of America. Juicy, lovely, and affordable!"

The woman smiled, white teeth through red, red lips.

"So when the Supermobile comes through town, when you arm yourself up and venture out to market, ask for it by name. ANIPROTEIN. Changing your life — without *you* having to change at all."

Sputo handed the box back to the woman. She walked off-stage, her pert, thong-covered ass wiggling back and forth provocatively.

"Sputo?" MacKay called.

"Yes, bubby?"

"All that meat," MacKay said slowly. "Where does it come from?"

Sputo hesitated.

"Aah," he said finally, "why you wanna ask questions like that? It's fat-riffic and juicy-licious!"

MacKay opened his mouth to inquire further, but abruptly Wellington played the theme music. "Back after this," the Englishman thundered.

Dog leapt up from his chair, vaulted over the startled Miko, and grabbed MacKay by the arm. He tugged him quickly off-stage, away from the bandstand and Wellington.

"What? What?" MacKay asked.

Dog pushed him into an alcove backstage, next to a lighting console. The monkey reached furiously into his vest, pulled out a cigarette, and lit it.

"Listen, you're supposed to be my spirit guide here. How about a little—"

"You're doing it all wrong," Dog said.

He puffed furiously while MacKay stared.

"You can talk," MacKay said.

"If you're going to go all expository on me every time something new happens, we'll never get through this." Dog's voice was measured, low, intense. He looked nervously, side to side, as he talked.

"Sorry."

"I'm not supposed to do this — I'm just supposed to grunt and give you vague guidance," the monkey continued. "But I can't just stand here and watch you screw this up."

"Screw what up?" MacKay gestured at the stage. "What *is* all this?"

"You've got to go with the flow more. Shooting the rhino – that was a major violation. It wasn't in the script."

"It was gonna kill Sputo."

"Maybe. Maybe not. It doesn't matter."

MacKay glared at him. Dog sucked in smoke, blew it out quickly.

"You've got to play this through to the end – that's how a Dreamquest works," Dog continued. "Everything happens for a reason. Everything is significant."

Dog looked towards the backstage area, nervously. MacKay followed his gaze, and caught a vague glimpse of those malevolent eyes and teeth again, waiting in the shadows.

"Oh, shit," Dog said. "I'm gonna be food."

"How long have I been here?" MacKay asked. "I've got to get out. Grandmother Spider could be up to anything by now."

"Forget Grandmother Spider," Dog hissed. "She's not important – she's as much a victim as the rest of us." He blew out a long, manic puff of smoke. "In her own way, I think she's trying to help you."

MacKay grabbed Dog's spindly front leg, pulled him close. "Those – *things* backstage," he whispered. "What's going on?"

"I gotta go." Dog threw the cigarette to the floor, stamped it out. "Shit, we're all food sooner or later, right?"

MacKay shrugged helplessly.

Dog started off into the black backstage depths. "Remember," he called back, "everything is a clue. Everything. *Play it through.*"

Then Dog was gone.

The music came up, and MacKay hustled his ass back onstage.

"Looks like Ed's off in the bloody tank again, Ratcatcher." Wellington played a rimshot noise, and the audience laughed.

MacKay said nothing. Seated at his desk – his huge, protective desk – he thought he still heard screams from backstage, where Dog had disappeared.

Sputo and Miko had, inexplicably, switched seats. They both looked at him, now, to lead them into the next segment. Sputo's arm was in a cast; he puffed hard on his cigar.

"Well," MacKay said. He looked at his next index card, which read, cryptically: VAVAVOOM! "It looks like we've got a very special treat up next—"

"Excuse me. Ratman, old boy?"

MacKay looked over at Wellington, startled. "Yes?"

"I'm sorry to interrupt, Ratcatchah. But… could I possibly handle this next introduction?"

The Englishman, MacKay noticed, was back to his stage persona – the annoying announcer-slash-bandleader. He sat at his drum set, wearing a big, brightly-coloured sombrero.

MacKay waved him on. "Knock yourself out, Alastair."

"Good show!" Wellington stood up, leaned forwards with a disturbing leer. "Ladies and gentlemen… we've come to the truly *adult* portion of our programme. Our next act is the type of lady your grandfather told you about, while your parents were out of the room. She's the type of vixen who drives men to war, who makes a young boy's voice drop two octaves. Her hips are registered as deadly weapons in May-hee-co."

The audience twittered expectantly.

"May I present to you that luscious lady of song… the queen of young men's dreams and old men's fantasies… the Latin bombshell… *Miss Mia Sangre!*"

MacKay's head jerked up in shock.

And that was *before* he saw her.

Mia strutted out to centre stage, hips swaying provocatively, breasts bouncing with each step. She wore a very short, red-blue-and-green skirt, with a frilly hem just inches below her waist. Two coconuts covered her breasts, tied with scratchy-looking rope twine. Her black go-go boots had a snakeskin pattern on them, and she carried a big, old-fashioned microphone trailing a long cord. Her makeup was caked on heavy and trashy: red lips, over-rouged cheeks, an abundance of blue eyeshadow.

She looked like she belonged on a fruit carton.

The audience went wild. Smiling, Mia crossed the stage, back and forth, blowing kisses to them. Then the stage lights dropped, and a bright white spot picked her out. She faced forwards, expectant.

Wellington tapped one drumstick lazily, setting up an easy Latin rhythm. Behind him, three trumpet players – also in sombreros – raised their horns and blew.

When Mia sang, she sounded like a baby doll with a heavy accent. She pouted and kissed at the audience, shaking her fringe right, left, and forwards again.

> *"I like jou*
> *Oh jes I do*
> *I like the things you know*
> *I like the way you go*
> *To work in the mor-neen*
> *Working very hard*
> *I like your credit card*
> *That buys me many theengs!*
> *And that is why I seeng*
> *I… like… jou!"*

Mia lowered the mike, and Wellington and the Patties glided into a mariachi-laced instrumental bridge. Then Mia launched into a high-heeled run, girly-style, arms flailing. She sprinted past Sputo and Miko and somersaulted onto MacKay's desk. She began to dance furiously, grinding her hips, staring down at him with vacant, flirty eyes.

Sputo leaned towards Mia and yelled "Go baby go! God, I wish I had legs!"

Miko looked straight up her skirt, then down at his own groin. "I'm startin' to get three-dimensional here, yo."

MacKay felt as if he'd passed into some sort of clinical shock.

He met Mia's eyes, and felt a deep disgust. He started to reach up and pull her down, but then he remembered Dog's words:

Play it through.

As the bridge came to an end, Mia slid off the desk and strutted back to centre stage.

"I like jou
Jou better bet I do
I like jour frilly pants
I like the way you dance!
Straight… to the jewellery sto'
When… I am feeling low
And when I see those di-monds
I just have to buy-dem
Then for you I shimmy
Shimmy whimmy jimmy
Up and down, nice and tight"

MacKay shook his head, trying to clear it. When he looked up, Mia was – alarmingly – beginning a new march towards his desk.

"And for at least one night"

Mia leaned down in front of Sputo, scratched his chin. His cigar bobbed up, erect.

"I"

She ruffled Miko's head. He stared at her wiggling ass.

"Like"

Finally she plopped down, on her back, on MacKay's desk. Reaching out a finger, she touched his nose and smiled.

"Jou!"

The audience burst into applause and catcalls.

Wellington reached up, pulled off his sombrero, and tossed it lustily into the crowd. "Ladies and gentlemen," he said, "Miss Mia Sangre, the Latin Bombshell!" He leered over at MacKay. "By Jove, I believe she *likes* you, Ratcatchah!"

Mia was still sitting on the desk, curled up against him now. "But of course, Olly-stair," she said, her voice squeaky. "The song, she said so, no?"

MacKay lifted Mia's arm off his neck. "That was, uh, terrific, Mia."

Sputo growled out a low laugh. "Whatsamatter, MacKay? Don'tcha like the ladies?" The audience laughed.

"Don't even play," Miko said. "My man Ratcatcher's all about it."

Wellington laughed then, a very unpleasant laugh. "You know what I think? I think—"

Clang Clong Clang!

"It's Balled Eagle Time!"

MacKay and Mia looked up fearfully. She hugged him close.

The bird swooped down. Its disturbingly intelligent eyes looked straight into MacKay's, as if it were trying to tell him something. It took an effort for him to look away.

Taped to its sac were the words: VACAS MUITAS.

"What the bloody ruddy bollocking Hell does that mean?" Wellington asked. "Piss off, Eagle. Come back when you're ready to speak bloody American!"

Eagle turned and swooped at Wellington, fixing him with a deadly glare. Wellington flinched, and MacKay tensed for violence. But then the eagle saluted and disappeared up, into the wings.

"That's right," Wellington said quietly, shaken. "Remember who pays your bloody salary." Then he let off a drum flourish and turned back to the audience. "As I was saying… do you know what I think?"

"WHAT?" the audience replied.

"I think the Ratcatchah should give Miss Mia a big, sloppy kiss."

Wild applause. Sputo whistled, and Miko let off a loud whoop.

MacKay looked into Mia's face, scant inches from his own. She looked back, all flirty, trashy, and made-up. A perfect coquette, an ingénue born, grown, and surgically enhanced for just one purpose: to perform onstage.

Mia was a beautiful woman, and through the dream-fog, MacKay vaguely recalled that they'd slept together. He realised that he'd even hoped, unconsciously, that she might be a kindred soul; a life-partner who shared his passions, who wouldn't try to tame him or convince him to give up the dangerous existence of a Sanctioned Op.

But this – this was all wrong. Mia wasn't a woman here; she wasn't even a person. She was an image, a pose, the creation of a talent manager. Like Sputo with his dumb jokes and his protein business, or Miko with his put-on slang and fraudulent charity. An angle. A phoney.

A lie.

Mia looked away from him, out to the audience. "Hwat do jou think, hah? Chould I do it?"

The audience cheered.

Mia puckered theatrically, and leaned in to him. Grimacing inside, MacKay closed his eyes. For just a moment, he thought he heard Dog screaming, off in the distance.

Then the theme music swelled. MacKay opened his eyes just in time to see the curtain slide shut.

Mia pulled her lips back and shot him a look of total disgust. "Thank fucking Christ." She folded up her legs, jumped to the floor, and stalked away.

Miko and Sputo were lined up before his desk, shifting back and forth, waiting to thank him. But Wellington's voice cut through the room, disturbingly devoid, now, of any trace of a British accent.

"That's a wrap, everyone. Thank you. MacKay… all I can say is, you better get your shit together before the next episode. I'm tired of carrying you."

But MacKay wasn't listening. All around him, the set was growing dim.

He'd already moved on to his next vehicle.

vi

"Mia?"

"Mmm?"

"What's, like, *this*?"

Mia turned in the uncomfortable metal chair and looked up at the trailer's kitchen area. Cristina stood, arms folded, leaning on the sink. Next to her, Britney held out a small chicken bone, accusingly.

"It was in your jacket."

Mia glared at her. "And why exactly were you looking through my jacket?"

"Well, excuse me for thinking you might have an inhaler or something in there!"

"Britney… have you ever seen me use an inhaler?"

Cristina pushed past her friend and sat down opposite Mia. She took Mia's hands in hers. "Listen, Mia. You know us. We're not here to judge."

"Oh, totally not," Britney agreed. She twirled the chicken bone between her fingers.

"But if you've got a *problem*… something you need to *tell* us… well, that's what we're here for."

"We're like sisters," Britney beamed.

Mia rose, snatched the chicken bone from Britney's hands. She was feeling much better, she realised.

"It's nothing." She dropped the bone down the sink and thumbed on the waste disposal. A deafening grinding noise filled the trailer.

Mia decided to change the subject. "Cris… a few minutes ago, when we were outside. Did you… did you *see* something? Out in the desert?"

Cristina's eyes went wide, in mock shock. "Duh! Yuh."

"What, exactly?"

"*You* know."

Britney and Mia both stared at her for a second.

"Uh, no, girl," Britney said. "We don't."

"The… you know! The oasis and the tents and stuff."

"Oasis?"

"And the big machines." She paused, puzzled. "You didn't *see* it?"

Mia thought back, and remembered her brief flashes of sight. "I think I did," she said softly. "For a moment."

"Well," Britney said haughtily, "I have like *no* idea what you two are talking about."

Cristina looked panicked. "But it's right *there*."

Mia paced the short length of the room. She pulled aside the window shade, just enough to see Grandmother Spider and

MacKay. They still sat on opposite chairs, unmoving, facing each other. Grandmother's motorcycle sidecar stood next to her, leaning against another trailer.

Beyond them: nothing but desert.

She turned back to Britney and Cristina. "I have an idea," she said. "You two go outside. I want you to ask Grandmother Spider to show you a little trick she uses to keep her sidecar from being stolen."

The girls looked at each other. "'Kay," Britney said. "What about you?"

"I'll be there in a minute." As the girls reached the door, she added, "Don't say anything about the... whatever. Oasis."

Frowning, they left.

Mia walked back to the window and waited.

Soon she saw Cristina and Britney approach Grandmother Spider, outside in the heat. She could just make out their voices through the trailer wall.

"Cool sidecar!" Britney said.

Grandmother Spider said something unintelligible. I'm not receiving her telepathy in here, Mia realised. That explained why her headache had gone away, too.

"Bet you have to hide it from gangcults," Britney continued.

Cristina kept darting glances at the desert, but she said nothing.

Grandmother Spider gestured towards the sidecar. A multi-coloured energy web — stronger than the one Mia had seen her project before — wafted out, and the cycle vanished from view.

Mia let the window shade drop. She sprinted to the door and opened it silently. Then she crept out of the trailer, down to the ground, and over to her cycle.

Britney's voice came, faintly, from beyond the trailer. "Cooooool!"

Mia unsnapped the combat laser from the front of the bike and hefted it on her shoulder. She thumbed the controls to a wide-angle beam — barely enough to cause a bad sunburn, but enough to cover a large area.

When she rounded the trailer, Britney was touching the invisible sidecar. MacKay just sat, rock-still, eyes closed.

Grandmother Spider saw the gun, and her eyes narrowed. *Young lady. What do you think you're doing?*

"Brit," Mia said. "Stand back."

The spider scuttled forwards. There was an edge in her voice. *If you're thinking of intimidating Grandmother Spider, you may want to think again. She can defend herself when—*

Mia sighted, took aim, and squeezed off a quick burst in the direction of the sidecar. It shimmered, wavered in a multi-coloured haze, and was visible once more.

That, Grandmother Spider said, *was rude.*

Mia turned around, aimed the laser straight at the desert plain. All she saw was flat ground, a few cacti. For a moment, she wondered if this was crazy.

Then she pressed down on the firing pin, and held it.

The laser shot out wide, a faint red aura in the bright sun. Mia kept a steady aim at just a slight upward angle. The beam faded at a distance of a few metres.

Stop that! Grandmother Spider said, in her mind. *Stop that this instant!*

Mia held her finger on the pin. She peered over the gun, squinting in the sunlight. She thought she could see… *something…*

Then a stabbing headache hit her: Grandmother Spider. Mia ignored the pain, kept firing.

"Ohmygod!" Britney said.

A gigantic, multicoloured pattern shimmered in the desert air, like a wide-angle rainbow. Bright lights sparkled where Mia's laser hit it. Then it was gone.

Mia lowered the laser and stared.

"Whoa," said Britney.

Where the desert had been, an entire community stood. Palm trees and pools, tents and humvees. Giant, bizarre machines and strange, barbed-wire enclosures, reminiscent of POW camps. A spidercopter landing pad.

Like Cristina had said: an oasis.

"Oh, bother," Grandmother Spider muttered.

Mia gestured at the settlement. "Cocoa Niño, I presume."

Then she saw the soldiers.

vii

THE LITTLE SCREEN shimmered, and a starfield appeared. Suns, moons, nebulae; they wavered from black and white to colour, and back again. Halting, off-key music, like a symphony recorded on warped vinyl, swelled.

This must be the part of the Dreamquest, MacKay thought dryly, where I watch TV for a while.

Words fanned out onto the screen like a comet tail:

THE ADVENTURES OF RATCATCHER!

Then came the narration, like a prepubescent boy deliberately pitching his voice down:

"The Adventures of… *Ratcatcher!*"

Didn't see that one coming, MacKay thought.

More comet-tail lettering:

AND HIS PAL DOG-BOY!

"And his pal Dog-Boy!"

MacKay shook his head, looked around. He sat in a hard, vinyl-upholstered chair, one of two facing the screen. Beneath the screen was a row of dials and oscilloscopes, none of them active. The walls on either side were covered with big, cheap-looking murals of space scenes; a couple of old-style subway straps hung from the ceiling. Behind him, a thick, dark curtain covered the back wall.

If you squinted, it looked like the inside of a spaceship. But a ship from a world where no one had heard of spidercopters, space shuttles, or CGI special effects.

Everything looked very 1950s, he suddenly realised. A time when the lies were a little easier to believe.

He turned his attention back to the screen, hoping for clues.

"Tonight's episode: *American Meat!*"

"As you recall, Ratcatcher's young friend Dog-Boy had been kidnapped by the evil AniMen, who have established a secret base somewhere on the planet Earth itself!"

Pretty sloppy homeland security, MacKay thought.

"Now he has flown his rocketship clear across the galaxy in pursuit…"

The screen faded to an image of a spinning globe, continents clearly visible, countries demarcated by distinct colours. Apparently on this show, the Earth had no atmosphere.

"EARTH – ORBIT – ESTABLISHED," said a toneless computer voice.

"Thank you, Canz," MacKay said.

"SHOULD – I – PREPARE – FOR – LANDING?"

"One moment," MacKay said. Just like before, on the talk-show stage, he could feel himself slipping into character, swaggering a bit. "I think I need some food first."

As soon as he said it, he could smell barbecue. His mouth watered.

MacKay looked to his left, and saw a slot in the wall. A big red button next to it read "food". He smiled and pressed it firmly.

The wall-slot made a grinding noise and shook a bit. Then, with a clatter, a chipped bowl slid out of the slot.

MacKay frowned, picked it up. He dipped the spoon into the bowl, lifted up a small helping of thin, grey gruel. Tofu bits floated in it.

As if on cue, two young people – a man and a woman – pushed their way through the curtain. The boy sported frosted orange hair; the girl's was pink. They both wore all black, down to their regulation space boots.

"Professor," the young man said. "I'm surprised you can think of food at a time like this."

MacKay smiled at him. "A growing boy has to keep up his strength." Then, for some reason, he pointed at the screen in front of him. "That's important, kids."

The girl seated herself in the second chair and punched a few buttons. A punched ticker-tape clattered out of another small slot, in front of her. She picked it the tape and frowned at it.

"Eighty-two point three o'clock local sidereal time," she said. "We're cutting this one pretty close."

"We'd better prepare for landing, professor," the young man said. "Are you ready?"

Confused, MacKay nodded.

The young man punched a button behind MacKay, and more ticker-tape spat out of the wall. "Coordinates VM-slash-B punched in."

"DO – YOU – REQUIRE – ASSISTANCE?"

"We'll handle this one manually, Canz," the young woman said. She lifted a flap in front of her and pulled up a small, round steering wheel. "Stand by for descent."

There was no sensation of motion, but suddenly the young man and woman both lurched to the left. MacKay looked over at them, puzzled. When they lurched back to the right, he shrugged and lurched along with them.

He glanced at the screen. It showed grainy, stock footage of an airplane's descent through the atmosphere.

Then there was a slight bump, as if a big hammer had been slammed down a few metres away.

"Touchdown," the woman said.

MacKay frowned. This was a much less convincing illusion than the talk show or the suburban house.

"Well, professor," the young man said. "I guess it's time we got you suited up."

THE BANDOLIER HUNG LOW across MacKay's chest, studded with ammunition. He hefted the laser rifle; he'd never fired one before. Idly he wondered why he needed a hundred rounds of machine-gun bullets for it.

The young man, fastidious in his black turtleneck, handed MacKay a heavy box the size of a hardcover book, stamped with an atomic-power symbol above a speaker grate. "Take this communic-box," he said. "We probably won't be able to talk to you, but just in case."

MacKay frowned at the thing, tucked it into his camouflage vest. "Where are we again?" he asked. "I didn't catch the landing site."

"Never mind that," the woman said. "The AniMen are deadly foes. They've unlocked the secrets of DFM – Diode-powered Fission Microwaves. They'll use 'em on Dog-Boy if they get the chance." She paused. "Or on you."

MacKay grimaced. Despite the absurdity of the situation, he felt a strange sense of urgency. He still recalled Dog's screams on the talk-show set, and the monkey's subsequent disappearance. Out in the real world, Dog had been his best friend for years. MacKay had to find him.

The young man was frowning at a big, bright red ray-gun with a big fin on top and a lightning bolt on the side. "You want this?"

"I–"

"You're right. Forget it." He tossed it to the side.

"Listen," MacKay said. "If you could just–"

"No time." The young man hustled him to the door. "God knows what they could be doing to Dog, even now. You've got to save him."

A hatchway swung open, and MacKay stepped out.

He was in a cavern, dark and dripping, all stalactites and stalagmites. Pale orange light shone from a few torches fitted into the walls at irregular intervals. Caves branched off in several directions, some of them barely wide enough to fit a man.

"Hey," MacKay said. "How do you land a spaceship in a cavern, anyw–"

But when he turned to look back, the ship was gone.

MacKay looked down at himself, at the space boots, cinched belt, bandolier, and camo vest. I look, he thought, like the bastard son of Rambo and Captain Video.

The cavern was quiet. Faintly, very faintly, he thought he heard Dog's cries of agony, echoing through the tunnels.

He started down one narrow cave, laser drawn. The screams grew louder. He crept a few hundred feet; nothing. No one passed him.

Then he saw light up ahead, and shrank back into a corner.

The prisoners were strung up, crucified against the walls. Some had bruises and welts all over their bodies; others bled from a thousand tiny puncture marks, into basins on the floor. A few had misshapen limbs – tiny hands or vestigial heads – growing from their stomachs or backs. And still others –

Still others had been sewn together, forming a daisy chain of human agony against the back wall.

MacKay felt bile rise in his throat. It was just like the slaughterhouse he'd seen in Miko's video and, briefly, in the suburban refrigerator. But these were *people*.

White-robed lab attendants roamed among the victims, taking notes on clipboards, administering injections. They wore surgical masks and goggles – MacKay couldn't see their eyes. And surrounding the perimeter, soldiers marched back and forth, armed with machine guns. The soldiers' uniforms were adorned with some odd crest at chest level, but MacKay couldn't make out what it was.

He wanted to scream; he wanted to attack; most of all, he wanted to *wake up*. But again he remembered Dog's words: *Play it through*.

He pulled out the bulky communic-box and pressed down on the atomic symbol. "Hello?" he whispered. "Can anybody hear me?"

Static.

He tossed the thing to the ground, and then grimaced as it struck a little too loudly. I guess we're not in the fifties anymore, he thought.

Suddenly he realised that Dog was not among the victims here; they were all human. If he found the monkey – his spirit guide – MacKay stood a better chance of deciphering this Grand Guignol and getting the hell out.

Casting a final glance back at the Nazi-inspired nightmare chamber, MacKay moved on down the corridor. He tensed for a confrontation with the soldiers, but they ignored him, just staring straight ahead as they marched. The lab-suited men didn't even glance his way, either.

He could definitely hear Dog's screams now, louder than before. He hurried down the corridor, faster now. He stumbled over a rock, recovered his footing. Then he rounded a corner, a little too fast–

And almost collided with Mia.

Tears rose to his eyes; he couldn't conceal his relief. "Mia!" he exclaimed, and hugged her. He buried his face in her black-clad shoulder…

Then realised that something was wrong. For one thing, Mia was several inches taller than usual. For another, she smelled different.

She smelled of leather.

Real leather.

He broke the embrace – but too late. A bullwhip slapped across his face, knocking him to the floor.

MacKay looked up, stunned. Mia stood over him, legs soaring upwards from six-inch heels. Her face was a study in hatred, and her body – her lovely, alluring body – was sheathed, neck to toe, in tight, genuine, cured, black leather. The skin of a once-living creature.

"You," she hissed, and a smile crept slowly over her hard features. "What a nice surprise."

Her whip cracked down again, knocking the laser from his smarting hands. Despite himself, MacKay cried out.

"Your timing is perfect as usual, MacKay. I was running out of… subjects."

Then he looked behind her.

Strapped to the wall were four men, stripped naked, all barely conscious. The first had a slight bulge on his neck. The second had apparently grown a ring-like tumour around his throat; it was discoloured, turning dark. On the third, the same growth was clearly visible as a black choker, protruding out from the neck.

And a fully-formed, organically-grown dog collar clutched the fourth subject's throat with hard silver studs, growing out into a perfect leather leash."

Mia grabbed the man's leash, tugged on it. He moaned in pain.

"My special project," she said. "Making America safe from terrorism."

Mia fingered the helpless man's collar with long, red nails. "You've heard of DFM – DNA-based Faunic Manipulation?" She smiled at MacKay. "It can do just about anything."

MacKay had just begun to think about rising to his feet when Mia's whip flashed out again, ripping his vest and knocking him painfully to the ground.

"If you can think it, imagine it, fashion it from leather… we can grow it straight out of your body. Your nasty, diseased, *sick* body." She picked up a hypodermic full of roiling black liquid, waved it in front of him. "Of course, when we're ready to bring the product to market, I think Discipline For Men might be a better brand name. Don't you?"

Then, smiling, she indicated a fifth spot on the wall, waiting with manacles open. Empty.

"I'm so glad you happened by, MacKay. Most of my guinea pigs are so weak. I can't wait to see the response I get…" She leered, lip curled, at his crotch. "… from a *healthy* subject."

MacKay remembered a phrase that Miko – the real Miko – had said to him: They Abu Ghraib you ass. Nobody never see you again.

Suddenly, barely thinking at all, he kicked out hard, knocking Mia off her feet. Then he scrambled to his feet and ran.

She recovered quickly; her flashing whip nicked against his foot. But he kept moving.

"MacKay! You bastard!"

Glancing back, he saw her sprinting after him, just a few feet behind in the cave. But she was having a rough time in those heels. She stumbled, fell to her knees.

"Liar! Hypocrite!" she screamed. *"Killer!"*

He ran.

Dog's screams were louder now. But despite the horror all around – despite the shock of Mia's Nazi-like experiments – all he could think about was how incredibly, breathtakingly hot she looked on her knees in skin-tight black leather and six-inch heels.

MacKay had no idea what was going on in the real world. But he kind of hoped Grandmother Spider wasn't staring too closely at his groin.

He shook off the image, focused on Dog. He'd come all this way, endured horrors, humiliations, and the betrayal of one-time friends. He'd lived through suburbia, stardom, and the worst depravities of human experimentation. If he couldn't find Dog, what was it all for?

A dark spatter on the cave floor caught his eye. Blood. He reached into his vest, pulled out a large analyser-device left over from *The Adventures of Ratcatcher*. He pointed it at the blood; it zinged and beeped for a moment. Then a small sheet of paper came lurching out of a slot.

He ripped it free, looked at it. A fuzzy, dot-matrix photo of Dog stared back at him. Below it was the text: DOG-BOY: 99.44 PER CENT ACCURATE MATCH.

MacKay tossed away the analyser and the paper, and ran on.

The blood-trail continued. MacKay stumbled over a bump in the floor, and then noticed one, two, several more up ahead. But they weren't bumps; more like arced, bony strips curving up the sides of the passage, and all the way across the floor.

Like ribs.

Something viscous fell on his forehead. He daubed it off, and looked up. The stalactites on the ceiling were dripping red now, and the rib-things stretched all the way around.

Dog's screaming grew louder.

Suddenly the cavern widened, and MacKay saw him.

In the centre of the chamber, Dog hung strapped to a huge, bone-like stalagmite growing out of the ground. Veins, arteries, mechanical tubes poked into his body, stretching off into the chamber walls – draining him dry. His fur had been shaved, and his skin was translucent. MacKay could see his internal organs; some of them looked bruised or dried up. One of them – the liver? – seemed to have a tiny head growing off of it, like the experiments MacKay had seen in the outer room.

The monkey's howling filled the chamber; his eyes were squeezed shut. MacKay walked up to him.

"Dog," MacKay said softly.

The monkey opened one swollen eye, wincing at the effort. He looked down at the tubes penetrating his chest and arms, and screamed again.

MacKay's gaze followed the tubes into the walls, watched Dog's blood flow out into the larger torture chamber.

"The heart," he murmured. "You're the heart."

Dog twitched his head, motioning MacKay closer. MacKay moved in next to his mouth, ignoring the smell of decay.

"The body... eats the heart," Dog rasped. "Debt pays for more debt. Contradictions... mount up. Feed on each other." He closed his eyes. "Till nothing is left."

MacKay recalled something Dog had said to him on the set of the TV show. "We're all food sooner or later," MacKay repeated.

"Yes," Dog replied. "All... food."

MacKay closed his eyes and felt despair.

Then he felt the laser in his hand. And, as he had so many times, he shut down the doubts in his mind with an effort of will.

"We're not food today," he said.

MacKay sighted the nearest artery-tube and fired. Blood spurted all around the chamber; the tube whipped free, flopped to the floor. Dog twitched, and MacKay yanked the tube free from his body, blocking the wound with his thumb.

"This might hurt a little," MacKay said. He ripped his camo vest into strips and started tying them onto Dog's wounds.

One by one, he fired on the veins and arteries, yanking them out of Dog's body and stanching the wounds with bits of cloth. It was difficult, unpleasant work, and Dog howled in agony. But it had to be done.

If I can euthanise two dozen diseased pigs, MacKay thought, I can save my best friend.

Finally Dog was free. Two bits of gristly rope held him to the stalagmite; MacKay cut them and caught the weakened monkey in his arms.

Keek, Dog said faintly.

"Time to get out of here," MacKay said.

Then he heard the running footsteps. He set the monkey down gently in a corner, and he smiled.

When the first soldiers came round the bend into the chamber, he fired the laser straight into their eyes. Their eyeballs melted back into their sockets, and they fell to the ground, screaming and bleeding profusely.

He burned the legs clean off the next two. They pitched forwards, machine-guns skidding towards him. Now MacKay could read the logo on their uniforms: ANIPROTEIN.

He picked up a machine gun, and let loose.

MacKay lost track of how many he killed. For an hour, two, they kept coming. He killed them in every way possible. He shot them in the gut and left them to bleed. He blasted them in the head till their brains flew out against the walls. He burned their throats shut with the laser rifle and watched them suffocate. Once, when his machine gun was empty, he charged and batted the gun straight into a man's solar plexus, then stomped his head till he heard the skull crack.

Finally, an eternity later, he stood amid a mountain of bodies. Nothing moved, nothing lived, nothing breathed. Nothing but him and his best friend, Dog-Boy.

And he felt great.

"Guess you're right, Mia," he gasped. "I am a killer."

Gingerly, gently, he helped Dog to his feet and leaned the monkey against his own body. Dog flinched, moved slowly; every inch of his body was bruised.

"Come on, pal," he said. "Let's get out of he—"

Then he heard a strange voice.

"What the hell's wrong with *him*?"

MacKay looked up and around, in alarm. Somehow, he knew, the voice didn't belong here. It wasn't part of this cavern, or of *The Adventures of Ratcatcher*. It wasn't a guest on *The Ratcatcher Show*, or a salesman come to call at his suburban home.

It wasn't part of the Dreamquest at all.

"I dunno," another voice said. "Let's sort him out later."

Then MacKay felt a sharp crack on the head. He struggled to stay conscious; then he struggled to wake up. But the second blow made both options impossible.

For a moment, he thought he saw Mia – the real Mia – standing over him. She looked down in honest concern, and he felt ashamed. She wasn't a nervous housewife or a slutty singer or a jackbooted Nazi sex-queen. All of those, he realised suddenly, were fantasy images; extreme roles that men cast women in, half lustfully, half hatefully. Things men wanted and feared, all at once.

He opened his mouth to say something – to apologise to her. But no sound came out. All he could hear, as he slipped away, were Dog's words, echoing over and over in the torture chamber of his own heart.

Sooner or later, we're all food.

part seven
unnatural acts

I

THE FIRST THING MacKay felt was the heat. Then the chains, scraping against his metal collar and wristbands.

Then he heard the voices.

"Oh, girl! You were so totally right about this."

"Yuh. Thanks."

"I'm so totally sorry I doubted you."

"Oh, that's super-nice of you! It's cool."

"No, really. I feel awful."

"I love you. I'd like to hug you right now."

"Me too. Totally."

"Stupid handcuffs."

Well, he thought, whatever the hell's going on, this is like jumping into a pool – might as well do it all the way. He opened his eyes wide.

The sun beat down; he was back in the desert. Two slim girls with torn Mad Cow jackets were chained in front of him. The group was being marched along by a small line of heavily-armed soldiers. Tents, tanks, and strange weapons stood clustered around the sandy landscape. The soldiers wore battered, used uniforms that looked oddly out of date, as though they'd been salvaged from abandoned army bases.

MacKay jumped as a voice spoke from just beside him, down low.

"The young man has rejoined us," Grandmother Spider said.

MacKay's chains jangled, and he felt a familiar gloved hand on his shoulder. He turned his head, and saw Mia. The real Mia.

She smiled apologetically, held up her chained wrist. "I, uh, I guess I found Cocoa Niño."

Her face was done up in her usual, Goth style, makeup a bit smeared. Her leather jacket was torn. Her lip had a small cut on it.

She was beautiful.

"Mia," he said, and stopped in his tracks. She looked at him quizzically. "You were right," he continued, finally. "I... I am a..."

A soldier smacked him on the arm.

"Keep moving. The General wants to see you."

Mia smiled at MacKay. "It's okay," she said.

He turned around and resumed walking.

To the group's right, a pile of boxes and machinery stood behind a barbed-wire enclosure. An ammo dump, MacKay realised. If this really was Cocoa Niño, then the army belonged to ACTS – Advanced Covert Theological Storm. And apparently, they were armed for a war.

MacKay couldn't trust everything GenTech had told him. But apparently that much, at least, was true.

"Where *are* we?" he asked.

"The trailers are back that way, about half a mile," Mia replied. "This was all shielded... one of Grandmother Spider's tricks."

The creature scuttled up close to MacKay, her arms sparking; he flinched away. "Many tricks," it said. "Did you learn anything from your Dreamquest?"

He frowned. "Stay away from me."

The spider humphed a little, moved off. She wasn't chained, MacKay noticed.

One of the girls turned to look back. "Hey Mia, have you — oh, look! The killer's awake."

The other girl smiled and waved, chain clanking on her impossibly thin wrist. "Hi killer!"

"Look up ahead, Mia and killer. What *are* those things?"

MacKay peered over the girl's tiny shoulder. And saw a very strange sight.

Five soldiers — three men, two women — were hard at work with chisels and sanders, polishing and chipping away at three huge stone sculptures. As MacKay drew closer, he saw that the sculptures were actually giant heads... busts of a sort, sitting right out in the open on the sand. Like the mysterious statues on Easter Island.

The soldiers hustled them past quickly, but MacKay took in as much as he could. One woman was polishing a large, cartoon rodent's nose. A man stood on a rickety scaffold, sculpting feline ears. The third sculpture seemed to be a dog of some kind. Two more soldiers stood guard, eyeing the captives stonily as they walked by.

MacKay cast his mind back to the briefing at Fuzzies, Inc. He remembered the words of Five-A, the faceless GenTech exec: "A dog, a cat, and a large mouse."

One of the girls pointed to the cat statue. "I love my little Whiskerfluff, back home," she said. "But that's just ridiculous."

MacKay turned to watch as they passed the giant stone dog. Mia caught his eye. "What is it?" she asked.

"Later," he said.

The dog-head stared blankly into the sun; its tongue hung out of its mouth dully. MacKay tried to remember... how had Five-A, the GenTech security man, described the missing animals? Far greater intelligence, and range of emotional response, than before.

Cocoa Niño's sculptors didn't seem to be the finest in the world, but if this likeness was anywhere near accurate, MacKay had a feeling these creatures were no intellectual threat to Sputo or Miko.

Which meant there had to be some other reason why a cult was erecting twenty-foot-high statues to them.

The soldiers led them to a row of large, high tents, blocking the remains of the compound from sight. The lead soldier, a stone-faced man with a case of permanent acne, disappeared into the largest tent.

One of the girls rubbed her wrist, near the manacles. She held it up to the nearest soldier. "Hello? *Moisturiser?*"

He ignored her.

The lead soldier reappeared. "Just these two," he said, pointing to Mia and MacKay. "The general says to take the others to a holding tent. We'll deal with them later."

The second girl smiled, shuffled over to rub up against a young soldier. "Holding tent," she said. "What does that mean?"

Sweating a little, the soldier stole a guilty look at the girl's body. Then he looked, pleadingly, at his commander.

"Get moving," the commander said.

Grandmother Spider made a low *tut tut* noise.

The soldiers disengaged the girls from the chain, and led them off. They turned to wave back.

"Bye, Mia!"

"See you soon!"

"Have fun with the killer!"

The commander held the tent flap open. MacKay and Mia exchanged a glance, and then shuffled inside. Grandmother Spider followed, arms sparking.

The tent furnishings were bare – just a few folding chairs and cots – except for one item: a huge, ornate, wooden desk covered with papers. Behind the desk, a man sat hunched over, squinting at an old-fashioned adding machine with a white tape trail. As MacKay watched, the man held up a sheet of paper, peering at it against the light, his mouth open. He wore small glasses and an expression that suggested he was studying something carefully, and would get to you when he got to you.

MacKay recognised him from the Fuzzies briefing. "Caisson," he said softly.

No doubt now. This was ACTS.

Caisson wore a general's uniform, and was flanked by two aides in military dress. His eyes bore telltale crow's feet; MacKay suddenly realised the man was quite old. Clearly he'd had Zarathustra treatments.

Caisson didn't look up. "You can go, Grandmother Spider," he said.

The spider shifted a bit on eight legs. "Grandmother Spider has much to tell you, General. She can—"

"No, that's... you can go."

Grandmother Spider hesitated. "These captives are—"

Caisson looked up now, fixed beady eyes on the arachnid. "We appreciate your efforts, Grandmother. Please see to your charges now." He paused ominously. "We'll deal with you later."

One of the soldiers held the tent flap open. Grandmother Spider looked up at MacKay. He shrugged.

Like a trained dog, she scuttled out.

Caisson ruffled a paper irritably, handed it to an aide. "What is this — numbers? I don't do numbers." The aide took the paper, folded it discreetly, and put it in a jacket pocket.

Then Caisson looked up at MacKay. He smiled a mean little smile that was apparently meant to be disarming. "Batton 'Rat-catcher' MacKay," he said. "So you're the man they sent to recover my animals."

MacKay shrugged; he couldn't think of a reason to deny it. "Just a job," he said.

"Just a job?" Caisson stood up. He walked around the front of the desk, squinting harder at MacKay. "This is anything but a *job*, MacKay. It's a full-on crusade."

"I meant *my* job," MacKay said dryly.

"See, that's where you're wrong. The second you crossed me — the moment you came after me, screwed around with my property — you became part of the crusade." He paused. "Question is, which side of it are you going to be on?"

"Maybe you should tell us about it," Mia said.

Caisson looked her up and down, like a CEO trying to decide whether to risk sexual harassment. "Maybe I should, Miss Mia Sangre. Former leader of the Mad Cows."

He knows a lot about us, MacKay thought. He glanced at Mia; she was thinking the same thing.

"Let me tell you about life, people." Caisson perched on the edge of the desk, crossed his arms casually. "This is an old favourite of Don's. In life, there are... well, there are known knowns. These are things we know we know. We also know there are known unknowns; that is to say, we know there are some things we do not know. But there are also unknown unknowns – the ones we don't know we don't know."

MacKay shook his head, already bewildered.

"Give you an example," Caisson continued. "Take warfare. I spent a lot of time in public service. When I was running Defense, I had colonels, I had majors, I had generals, all telling me you need troops. You need people on the ground, they said. You need numbers – otherwise the third worlders, the mud-people, they'll run right over you.

"That, to them, was a known. A known known, I guess.

"I said, poppycock! We've got technology those people can't imagine. We've got guided missiles, we've got tanks, we've got good old American know-how up the wazoo. You don't need a big, clumsy army. What you need is to strike with pinpoint accuracy, with a few men. And you can win any war, anywhere, anytime."

MacKay frowned. "Is that how you intend to conquer America with a hundred men?"

Caisson pointed a finger at MacKay, jabbed him in the chest. The man's pinched smile was truly frightening.

"That's *precisely* how, my friend."

Okay, MacKay thought. We've gone past mad now, to insanely delusional.

"Another example," Caisson said. "One of the big unknowns to me, in the old days, was religion. We used it, my friends and me; we manipulated it. People started to waver in their support, we just threw around the word 'abortion' a few times. Worked like a charm.

"But I can't say I really *believed* in religion. It was – kind of a known unknown to me. Or maybe an unknown known. Something to manipulate, something to pay lip service to. But not something I felt deep inside.

"Until I found God."

MacKay frowned. "The holy trinity?"

Caisson smiled his little smile again. "Right! I see Fuzzies briefed you well."

Mia looked thoroughly puzzled.

"The animals," MacKay explained.

"The animals," Caisson confirmed. He leered at Mia again. "You're quite the animal lover, Miss Sangre – when it suits you, anyway. Didn't you meet Mister MacKay here while trying to save some pigs from the slaughterhouse?"

Mia stared him down. "I've never heard of you before," she said. "Where do you get your intelligence?"

"Intelligence? I don't do intelligence." Caisson motioned to an aide, who stepped outside. "I do infiltration."

The aide walked back in, accompanied by a figure very familiar to Mia.

"Jefe," she said.

The young Mad Cow stood, posing aggressively, a slight smirk on his face. He looked faintly ridiculous in his ACTS uniform, all spit and polish over sewed-up rips – sustained, presumably, by its former owner. In a *real* war, MacKay thought.

"Hey Mia," Jefe said coolly.

MacKay grimaced. "Some gang you've got," he muttered.

"Shut up," Mia replied. "Jefe – what's up with this?"

"What's up? What's up is you're not in charge anymore. Of me, anyway."

Caisson stepped forward, put his arm around Jefe. "This young man has pledged his heart, his trust, his life to the Advanced Covert Theological Storm," Caisson said proudly. "He knows the truth when he sees it – the future of this once-great nation."

"A known known," MacKay said.

"*Shut up,*" Mia repeated. She turned back to Jefe. "So you sold us out."

Jefe walked up to Mia, spoke right in her face. "That's right, *Meeee*-a. Just like you sold us out to Thalamus, five years ago."

Mia sneered at him. "You all voted on that."

"Yeah. 'Cause we *trusted* you."

"I did what I did for—"

"For the good of the cause, right?" Jefe snorted. "You just wanted the benefits, man."

"Not for me," she said. "For all of you." But MacKay heard her voice falter.

"You lie." Jefe stepped back, paced around; MacKay could tell he was working out some long-suppressed anger. "You always lie. Everybody lies."

"Jefe, listen to me. This man is crazy. He's told you a bunch of—"

"What, Mia? A bunch of *lies*? Tha's good, coming from you."

"Son," Caisson said. "Perhaps you should appeal to her… *vegetarian* spirit."

Jefe paced back and forth, thinking. Then he looked up at Mia. "You say you believe in the — whazzit — sanctity of animal life, right?"

"I — right."

"Well, that's what this is about, Mia! These three animals — they're sacred, man. They're *holy*."

Mia frowned. "I believe we don't have the right to take an animal's life for food, Jefe. That doesn't mean I believe they embody the spirit of God."

Jefe stared at her with undisguised hatred. "You are such a hypocrite."

Mia flinched, looked down.

"Perhaps we should show them," Caisson said brightly. "Does that sound like a good idea, son?"

Jefe smiled. "Yeah. Show 'em the ritual."

Caisson ushered them to the tent flap. As the soldiers ushered them out, Mia walked past Jefe. She looked him straight in the eye.

"So you and Shank. That was just part of your cover? Your infiltration of my gang?"

Jefe backhanded Mia across the face. She stumbled back, held partly upright by the chains.

MacKay tried to move on Jefe, but the chains pulled him down onto his knees, next to Mia. He stumbled, reached for her.

"You shut up about her," Jefe snarled. "If you were a better gang leader, she'd still be alive."

"Hey. Hey. *Hey!*" Caisson said. "Deal with this... this pettiness on your own time. I don't do pettiness."

MacKay pulled Mia to her feet. Her cold eyes were fixed on Jefe, and he knew, sooner or later, she would have her reckoning.

First, though, it was time to meet the holy trinity.

II

THE SUN WAS sinking low as Caisson led them, still shackled, to the other side of the big row of tents. Mia and Jefe walked at opposite ends of the group, separated by soldiers, glaring at each other periodically. MacKay had forgotten that Mia was, first and foremost, a gangcult leader. He'd seen some examples of gang betrayal, and the resulting vengeance, before, and it was never pretty. Religious soldier or no, Jefe had better watch his ass.

As they passed through another empty desert area, MacKay noticed a small group of tents off to one side, surrounded by a high razorwire fence. A few women and children peered out through the fence, watching the captives march by. Their eyes were blank, bored.

"Is that the holding area?" MacKay asked.

Caisson laughed. "No, no, son. That's the civilian zone. Where the soldiers' families live."

MacKay looked over at the cramped, enclosed area. "Behind barbed wire?"

"It's for their protection." Caisson cocked his head, squinted at MacKay. "You see – our soldiers – most of 'em are men – they have to be on call 24/7. They live in barracks, over there." He pointed to another clump of tents – an unfenced group. "Since they can't spend much time with their loved ones, they want to make sure they're safe."

"Why would they bring their families here at all?"

"So they can live in peace and freedom. That's what ACTS is all about."

MacKay cast a last glance back at the civilian zone. A little black boy with no shoes eyed him suspiciously.

Jefe was marching out in front now. Caisson called to him: "Whoa whoa whoa, stop! You're almost on top of it."

Jefe stopped dead.

MacKay looked up ahead, but saw nothing. In the distance, the air shimmered: another shield.

"Grandmother Spider," Caisson called. "Come on out, please."

The air directly before them wavered, rippled through various colours. Grandmother Spider, expression blank, shimmered into view. And a few feet past her, MacKay finally saw the objects of his quest.

The dog and cat were both human-sized, and bore blank, dull expressions; their mouths were almost undetectable. The mouse was a bit smaller – about four feet tall – but, like Miko D, proportionally much larger than the others. They were shaggy, dirty-looking creatures, wandering aimlessly around a cactus. All three were bipedal, walking on two legs.

And all three appeared to be congenital idiots.

MacKay walked up close to the group. "Careful, young man," Grandmother Spider said. "There's another force field there. An invisible one, to keep my children safe."

Cautiously, MacKay reached out a hand, and felt a sharp shock. He pulled back.

Keeping a careful distance, he stared at the cat, which had come over to look at him. It cocked its head one way, then the other. It reached up a paw and licked it, then rubbed the paw on its face. It turned to look at the dog, briefly.

MacKay had been around dumb animals all his life. This, he knew, was a dumb animal.

"Grandmother Spider protects her children," the arachnid said proudly.

Still chained behind him, Mia stared along with MacKay at the animals. "They don't look very… advanced," she said.

Caisson smiled, and Jefe smiled along with him.

"Watch," Caisson said.

They turned back to the animals. The dog noticed the cat looking at MacKay; it stepped out from behind a cactus, walked up to the cat, and rubbed up against it in a disturbingly sexual manner. The cat purred briefly, then leapt away from the dog.

The cat strode over to the mouse, who was watching with dull eyes. When the cat got within a few feet, the mouse picked up a rock and threw it at the cat's head. The cat stumbled back, dazed, and tottered a bit.

This enraged the dog. It ran over to the mouse and knocked it down with a single swipe of its thick paw. Then the dog turned its attention back to the cat.

MacKay was utterly baffled. "*These* are your holy trinity?"

Caisson pulled out a MiniShredder, aimed it at MacKay. "Watch again."

Before MacKay's and Mia's eyes, the animals played out the exact same ritual a second time. The dog nuzzled the cat; the cat deserted it for the mouse. The mouse conked the cat in the head with a rock, and the dog knocked the mouse to the desert floor.

This time, though, MacKay thought he saw something… right at the very end, when the mouse hit the ground. The three animals stood in an equilateral triangle – and for just a second, a flash of fiery emerald energy erupted from the very centre of that triangle. Then it dissipated in the air.

"Again," Caisson said.

Once more, the dog pressed itself against the cat. The cat repeated its previous motions, and so did the dog and mouse. When the dog smacked the mouse down, a larger, more sustained flash of green energy flared upwards.

Puzzled, MacKay glanced over at Mia. She was watching the energy with what seemed a mixture of alarm and dread.

The fourth time the mouse hit the ground, the energy flared upwards and stayed. It hovered, rose, grew larger. There was a slight flash as it passed through Grandmother Spider's energy barrier.

MacKay took a step back, almost knocking Mia down.

The energy bolt moved back and forth over them for a moment, as if considering its next move. Then it stabbed out to engulf Caisson. He arched upright as though struck by lightning, twitched for a moment.

Jefe smiled. The soldiers watched, expectant.

Caisson straightened, out of his usual hunch. He smiled, an unearthly smile. His eyes seemed to glow yellow, and a slight green aura surrounded him.

"Now I am filled with the Great Holy Spirit of the Trinity," he said, voice booming. Then he laughed dryly. "Or some shit."

Mia grabbed MacKay, hissed in his ear. "That's Nihilo."

"What?!"

"Project Nihilo – I told you about it before."

Caisson looked around, grimaced. "Back in the fuckin' desert, huh?" He shrugged, rippling with energy. "Might as well make the most of it, I guess."

MacKay leaned in close to Mia. "How do you know? And what is Nihilo, anyway?"

"I don't know. And I don't know."

Caisson pointed sharply down at the scuttling Grandmother Spider. "You. Ugly thing. I thank you – uh, I mean *your* God thanks you for protecting his Trinity."

The spider smiled tentatively. "Grandmother protects all her–"

"Yeah, yeah. Whatever. Always thought six would have been a better number myself but sextet just doesn't have the same ring to it." He cast his eyes around, focused on Mia. "You look familiar."

Mia grimaced. "I, uh, I don't think so."

"Have we slept together?"

"I think I'd remember that."

"'Cause I was pretty fucked-up for a few years there." Caisson looked around, noticed the soldiers, and Jefe, staring at him. "Hey, God works in mysterious ways." He clapped Jefe on the back, almost knocking him down. "You my boy."

Jefe smiled like a little kid. "Thanks, God."

Caisson pointed at Mia and MacKay again. "The general tells me you two are infidels. Not yet committed to the, um, Holy Cause of God."

MacKay didn't know what to say. "Well, we're, uh, we're still thinking about it. You don't want to choose the wrong religion."

"And wind up in Hell," Mia added.

"Whatever. Tell you what." Caisson walked right up to them, and MacKay smelled a faint odour of ozone. "I am a merciful god. So I'll give you till the morning to decide to join up with my excellent friends, ACTS. How's that sound?"

"Uh… okay," MacKay said.

"Pretty goddamn generous and merciful, am I right?"

"Good God," Mia agreed, nodding.

"Awright. If you don't join us at sunrise, we'll have to put you to death. Nothing personal — it's just, we can't have agents of, erm, Satan runnin' around this shithole. Holy place, I mean." He gestured to the soldiers. "Am I right?"

The soldiers applauded. Jefe was the loudest.

"Cool! Okay, take 'em to the holding tents."

The soldiers grabbed MacKay's chain, started leading him and Mia back towards the compound's centre.

"Hey Mia," Jefe called.

MacKay and Mia stopped, turned to look back.

"Don't pull none of your crafty escape shit," Jefe continued. "I see you creepin' around this place at night…" He pulled out a big knife, sliced it across the air in front of his neck.

Mia glared, but said nothing.

The soldiers pulled them back, resumed the march.

Behind them, MacKay heard Caisson's booming, inhuman laugh. "You crazy kids. God loves all his children." Pause. "Except that repulsive little spider-bitch. Can we get that disgusting thing out of here?"

▥

"WHAT," MacKay asked again, "is Nihilo?"

No response. He lay on the cot, stared at the tent flap. It was dark now, and the only light came from distant torches outside.

MacKay and Mia had been thrown in here, their chains locked to the cot. Exhausted, they had both fallen into an awkward, troubled sleep. Now they were curled up together, with her still positioned behind him. He would rather have been the one spooning her, but a bit of frustrating experimentation had shown that their chains would not allow that.

"I mean, I kind of understand psychic powers," he continued. "Grandmother Spider pulled a real ambush on me, threw me into that Dreamquest. And something strange definitely happened back there with the animals — no question.

"So… is *that* what this Nihilo is? Some kind of experiment in…"

Mia twitched, grabbed his side awkwardly.

MacKay turned to look at her. Her eyes were open, staring glassily. She twitched again, fingernails clutching at the air.

"Hey. Mia!"

She tried to bolt upright, yanking against the chains. His weight pulled her back down.

Then she shook her head, looked straight at him. "MacKay?"

"Yeah."

"What… where was I?"

"Not here, that's for sure." He hesitated. "Was it the visions again?"

"Yeah." She tried to bring a hand up to her head, but got tangled in the chains. He reached up and brushed the hair out of her eyes. "Thanks."

"What did you see?"

She sighed heavily. Slowly, together, they sat up. "Same as usual. Animals strapped to walls, grown together into monstrosities." Her eyes went wide. "Humans, too. That's a first."

"Not for me."

"Mmm?"

Briefly, he told her the highlights of his Dreamquest, leaving out the various versions of her that had peppered the vision.

"Seems like you were in there for a long time," she said.

"It felt that way."

"And there were little… what? Clues along the way?"

He thought for a moment. "For some reason, I keep thinking about the words the eagle had taped to him. During the talk-show sequence." He looked at her. "What does 'exsanguination' mean?"

"It means to drain blood."

"Oh. Well, that's fairly obvious." He thought harder now, trying to remember... "What about 'Vacas Muitas'?"

She looked puzzled. "Vacas is Spanish for cows, but I don't know... how do you spell the other word?"

He spelled it.

"I don't think that's a Spanish word. Portuguese, maybe?"

He shrugged. "I barely know English." He tugged at the chains. "I guess we should be trying to figure a way out of this."

She nodded. "Yeah. Whatever that thing was that jumped inside Caisson, I'd like to be away from it. As quickly as possible."

"Now, that's what I was just talking about. While you were out." He hesitated. "You... what? Recognised that energy from your time at Thalamus?"

"I'm not sure I can explain it. I just know."

"You said it was 'Nihilo'. That word popped up in my Dreamquest, too. What is it? Some kind of Thalamus experiment in psychic energy?"

"I don't know what it is. But I know I've felt it before."

"In the Thalamus offices."

"Yeah. And also..." She looked down. "This is hard to talk about."

He stroked her shoulder delicately. "Mia, we've known each other for less than a week, and we..."

She smiled. "We've already had a lot of ups and downs."

"Yeah. But I... I want you to trust me." He smiled, very sincerely. "I don't see how else we'll get out of this."

They stared into each other's eyes. And at that moment, he knew there was something real between them. Something that wouldn't just fade away when the last dog – or vegetable protein substitute – was hung.

"I want that too," she replied. "That's why this is hard. I... I've felt that energy before... when I slept with Hank."

MacKay didn't know what to say.

"I think… whatever it is… it belongs to Thalamus." She sighed. "Hank belongs to them too, I guess."

MacKay got up to pace away, then remembered the chains. He took her hand instead.

"Okay. Let's say I believe this for a second. What is this Thalamus… energy… doing inside three Fuzzies animals? Fuzzies, which is owned by GenTech?"

"Oh, my God," she said, eyes wide. "It all makes sense."

"That's not exactly what's running through my mind right now."

"Listen. Listen." She clasped his hand. "GenTech, Fuzzies, whatever; they've been spying on Thalamus."

"Sounds like standard corp operations."

"Whatever Nihilo is… a weapon, an artificial intelligence… GenTech has stolen it. Part of it, anyway. They've stolen it from Thalamus and put it into their experimental animals."

MacKay stared, blankly.

"That's what's special about the Cocoa Niño animals – they're full of Nihilo. And that's why Fuzzies lied to you, told you the older animals were less intelligent. They couldn't tell you they wanted their *new* specimens back because they'd stuffed them full of a competitor's property.

"Caisson thinks Nihilo is God. GenTech wants their animals back. And Thalamus wants their *experiment* back." She paused. "This is all just a big corporate turf war!"

"I–"

"Back when we first met Grandmother Spider, I could see… flashes of Cocoa Niño, out in the desert. When you couldn't. That's because I've been close to the energy before – close to Hank."

"Okay. But–"

Suddenly Mia sat upright, yanking MacKay along with her. "That little bitch!"

"Ow!"

"She slept with–"

"Listen," MacKay said, taking her by the shoulders – an awkward move around the chains. "I can buy the turf war. I believe that Thalamus and GenTech have pitted us against each other for some reason. But isn't it possible there's a simpler explanation for the rest?"

"Such as?"

"Let's see: Caisson's crazy. The animals are wired funny. Grandmother Spider has telepathic electrical powers that make people see things." He pointed to his own head. "The last part, I can vouch for personally."

"I don't know, MacKay."

"Neither do I. And you know what?"

She sat, looking at him, waiting.

"I don't really care." He tugged against the chains, felt a rage growing inside him. "You told me once – accused me of liking to kill things."

She stroked his hair – a very tender, un-Mia gesture. "MacKay–"

"No, you're right. I do like to kill things. I learned that in the Dreamquest, too." He hissed air out between his teeth. "Not for fun, not all the time. But when necessary. And I'm ready to go kill the entire ACTS goon squad if I have to."

For a moment, he thought he'd gone too far. He remembered the disgusted look she'd given him, back at the I Heart Florida compound, when first confronted with his bloodthirstiness. I've blown it, he realised. The best thing that ever walked into my life, and I've just thrown it away. By being too honest.

Then Mia smiled. "I'm with you."

He smiled back.

"We'll figure out the rest later," she continued. "But first, we have to get free."

"Right. Yeah. What's our plan on that?"

"Well–"

An explosion shook the ground, lit up the predawn sky. Its glow shone through the thick canvas of the tent.

"What the hell was–"

Another boom. The cot rattled.

"That's not the direction of the ammo dump," MacKay said. "I think ACTS must be under–"

Keek! Keek!

MacKay turned, smiling, to see a familiar, friendly face peek through the tent flap. Dog scampered in – normal-sized, MacKay was relieved to see, and metallic. He jumped up into MacKay's lap, nuzzled both MacKay and Mia.

"Buddy!" MacKay said, fighting back tears. "I was wondering when you'd turn up." He realised he'd been very worried about the monkey – irrationally so, since the events of the Dreamquest.

The monkey jumped excitedly, then held up a small, solid bolt-cutter.

"Isn't he, like, cool?"

"He freed us, too!"

"He's the best monkey *ever!*"

Mia looked up at Britney and Cristina, both standing in the tent doorway. She didn't seem entirely happy to see them.

Another blast, outside, rocked the compound. Now MacKay could hear soldiers shouting. He saw them silhouetted against the predawn sky, running towards the explosions.

MacKay pointed his thumb outside. "This your doing?"

Dog shrugged, shook his head.

Carefully, MacKay cut through his and Mia's chains. They'd be stuck with the manacle-bracelets for a while – as, he noticed, the girls were – but at least they could move.

"Come on."

As they headed towards the tent flap, Mia paused. She laid a hand on Cristina's shoulder.

"Mia? Whazzup?"

Face still blank, Mia punched Cristina in the stomach, hard. The girl grunted, gasped, and went down.

Britney, MacKay, and Dog just watched. Slowly, as Cristina tried to catch her breath, Mia reached a hand down to her.

"Wh… wh… what was, like, *that* for?" the girl said.

"Tell you later, babe," Mia said, pulling Cristina to her feet. "Right now, we better go."

Cristina looked at her, nodded. Together, the odd fivesome – monkey included – crept out into the still-dark desert morning.

Dawn was just beginning to break as they threaded their way among the closely-packed holding tents. The soldiers were all gone; MacKay could hear them, yelling and running frantically, in the distance.

He glanced up. Five large, black troop-carrier spidercopters hovered above. A hiss came from one, and another explosion erupted on the ground, a few thousand feet away. MacKay grabbed Mia, and the girls clutched each other.

Keek! Keek!

"That – that hit near Caisson's tent," Mia said. "Where we met him yesterday."

"The centre of the compound." MacKay pulled Mia around the corner of a tent. He gestured back to Cristina and Britney. "Can we trust those two?"

"To help us, yes. To not sleep with my boyfriends… maybe."

"It's just – this compound is under attack. How do we know they didn't call in the troops? Whoever the troops are?"

Mia whirled on him. "Look. Those girls are nothing like Jefe. They–"

"*Jefe?*"

MacKay groaned. One of the girls had sneaked up behind him. It's easy to be stealthy, he supposed, when you weigh ninety pounds.

The other girl crept up, excited. "Jefe's *here?*"

Mia gave her a withering glance. "Crank down the hormones, Cris. He's defected – he's working with our enemies."

Cristina's face fell. "Aww."

"Ohhh," Britney said.

Mia frowned at her. "What's wrong with *you?*"

"It's just – it's so *romantic.*" Britney put her arm around her friend's bony shoulders. "Star-crossed lovers, Cristina and Jefe. Working on different sides of the–"

"Shut *up*! I don't like him *that* much."

MacKay pressed a hand to his temples. "Can we concentrate on the–"

"ATTENTION, BLIGHTERS AND BUGGERERS!" The electronically-amplified voice boomed out of the sky. "YOU

ARE NOW UNDER THE JURISDICTION OF GENTECH,
DON'TYOUKNOW. SURRENDER IMMEDIATELY AND
YOU WILL NOT BE HARMED. MARQUIS DE QUEENS-
BURY RULES!"

MacKay groaned. "Wellington."

Britney and Cristina were still teasing each other, oblivious.
Mia grabbed them each by an arm and said, voice low and measured: "Do. Either. Of. You. Know. *Where we might find some guns?*"

Keek! Keek! Keek! Dog pointed, hopped off.

They followed the monkey to a guard tent, now unmanned. The
camp's entire complement had apparently been called away to the
central administrative area, where the battle was taking place.

At the tent flap, MacKay hesitated. He looked up, and saw
two of the copters descending for a landing. The others seemed
to be lowering ropes; he could just make out figures shimmy-
ing down them, limned against the lightening sky.

A volley of machine-gun fire erupted from the ground. One
of the figures on the ropes twitched, lost his grip, plummeted
to the ground. The copters responded with lasers and rapid-fire
bullets. MacKay couldn't make out the situation on the ground
– the tents were in the way. But it didn't sound good. He could
hear the screams and gunfire from here.

Mia appeared at the tent flap. She and the girls were now
heavily armed. She handed him a G-Mek Rapide full-automatic
machine gun, ammo clip, a small pistol, three Gren-Aids – and a
shoulder-mounted rocket-launcher, equipped with a NeoGen
one-shot Ground-to-Air Missile.

He looked at the launcher. "Isn't this a bit much?"

She kissed him on the lips, hard.

"You need to be ready to kill things," she said softly.

"Thanks," he replied, utterly moved.

"Awwwwwww," Britney said.

"But," he continued, "I'm starting to think maybe we should
get the hell out of here instead."

Dog nodded. *Keek! Keek!*

Mia paused a moment, thinking. "Aren't you forgetting
something?"

He swallowed.

"The animals," she continued.

"The dog," he said.

"The mouse," she said.

He closed his eyes, defeated. "The cat."

Cristina looked up, excited. "There's a *kitty*?"

MacKay pointed towards the sounds of carnage. "We can't just walk out into a war zone, between two armies. We'll be slaughtered."

"ACTS isn't going to be any match for GenTech. And GenTech won't kill you – you work for them."

"That's a big assumption. But okay." He glanced up; the copters had fanned out to cover the compound. Presumably Cocoa Niño's invisibility-shield had been compromised. "They'd probably see us if we made a break for it anyway."

"Follow me," Mia said.

"Where are we going?"

"I just want to get to the edge of this group of tents. So we can see what's going on."

MacKay fingered his new machine gun. He followed her, weaving around the tents till they came to the open desert area.

The minute they stepped in front of the tent, a searchlight stabbed down from one of the copters, blinding them.

"DON'T MOVE, OLD BOY."

A rope slid out of the copter's bottom hatch and the portly, bushy-moustached figure of Alastair Wellington bounced awkwardly down it. Wellington wore a 19th century fox-hunting outfit, starched white shirt, black boots, and tight trousers that showed off his prodigious hindquarters.

Must be a sturdy rope, MacKay thought.

Wellington landed with a thud, brushed himself off. A couple of soldiers descended from other ropes, next to him. They wore odd, colourful uniforms.

"Well, well, dear boy!" Wellington exclaimed, thwacking a riding crop excitedly against his thigh. "At last I stand, side by side, on the field of battle with my staunchest ally–"

MacKay winced in anticipation.

"–the *Ratcatchah*."

The sun was coming up now. Wellington looked up at the copter, made a slicing-throat motion. The spotlight went out.

"I see you've found allies of your own," Wellington continued. He leered at Mia. "This one bears a Thalamus stamp."

"I'm currently unaligned," she said warily.

"So was I, once." Wellington frowned; a memory seemed to flicker across his face. "Perhaps you'd do me the courtesy of handing over your weapons."

Cristina and Britney looked at the soldiers, uncertain. Mia shrugged, threw her gun to a soldier. The girls followed suit.

MacKay cocked an eyebrow. "Me too?"

Wellington stared at him, and beneath the would-be-Englishman's affectations, MacKay saw the shrewd exec he'd caught a glimpse of once before. "I think we can trust you, Ratman, old boy. After all, you've a contract with us." Then Wellington smiled, clapped MacKay on the back. "You're just in time to see us recover our property and show these ruddy survivalist blighters what-for. And we owe it all to you, lad."

Dog jumped up onto MacKay's arm, peering at Wellington warily. "You followed me here?" MacKay asked.

"Quite."

"How?"

Wellington smiled, reached out to Dog, and in one quick motion, pulled a thin, transparent strip off the monkey's lower back. He held it up.

"We bugged your monkey, too," Wellington said.

MacKay frowned at the sheepish Dog. "Next covert job, you stay in the *fucking car*."

Another explosion rattled the compound. Wellington turned, made a sweeping motion towards the centre of the compound. "Come now – let's go."

Again the girls hesitated. Mia and MacKay exchanged glances.

"In for a penny," Mia said.

Britney and Cristina just stared at her, heads cocked quizzically.

"Let's go," Mia said.

The GenTech ground soldiers moved to flank them. MacKay shrugged at Mia, and together the group set off.

IV

MACKAY STUDIED THE GenTech troops. They wore protective helmets, combat boots, and baseball jerseys emblazoned with advertising logos reading Miami Snakeheads and Killer Bees — Reno.

Wellington glanced at him. "Pays the bloody bills," he said, and sighed. "Notice I'm not wearing one, old boy. First thing I had written into my contract."

Just ahead of them, a savage battle raged. ACTS soldiers had taken cover behind the giant statues of the animals, firing on GenTech ground troops and the copters above. They moved fast, and clearly they knew the terrain better than their attackers. But they were outnumbered and outgunned, and they were losing. Their bodies littered the ground, bloody in their antique army uniforms. GenTech ScumShredder fire had already lopped one ear off the giant sandstone dog, and the mouse's round nose was covered with laser burn-marks.

Wellington ushered MacKay's group carefully around the carnage area. His copter, above, paced them. At one point, an ACTS soldier broke and ran towards them. The copter cut him down with rapid fire.

"Slow and steady," Wellington said.

Cristina looked back at the fighting. "I don't see Jefe," she said.

The administrative tent area, in the centre of the camp, had been totally decimated by the initial clusterbomb strike. Struts, charred canvas, and bits of desk and paper littered the ground; the area smelled like a bonfire. As Wellington led them through it, MacKay noticed a few mutilated bodies.

"Ewww," Britney said, stepping over an arm.

"Most of the blighters evacuated, like we told them," Wellington said. "A few were just too bloody stupid."

As they crossed the sandy expanse to the animals' enclosure, MacKay could still hear the battle raging behind them.

"Chop-chop," Wellington said. "Time to wrap this up and retire back to the comforts of hearth and home. Or perhaps a good pub crawl."

MacKay glanced over at the civilian zone, which had so far escaped GenTech's attentions. A little girl with a dirty face spotted him, and ran for cover behind the tents.

Up ahead, a volley of shots rang out. MacKay ducked, but Wellington just shook his head and kept moving.

The animal preserve lay just ahead. In front of it stood a tattered, squinting figure in a ripped old military uniform, flanked by a single, very scared-looking soldier with grime all over his face. One of them had apparently just fired a warning burst into the air.

"Stop right there!" Caisson yelled. "Advanced Covert Theological Storm stands prepared to defend the Holy Trinity."

MacKay stared at the cult leader. He could just make out the three animals – peering, frightened, from behind the lone cactus inside their protective shield. He saw no energy rising up from them, nor any green aura around Caisson. Apparently Nihilo, whatever the hell it was, wasn't out today.

Wellington laughed. "Your cult is demolished, old boy," he said. He waved at the frightened ACTS soldier. "Are you going to defend your compound with *that*?"

Only when MacKay looked closer did he realise that the soldier was Jefe. He looked shell-shocked and very, very frightened.

Cristina squealed. "Cutie boy!"

Jefe winced.

Caisson squinted even more, his eyes seeming to push into the centre of his face. He gestured to Jefe. "You go to war with the army you have – not the army you might want." He paused. "Or wish to have at a later time."

"Listen to me, old sock. I really would prefer not to have to shoot you."

Wellington's group was no more than twenty feet from Caisson now. Caisson raised his machine gun, aimed it straight at Wellington.

Mia was staring at Jefe, hatred in her eyes.

"Not another step!" Caisson's voice cracked. "These animals represent the second coming of the Lord – and the only hope these poor United States have for a decent, prosperous, Christian future."

As if on cue, the dog stepped out from behind the cactus. It dug for a minute with its hind legs, squatted down, and took a prodigious dump.

"*These animals* are the property of Fuzzies, Inc." Wellington replied. Then, his voice dropping a bit, "A division of GenTech Corporation of North America. They have been stolen from their rightful owners – and we're recovering them."

The GenTech soldiers raised their guns. Quivering, Jefe lifted his as well.

Behind them, the combat sounds continued. The gunfire seemed a bit sparser than before.

Overhead, the copters whirred.

Jefe's wide eyes shifted to Cristina. "Cris, get out of here."

"Don't move," Wellington warned her.

MacKay hefted his machine gun, unsure what to do. Something had to break here. But Wellington wasn't going to leave without the animals, and Caisson was crazier than–

"*Daaaaaaaarrrrrrk seee-crets!*"

MacKay didn't need to look up. He grabbed Mia's hand; she grabbed Britney's, and Britney grabbed Cristina's. Cristina looked to Jefe, and he smiled, broke ranks, and ran to her. Dog jumped up on MacKay's shoulder, and they all tumbled to one side. The weight of the rocket-launcher almost tipped MacKay over, but he recovered his footing and crouched down with the others.

Wellington, Caisson, and the GenTech soldiers looked up, surprised.

"Oh, bollocks," Wellington said.

Balled Eagle screamed down out of the sky, faster than MacKay had ever seen him move before. But he wasn't heading for them. His trajectory was taking him past the group, towards that cactus–

The animals.

Caisson lowered his little spectacles, peered over them. "Satan?" he asked.

Eagle dropped lower: twenty feet, fifteen, ten. The cat, mouse and dog looked up, curious and a bit afraid. Then, abruptly, Eagle bounced off an invisible wall in the air, tumbling up and to the side.

"The shield," Mia said.

Dazed, unsure, Balled Eagle hovered in the air for a moment, ten feet above.

Wellington spoke into a device on his shoulder. "We have made contact with Eagle One," he said. "Please advise what armament we have that can *take down the ruddy blighter!*"

Balled Eagle shook his beak violently, looked back at the Cocoa Niño animals. He squawked, a loud, savage sound.

Slowly, MacKay motioned Mia and the others to a gradual retreat. They began backing away, across the sand.

Then MacKay noticed something very odd. Caisson had dropped his weapon and walked up to stand almost directly below Balled Eagle. His mouth was open in shock, and his squinting eyes were focused directly on the eagle's additional, hanging equipment sac.

"Ch-chief?" Caisson said softly.

Eagle's head whirled, violently, to glare down at Caisson.

Caisson spread his arms, then pointed at his own chest. "Chief – it's me!" he exclaimed. "Don! Remember?"

Eagle just stared.

Caisson waved at Eagle's sac. "I'd know those balls – I mean, I'd know *you* anywhere. Boy, you've changed. Remember all the fun we used to have? Invading countries? Lying to the press?"

All activity had stopped now; everyone stared at the bizarre tableau. Even the animals seemed transfixed, ogling the duo with big, gaping, cartoon eyes.

"We sure transformed the Middle East, didn't we? Just like we said we would. Go USA!" Caisson paused, confused, and looked around him. "I mean, sure, there were those little nuclear exchanges. And the USA's going through some hard times right now. But like we used to say — that's when you need to stand firm behind the Chief more than ever! Stop questioning! Right?"

Eagle pivoted towards Caisson, his beak pointing nearly straight down. He made a low, squawking, animal noise.

Caisson shook his head apologetically. "I'm sorry, chief. Is that bird language? I don't do—"

Then Balled Eagle dived.

MacKay had seen his share of violence in the animal kingdom. He'd seen cheetahs rip their prey to death with sharp teeth. He'd seen pythons squeeze the life out of squirrels before devouring them whole. He'd seen lions batter small mammals half to death before turning them over to their cubs to finish off.

But he'd never seen anything like this.

The first things Eagle went for were Caisson's squinty eyes. In two quick, precise motions, he plucked them out and spat them on the desert floor. Caisson stood, shocked and bleeding, for a moment. Then he screamed.

Eagle reared back, fluttering up a few feet, then came in for a second attack.

He pecked a hole in Caisson's stomach, and blood started to flow. He twitched back, then plunged his beak into the hole, and came out with a triumphant mouthful of intestines.

Caisson's blood spattered out in a frightening gush.

Eagle slashed at Caisson's feet. He ripped the jacket off his chest, and then slit his throat. He severed a hand in three quick motions — peck, peck, peck. He reached into Caisson's mouth and ripped out the man's tongue.

Mia's hand clutched at MacKay's chest absently. They stood together, watching in horror. Dog clung to MacKay's trouser leg with painful metal claws.

"I guess loyalty was a bit overrated in that administration," MacKay said.

Wellington was still talking into his shoulder. "How's things going back there?" Crackle crackle. "Good. Stand by a moment—"

Then MacKay heard yet another noise. Another familiar noise. Mad Cow motorsickles.

Hank and his two remaining Cows screeched onto the scene, skidding to a halt in a triangle formation around MacKay, Mia, Cristina, Britney, Jefe, and Dog.

A few feet away, Wellington and the soldiers looked at them in surprise. Then they turned their attention back to Balled Eagle – who sat on the desert floor now, picking pieces out of Caisson's corpse.

Hank dismounted quickly. His laser, and those of the other two, were all pointed at MacKay. Mia had told MacKay about those two – Wister-Hauser and Hauser-Wister.

"Well," Hank said. "Looks like only one person's armed here." Then he noticed the grime-covered Jefe. "Except you. Jesus. What happened?"

"He's not with us," Mia sneered.

Hank walked over to Jefe, fury in his eyes. "That true, ese? You just keep running out on people? That's what you do now?"

Jefe fingered his rifle, clearly too jittery to raise it.

"I thought you wanted to avenge your girlfriend?" Hank asked. "She'd be sick if she saw you now."

Fury rose in Jefe's eyes.

"Seemed like we understood each other," Hank continued. "That night in the bar. But you were just playing me – trying to get information. Right?"

Jefe snarled. "That's right, bitch. Corporate tool like you – think you're one of us?" He started to lift his gun. "Think you're *better* than–"

With his left hand, Hank pulled out a small pistol and shot Jefe in the gut.

Dog jumped. *Keek! Keek!*

Jefe doubled back, spurting blood.

"Item one off the agenda." Hank turned, murder in his eyes, to Mia. "Now for the main business of this meeting."

"Excuse me – old boy–" Wellington pushed his way into the circle. "You may have noticed we're in the process of assaulting this compound."

"Stay out of this, limey," Hank said. "This is gang business."

Wellington looked from MacKay and Mia, to Britney and Cristina, to Hank and his small group – and then, finally to Jefe's body, dripping blood into the sand.

"Righto," he said. "Carry on."

"Gang business?" Mia said. "Gang business? You call this a *gang*?" She gestured to Wister-Hauser and Hauser-Wister, both of whom had guns trained on her. "This isn't a gang. It's a jazz trio with lasers."

"Actually, Mia," Wister-Hauser said calmly, "jazz is a debased art form."

"True," said Hauser-Wister. "American in origin, yet infected by the taint of the lesser races."

"Still. The analogy is not without… "

Hank ignored them. He walked straight up to Mia, poked her in the chest. "This *would* be a gang. If you hadn't let so many people get killed on your watch." He counted off on his fingers: "Chester, Brutus, Shank… "

"Jefe," she countered.

"Thalamus made a big mistake leaving you in charge of the Mad Cows, Mia. This entire mess is your fault."

MacKay glanced over at the Cocoa Niño preserve. The animals were twitching, running about now. All the shooting and killing seemed to be stirring something up in them.

Mia had noticed it too. Still looking at Hank, she pointed to the preserve. "You want to see a mess? Stick around a few minutes."

"Nice try, Mia. I'm not taking my eyes off you."

Mia rolled her eyes. "Jesus, Hank."

MacKay watched as the Fuzzies cat walked, on two legs, up to the edge of the force field. It reached out a paw, received a shock, and retreated back.

A few feet away, Wellington and his baseball-uniformed soldiers watched the gang squabble, amused.

"I killed Jefe," Hank said, teeth gritted. "I can kill you too."

"At least Jefe believed in something," Mia replied. "If you kill me, what'll it be for?"

"It'll be – hey!"

MacKay broke and ran. He knocked Wister-Hauser down and vaulted over the Cow's cycle. Then he sprinted past the surprised Wellington, making a wide arc around the animals.

"Kill him!" Hank yelled.

Wister-Hauser and Hauser-Wister both aimed lasers at MacKay. But their beams sputtered and died against the animal preserve's shield.

MACKAY STOPPED, EXHALED in relief; he was winded from running with so much armament on his body. He'd managed to circle around the preserve, placing its curved, invisible shield between him and the Mad Cows. But the advantage would only last a minute. Hank and Hauser-Wister were already running into a new position, where he'd be in a clear line of sight.

It was time for a big distraction.

MacKay thumbed the rocket-launcher's safety off, aimed, and fired.

The ground-to-air missile hit the GenTech spidercopter with a *konk*, then exploded in a fiery blaze. The copter listed, tipped, and exploded again as its fuel line went up.

Mia and the Mad Cows looked up, surprised. Wellington ripped a receiver out of his ear as feedback screeched from it.

"Bugger!" he exclaimed.

For a frozen moment, the copter hung tilted in the air as fire licked up its sides. MacKay was glad for its tinted windows – he didn't really want to have to look at the pilot right now.

Then it began to fall. Straight towards the animal preserve.

"Bugger," MacKay said quietly.

The massive airship plummeted, straight down towards the Cocoa Niño animals. They stood still, staring up at it like the idiot-savant creatures they were.

Even Balled Eagle looked up from his carrion-feast, squawking once.

Then, at the last minute, the flaming spidercopter hit the shield – and skidded off it, sparks flying. It slid down the side of the invisible shield like a pebble skimming down the side of a dome, electricity and fire erupting in its wake.

The Mad Cows scattered. Wellington motioned his soldiers to retreat.

"All forces!" he yelled into his shoulder. "Converge on my position!"

When the spidercopter finally hit the sand, it went up in a huge, fiery blaze.

The shock knocked MacKay to the ground. He shrugged off the heavy, now-useless rocket launcher and looked up, to where Mia and the others had been. But all he could see was thick, black smoke. In the other direction, the Cocoa Niño animals still stood safely behind their shield, watching.

The dog walked up to the cat, nuzzled it. The cat moved away.

"Uh-oh," MacKay said.

Then the air next to him shimmered in multicolour, and Grandmother Spider appeared. Her arms sparked wildly; she looked pissed off. "Why is everyone trying to harm Grandmother's children?" she asked.

"Sorry, Granny. Accident."

Behind the shield, the mouse threw a rock at the cat.

The smoke was subsiding now. MacKay could just make out Wellington, coughing on the ground; a few GenTech soldiers crawling from the twisted wreckage of the spidercopter; and an army of other GenTech soldiers and a few ragged ACTS survivors, running towards them from the other side of the camp. The two remaining Mad Cows, Wister-Hauser and Hauser-Wister, stood pointing at the wreckage and arguing, in a very calm, philosophical manner. Britney and Cristina were on their knees, frantically daubing moisturiser on each other's soot-blackened face.

And over by the far end of the copter, Mia stood over Hank, pointing a gun at his head.

MacKay wanted to run to Mia. But his attention was captured by the animals.

The dog swiped out with a thick paw, knocking the mouse down. Then the dog walked back over to the cat, rubbed up against it again.

And the energy began to rise.

★ ★ ★

V

MIA LOOKED DOWN at Hank as she aimed the MiniShredder at his forehead. She tried to ignore his blubbering.

"This is really… Mi, you don't think I was serious!"

"No, Hank. You're not a serious person."

"We can work this out. I'll refer the whole matter to Human Resources!" He scrunched his eyes shut.

She wondered what she'd ever seen in him. And yet… "I guess I owe you a favour, Hank."

He looked up at her hopefully. "Yeah?"

"Yeah. Getting burned by you gave me the insight to see things as they really are."

He raised himself up by his elbows, clearly confused. "Well," he said, "yay me, right?"

She looked at his stupid grin, his too-polished jacket, and the snorting Mad Cow insignia on its breast. And, as she had before, Mia found herself thinking back on her life with him. She thought of too many days spent in airless Thalamus conference rooms. Too many nights under Hank's grunting bulk, hoping it would all be worth it.

Then she thought of her visions. Of generations of animals, grown to live and die in pain. Of the millions of Americans who lived in wilful ignorance, not wanting to know what horrors supported their fatty, debased lifestyle. Of the corporations that encouraged those horrors, in the name of profit. And, most of all, she thought of the ordinary men, the thousands of faceless men and women in offices all over the country who made it all possible. Who greased the gears with blood, raped the world and transformed nature into an endless slaughterhouse of pain. All without ever dirtying their own, delicate hands.

She looked down at Hank. She remembered the one thing she'd always liked about him: his touch. His soft, uncalloused hands.

Once again, she remembered the words of Professor Wan's grad student: "The reality of life around you would be too great a shock to bear."

And then she thought of something else. Something MacKay had said: "Sometimes, you just gotta put an animal down."

She fired.

When it was done, she looked up. She knew she should be stunned, maybe even shell-shocked at having killed a former lover. She should also be tired, having just closed a long, dark chapter in her life. But she wasn't any of those things.

She felt great.

She searched the smoke for MacKay. There he was, standing with Grandmother Spider. Mia started in their direction, hoping the arachnid wouldn't be any trouble.

Then she noticed the Cocoa Niño animals, running around wildly. Nuzzling, throwing rocks, falling to the ground... over and over again. And above them: the familiar column of crackling, green energy, reaching for the sky.

MacKay barely had time to register Mia running to him – when a loud, inhuman *screeeeeeeech* made him turn to his left.

Through the clearing smoke, MacKay saw Balled Eagle rise slowly from the sliced-and-diced remains of Caisson. Barely enough remained of the former cult leader to identify; he in no way resembled a human being.

Then, as if on cue, the spidercopters descended. Mia darted away to avoid them, and MacKay lost sight of her. He checked his machine gun and sidled around, between the copters and the animal preserve. Grandmother Spider scuttled along next to him.

MacKay glanced at the preserve. The animals were still engaged in their ritual, and the energy was rising. He turned to Grandmother Spider. "Is your shield still active?"

Grandmother Spider nodded. "Yes, dear."

"Can you keep that energy inside?"

Her brow furrowed. "I've never tried, dear. Is it important?"

"Yeah."

She looked at him for a moment. "You stole the sun for Grandmother," she said slowly. "And you travelled the Dreamquest. Did you learn what you needed to know?"

MacKay hesitated. "I... I think so. Most of it. Yes."

"Then Grandmother trusts you." She turned to the animal preserve and held up four arms, crackling with power.

Electricity flashed from her in thick bolts, reinforcing the field around the animals.

Meanwhile, Balled Eagle hovered, twitchy, ten feet off the ground. The four huge copters surrounded him and descended, touching ground in a gigantic cloud of dust and noise. As MacKay crept forwards to watch, soldiers poured out of the copters, all wearing the GenTech demi-baseball uniforms. Some of them, he noticed, actually carried bats.

And four of them carried the biggest, nastiest-looking laser cannon he'd ever seen.

Wellington stepped forwards, between the copters, gesturing theatrically at Balled Eagle. He looked like a ringmaster for some demented Victorian circus.

"Give him what-for, lads!"

The GenTech soldiers frantically pressed buttons on the laser cannon – and a strangely-shaped, flat beam stabbed out. It struck the startled eagle straight-on – and before he could even react, his hanging sac was severed. Neatly, cleanly. Like a surgical incision.

When it struck the ground, Wellington jumped back, eyes wide.

Eagle stared down at his fallen bits for a moment, paralysed with pain and shock. Then he howled, screeched, and looked to the sky. His eyes focused on the rising sun, and he thrust towards it like a bullet. Soon he was lost from sight.

Wherever he is, MacKay thought, I hope he's not licking his wounds.

Wellington had stumbled over to MacKay's side. MacKay heard a voice from the exec's shoulder-radio: "Should we chase him, sir?"

"Negative," Wellington replied. "Blighter shouldn't be any more trouble now."

A GenTech soldier, with sergeant's bars on his New Jersey Snipes shirt, pushed through the copters towards Wellington. Behind him, five more soldiers hustled a clump of dejected, bruised, chained ACTS commandos along. They detoured carefully around Caisson's bloody remains, then stomped, unaware, on one of Eagle's discarded testicles.

"Sir!" The sergeant saluted Wellington. "We've rounded up the remains of the cultists, sir. Resistance is effectively stopped." In the distance, a volley of Shredder fire rang out. "Effectively."

Wellington grimaced. "Bully." Then he heard something, turned to the animals, and noticed the thick, green column of energy. "What the bloody– Ratcatcher! Is this your doing?"

MacKay cast a glance at Grandmother Spider, who was still busy reinforcing the field. The energy stopped at the top of the invisible dome now, contained. "No, Wellington," MacKay said. "I can confidently say that it is not."

Wellington pointed to Grandmother. "What's that blasted thing doing?"

MacKay stepped between them. "She's containing the–"

"Sergeant!" Wellington pointed around MacKay, at the spider. "Take that bloody animal out!"

Mia ran up. "No!" she yelled.

"No!" MacKay echoed.

Three GenTech soldiers raised their Shredders and fired, rapidly. Their aim was true: Grandmother Spider spasmed, twitched, sparked madly. Dark ichor spurted from bullet holes, and she shrieked, a high-pitched sound with the agony of generations in it. Then she slumped to the ground and was still.

"Bloody savages," Wellington muttered.

"You fucking… *American*… idiot!" MacKay said.

Wellington cocked an eyebrow at him. "That does sting, old bean."

But MacKay had stopped listening. With Grandmother dead, or at least unconscious, the energy-barrier around the animals was dissipating, sparking out of existence. And the green energy was rising higher, out of control.

The mouse hit the cat with a rock. The cat hit the ground.

Wellington placed a hand on Mia's shoulder. "I say, young lady… the Ratcatcher there seems a bit upset. Might I prevail upon you to tell me exactly what that queer electrical discharge is?"

She glared at him. "It's called Nihilo."

Wellington's eyes went wide. "Oh, crap. I mean bugger."

MacKay looked at him, sharply. "Do you know what Nihilo is?"

Wellington frowned. "I… "

The Nihilo-energy flared up, over the group. It arced over the downed spidercopters and whipped around, surveying the scene. Then it dipped down low, between the copters, and stopped just above the chopped remains of Donald Caisson, leader of ACTS.

MacKay knew it was impossible, but he swore he saw the energy *sniffing* at Caisson.

Then it whipped back up, sharply, angrily, and made a bee-line straight for Wellington.

"Aaah, *nuts*," Wellington said. In that moment, he was every inch the boy from Newark.

Then the energy hit him, and he wasn't much of a boy any more. Or a man, for that matter.

MacKay had seen this before, with Caisson; this time, he didn't hesitate. He raised his G-Mek and fired a round directly into Wellington. Then, without looking, he snapped another clip in and fired another.

The bullets struck home; Wellington staggered back. His limbs twitched, his body spasmed. But he stayed upright. And the green glow around him grew stronger.

MacKay fired a third round. By now, Wellington was a mass of blood-holes; his cheeks hung off in strips, bits of brain leaked out both sides of his skull. But he stood his ground, spread his arms, and laughed.

When MacKay loaded the fourth round, Wellington reached out a hand. Energy crackled from it, striking MacKay's machine gun with a powerful electric shock. MacKay cried out, dropped the weapon.

"You can stop that now, asshole!" Wellington said.

Mia started to raise her weapon, but Wellington cast a glance at her. "Don't try it, honey. I am a vengeful god, knowwhum-sayin'?"

Wellington rose up, levitating a few feet off the ground. Dripping blood and meat-parts, he surveyed the area: the one crashed copter, the four intact ones, the GenTech soldiers in their ridiculous uniforms with guns raised, unsure what to do next. Then he pointed down at the remains of Donald Caisson. "You fuckers sure made a mess out of my little cult." He looked around. "Doesn't matter. This place is gonna be mine, real soon."

Mia stepped forwards, frowning. "This place? You mean Cocoa Niño?"

Wellington smiled. "I mean *Earth*, swee'pea. Mine and my masters'. Starting with the great, God-favoured, almighty You-nited States of America."

"Why?" Mia asked. "What are you, anyway?"

MacKay glanced at her nervously. What game was she playing?

Then he noticed the GenTech soldiers with the laser-cannon – the one that had defanged Balled Eagle. They were setting up for another shot.

Wellington leaned down to Mia. "Maybe I can explain it to you, cutie," he boomed. "You're an American, right?"

"Right," she said.

"You claim to be a vegetarian – I can see that in *his* mind." Wellington pointed to his own head. "But you've got the lust, just like the rest of them. You need meat."

Mia drew herself upright. "That's a lie," she said.

"Oh, yeah? What about your big, juicy barbecue-orgy with the Ratfucker here?"

"Rat*catch*er," MacKay said.

"I didn't…" Mia had gone even whiter than usual. "How do you know about that?"

Wellington tapped his own head. "He had you bugged, remember?"

Mia looked down.

"It ain't nothin' to feel bad about. you need meat, I need meat – everybody needs meat. well, we don't *need* it – not really. Not to survive. But we *want* it."

Without even noticing, MacKay had placed his arm around Mia. She was trembling.

Wellington laughed. "'ANIPROTEIN – MADE IN THE USA.' You don't really believe any of that crap, do you?" He fixed Mia with a red-eyed glare. "If you knew – if you had any idea where your meat *really* comes from–"

The soldiers fired their laser.

Once again, the flat beam shot out – neatly bisecting Wellington at the waist. His top half tottered, and then toppled to the ground below.

Wellington's legs fluttered in the air. On the ground, his head propped itself up on its elbows. "Fuck me sideways," it said. "This is gonna take a minute."

"We've gotta move fast," MacKay said. He looked from the unmoving Grandmother Spider, to Mia, to Britney, Cristina, and the other two Mad Cows, just running up to them.

"Is it, like, safe?" Cristina asked.

"No," MacKay said.

Mia was stunned. "'Where the meat comes from'?" she repeated.

"I think we've got a more immediate problem." MacKay gestured over at Wellington. The possessed exec's arms were slowly, laboriously climbing up his lower torso, which still hovered in the air. "Whatever that thing is, it's not out of action yet."

Then he felt a soft touch on his shoulder. "Pardon me. I might be able to contribute a few insights."

MacKay turned, surprised – to see, hovering next to him with one wing on his shoulder, Balled Eagle.

Or, rather, No-Longer-Balled Eagle.

"Pretty stealthy," MacKay said.

The bird's eyes were clear, intelligent. "I find my mental faculties have suddenly cleared up a bit. No doubt as a result of my recent… loss." He waved a wing at his underside, where the sac-wound had been cauterised. By the laser, presumably.

"Great. Good to have you on the team," MacKay said dryly. "What have you got?"

"I've made some studies of Fuzzies over the years, and I believe I can answer some of Miss Sangre's questions regarding the growth and sale of comestible animal proteins." Eagle turned to MacKay. "But I agree with you that that entity is our first priority."

"And?"

"Whatever it is, its power clearly draws on sources beyond this place. Which means no one here has the power to defeat it." Eagle sounded, MacKay thought, like a college professor now. "Mister MacKay, your fighting ability is formidable... but limited to the purely mechanical. Miss Sangre, you and your erstwhile gangcult are likewise out of your depth. My own ferocity might have slowed it down, but I fear I cannot even draw on that depth of aggression anymore. And the less said about the GenTech soldiers, the better."

The soldiers looked around sadly, hefting bats and machine guns. They looked like a farm team that would never make the majors.

"No," Eagle continued, "only one creature here draws on the very core of oppressed America. Only one of us was engineered with the sheer power required."

He fluttered over, gently, and pointed a wing at the unmoving, bullet-riddled form of Grandmother Spider.

MacKay grimaced. "Is she even *alive?*"

In response, one of the spider's freakish eyes shot open.

"Ah. That's a little more like it." Behind them, Wellington adjusted his newly repaired waistline, then turned to face the GenTech laser squad. "So you bastards thought it'd be funny to cut me in half, huh? Like in that film, *Catch-22?*"

Energy shot out from Wellington's form, frying and scattering the GenTech men. Stray electricity hit the laser, shorting it out violently.

"Soldiers don't make out too good in that movie, either!" He turned back to MacKay's group. "Now, which of you big talkers is gonna be next to—"

Almost quicker than MacKay could see, Grandmother Spider leaned back on two legs, and blue energy poured forth from her, a thick current of electric death. Cristina and Britney jumped back, out of the way.

"Whoa!"

The energy struck Wellington as he hovered in the air, knocking him backwards. He shook his head, smiled, and fired back, a deadly green bolt tinged with something unearthly.

The bolt struck Grandmother, and she rolled back. But she maintained her assault.

"The *Native American*," Wellington taunted. "So noble, so wholesome, so linked to the earth. The emergency battery source for the Nation." He smiled. "Another natural resource down the shitter, I guess." And he fired another bolt.

The assault singed Grandmother Spider's fur, but she maintained her flow of current. "Grandmother – protects – her children," the creature gasped.

I've never seen her do anything like this, MacKay thought. It must be burning her out.

"*Grandmother* is still of this world. Me – I'm something else."

The surviving Mad Cows were hanging together now, watching intently. The GenTech soldiers backed away slowly. A few of them started retrieving their comrades' corpses.

"You're a dinosaur, Granny. A freak from an extinct country." Wellington smiled, but he seemed to be weakening. "Meat. Just like the rest."

Grandmother's eyes screwed up in an expression of pure hatred. "Not – *meat!*"

And her final bolt incinerated Wellington. He burned, screamed once, and crumbled into a wisp of mist and ashes.

Then he was gone.

Mia and MacKay exchanged glances, then moved as one to Grandmother Spider. But they knew what they would find.

She was hollow, empty. A part of the Earth now.

Another animal to be mourned.

          ut

THE GENTECH SOLDIERS quietly boarded the copters, dragging their prisoners along. At one point, a couple of ACTS commandoes made a run for it. A GenTech soldier sighted them with his Shredder, then shrugged and let them go.

Wister-Hauser, Hauser-Wister, Britney, and Cristina were sitting on the edge of a collapsed tent, frantically comparing notes. The girls gestured excitedly; the Germans made elaborate gestures, accompanied by tortured metaphors. MacKay had a sinking feeling they might be forming a new gang, any time now.

Dog jumped from Cristina's shoulder to Britney's, cluelessly following the conversation. The monkey had been shrewd enough to stay out of sight during the worst of the melee. MacKay just hoped he wasn't thinking about going off with the new, improved Mad Cows.

MacKay stood on a rock, his arm around Mia. Ever since the big battle, she'd been excited but distracted. She seemed to want to be with him, but not to talk. Not yet.

The eagle fluttered up in front of them, looked at the rock beneath their feet.

"Not high enough," he said. "It's very easy for Americans — good, well-meaning Americans — to lose sight of the bigger picture. Would you like a bit more perspective?"

MacKay frowned, puzzled.

Eagle hovered right over them, sharp talons hanging down. "Grab on," he said.

Mia looked at MacKay. They each grabbed a leg, and up they rose.

The desert air was hot and dry. The first copter was just taking off, rising into the sky ahead of them. Past the other three, MacKay could see the one he'd shot down, still smoking slightly. And past that, very small in the distance, the three Cocoa Niño animals, free of their enclosure, wandered off slowly in the distance.

Now and then, the mouse paused to hit the cat with a rock. But no energy rose up.

MacKay cocked his head at them. "Old habits," he said.

Mia smiled.

They rose up: ten feet, twenty now. MacKay looked to the other side of the compound, past the scorched line of administrative tents. He saw the ammo dump, which was now a crater — GenTech must have targeted it early. He saw the Easter Island statues, chipped and broken, the mouse's ears strewn over the bullet-riddled landscape. He saw the holding tents, the only untouched part of the compound.

No, he thought, and turned to the right. Not the only part. There was also the Civilian Zone.

Behind the barbed wire, a clutch of people stood, looking up at the eagle and his passengers. Pointing.

"What are they thinking?" MacKay whispered. "What do they believe they saw?"

He still wasn't sure himself.

"Eagle," Mia said. "You were going to tell us about Fuzzies, Inc."

"Ah. Yes." Eagle swooped sideways, gently. "Since going renegade, I've made a point of learning as much as I can about my creators. A few... high-placed friends in what remains of the federal government have helped me in that goal, over the years.

"Mister MacKay... did Mister Wellington tell you much about the history of Fuzzies?"

MacKay frowned. "I think he said he'd started it himself, and ran it privately for years. Until GenTech came in."

"Quite so. Fuzzies' core business – the creation of specialty AI-enhanced animals such as myself – depended on a certain general level of economic prosperity. As the infrastructure of America declined and the economy collapsed, people could no longer afford such luxuries. Wellington found himself with a large overhead and no income. He was forced to sell out to GenTech."

"He did seem bitter about that."

"GenTech promised him they wouldn't interfere with his work, of course. And then, as soon as the deal was complete, they stepped right in and took over. They stripped Fuzzies down and refocused its business entirely... adding staff to one key area that had, hitherto, been a very minor part of their R&D operations." Eagle paused. "Did you ever wonder why they had such a large headquarters?"

"Yes, I did."

"GenTech focused Fuzzies on one thing, and one thing alone: meat. Specifically, the growing of meat for food."

MacKay absorbed that for a moment.

"GenTech had identified a basic American need," Eagle continued, "one that people would pay to fill, even in these difficult times. Meat had become scarce, hideously expensive. If they could use Fuzzies' core technique — DNA-based Faunic Manipulation — to alleviate that shortage, they could make the company profitable again."

Mia's eyes were wide. "Aniprotein?" she asked.

"A fiction. A shell. A brand name, intended to propagate the lie that this meat was produced within the United States. That America was back on its feet again, taking care of itself. Feeding its own."

"Wellington, Nihilo, whatever," MacKay said. "It said that if we knew where the meat really came from—"

"Brazil," Eagle said.

Mia looked up sharply at him. "Brazil?"

"The operation is administered from Fuzzies' headquarters in Florida… but the plants are in Brazil. We couldn't have all kinds of monstrous genetic slaughter going on here in the US, could we?

"But parts of South America are even more unstable, lately, than this country. Thalamus has been raiding GenTech's Brazilian plants… the farms full of meat animals. That's heated up the war between those two corps. It's probably why GenTech decided to steal the essence of a top-secret Thalamus project."

MacKay frowned, thinking. Mia was likewise silent.

Eagle swung down now, towards the trailers at the edge of Cocoa Niño. He set them down, gently, next to the abandoned lawn chairs where MacKay had gone on his Dreamquest.

They stood, facing the hovering Eagle. He looked from one to the other, with kind eyes.

"I haven't known you two very long," he said. "But I can sense you have a rare and true connection. I also sense you haven't truly found your callings in life, either of you. Is that right?"

MacKay looked at Mia, a bit stunned. They both nodded.

"You're very… perceptive," MacKay said.

Eagle laughed, looked down. "I should have gotten rid of those things years ago."

MacKay smiled. "I've thought about it myself."

"Perhaps I can help you both," Eagle continued. "Consider it a gesture of atonement for years of mindless, destructive behaviour."

"Thank you," Mia said.

"Two words… "

They looked at him, expectant.

"*Vacas Muitas.*"

epilogue
vacas muitas, brazil

THE COMPLEX ROSE before them like a dozen giant, dull-green aircraft hangars. Barbed wire, electric fences, high-powered lasers mounted on every corner. As they watched, an automated truck whirred up to a gateway, docked at a delivery station. A large tube, like an airport jetway stained brown with dried blood, creaked out to meet it.

The truck took delivery. MacKay could just make out the words on the bottom of its licence plate: The Lone Star State.

The truck moved out; the gate hissed shut. As the truck drove away, it bumped over the rotting bodies of a few Thalamus soldiers. More corpses littered the forest outside the walls, remnants of a raid some weeks ago.

Mia trembled slightly next to him as they sat crouched in a tree. "This is weird," she said. "It feels like facing my greatest fears."

"In a way, it is," he replied. "Or your visions, at least."

"What's in there?"

"We're about to find out." MacKay's HanHeld beeped, and he thumbed it open. "Dog, you in?"

Keek! Keek!

The HanHeld screen flickered to life. Dog's camera began broadcasting flickering, shadowed images. MacKay made out a headless creature, propped upright permanently in a pen; a cow with no face; and a thin, stringy, unidentifiable animal, front paws strung up to a high ceiling, blood dripping slowly from its feet. Its face was a mask of agony, and very, very humanlike.

He and Mia exchanged a look. That was a new one.

The camera angle tilted, and then MacKay saw the Machine. Cold, iron, immense. A huge, grinding mass of gristle-soaked gears, with a nozzle like a vacuum cleaner, but big enough to feed a boar into. Ready to chop, dice, cure, process, and spit out meat in varying degrees of quality, for sale at different prices.

MacKay shivered.

Mia handed him an M-78, checked the ScumShredder ammo in hers. She clipped a revolver and three Gren-Aids to her belt. She looked over and noticed that MacKay had four on his.

"I guess this is our calling," she said. She was trying to remain sombre, but she smiled, excited despite herself. "To kill things."

He looked up from checking his Shredder, very serious. "I know it's mine. I learned it in the Dreamquest."

She nodded. "And I learned it at Cocoa Niño."

Then he reached over and took her hand in his.

She looked down at it, and nodded. Strength flooded into her – just like in her vision.

"Ready to go?" he asked.

"Yeah."

As one, they leapt out of the tree and charged.

FIFTY FEET AWAY, steely eyes watched the duo through binocular implants. Professor Wan reached up, clicked the bone next to his eyes, and shook his head.

He turned from his perch, in the observation bubble of his hidden mobile laboratory. A young woman in black, with frosty violet hair, came up behind him, handed him a glass of herbal tea. A young platinum-blond man, also in black, passed him two packets of sugar.

"Is everything all right, Professor?" the woman asked.

"Yes, grad student." He smiled coldly. "Just another pair of misguided souls, in need of education."

"Should we stop them?"

"No." Professor Wan turned to them; it was part of his obligation, he always reminded himself, to teach the young. "Americans have a great deal of difficulty accepting the source of their protein. These two have been forced to confront the reality... and have chosen to destroy it."

The young man frowned, puzzled. "But should we not step in?"

"We must let them find the true path. I dream of a future where Man holds dominance over all other life, shaping it to his will. Where no human shall ever go hungry; where all will serve us."

He turned to look back at Mia and MacKay. "On that glorious day... they, too, shall be among the masters."

In the distance, MacKay's and Mia's Shredders rang out their destructive song.

"Let GenTech and Thalamus play their demon-guided games," Professor Wan continued. "They know the truth: every American needs his meat."

The young man nodded. The young woman smiled, licked her lips.

Then there was blood. And the gods were pleased.

ABOUT THE AUTHOR

Stuart Moore is an acclaimed writer of comic
books, novels, and screenplays. His comics
work includes *Firestorm*, *Stargate Atlantis*, *Lone*,
Para, *Justice League Adventures*, and the satirical
graphic novel *Giant Robot Warriors*. At DC
Comics, Stuart was a founding editor of the
acclaimed Vertigo imprint, where he won the
Will Eisner award for Best Editor 1996 and
the Don Thompson Award for Favorite Editor
1999. From late 2000 through mid-2002 Stuart
edited the bestselling Marvel Knights comics
line. Upcoming works include new graphic
novels with Tokyopop and AiT/PlanetLar, a
comics adaptation of the bestselling novel
Redwall, and more *Firestorm*. He lives in
Brooklyn, New York.